# ARABELLA AUSTIN

## Southern Sunshine

*Southern, Sassy, and Satisfying.*

ISBN 9781733776707 (ebook)
ISBN 9781733776714 (paperback)

www.arabellaaustin.com
southernsunshineseries@gmail.com

Author's/Publisher's Note
This is a work of fiction. Names, characters, places, and inci-
dents either are the product of the author's imagination or are
used fictitiously, and any resemblance to actual persons, living
or dead, business establishments, events, or locales is entirely
coincidental.
This book is not intended for readers under the age of eighteen
due to language and sexual content.

# Contents

CHAPTER 1 - Know Your Guns                                    1

CHAPTER 2 - Frenemies                                         9

CHAPTER 3 - Treat Friends like Family                        19

CHAPTER 4 - Loose Women                                      31

CHAPTER 5 - Conspiracies                                     43

CHAPTER 6 - Hell in a Hand Basket                            55

CHAPTER 7 - The Shirt Off Your Back                          65

CHAPTER 8 - Hard Work Pays Off                               77

CHAPTER 9 - Gather 'Round                                    87

CHAPTER 10 - Duck and Cover                                  97

CHAPTER 11 - Moonshine                                      107

CHAPTER 12 - Sugar Ain't just for Sweet Tea                119

CHAPTER 13 - Nobody's Perfect                              131

CHAPTER 14 - Battle Lines                                  145

CHAPTER 15 - Dirt Roads                                    155

CHAPTER 16 - Sneaky Varmint                                165

CHAPTER 17 - Mornin'                                       175

CHAPTER 18 - Shake a Stick At                          183

CHAPTER 19 - Small Town                                193

CHAPTER 20 - Crazy Heifer                              201

CHAPTER 21 - Afternoon Delight                         211

CHAPTER 22 - Table for Two                             219

CHAPTER 23 - Worn Thin                                 229

CHAPTER 24 - Drinkin' Beer and Tellin' Lies            241

CHAPTER 25 - The Shit Hits the Fan                     251

CHAPTER 26 - Bless His Heart                           261

CHAPTER 27 - Bless Her Heart                           269

CHAPTER 28 - Home                                      277

CHAPTER 29 - Their Beginnin'                           285


Epilogue                                               295

# CHAPTER 1

## Know Your Guns

"People think being Southern is simple. They assume an occasional y'all, darlin', droppin' the *g* off the end of a word, or listenin' to country music qualifies you for the Southern way of life. That ain't so. In fact, it's far from the way it is. Being Southern is something bred deep within you. The need to help your family, friends, and neighbors during the tough times. The ability to serve sweet tea at the drop of a hat, and be kind to one's elders. Respect for your family and friends and the capacity to see a need and act to meet it is imperative. Being Southern means going at a slower pace and enjoying the world around you. Sittin' down and havin' a home-cooked meal with your loved ones. There is also the required discipline to only say 'bless their heart' when people assume us Southerners are stupid because we talk slow. Being Southern is something you shouldn't take for granted."

Sunshine listened to G-Daddy's deep voice as he rocked her on his and G-Momma's front porch. She hugged him tight as she watched the chickens peck at the grass. Her G-Daddy was the sweetest. He helped her make mud pies, gave her sweets when her Momma wasn't looking, and kept her from getting a good many whoopings. He seemed to be trying to instill a lot of wisdom in her.

Sunshine knew what wisdom meant. She was ten now. She was intent on taking it all in when she saw her enemy-of-the-moment pull into G-Daddy and G-Momma's drive. Sunshine jumped out of G-Daddy's lap and stood on the top step. "What are you doing here, Duck?" She aimed her best sneer at the boy who used to be her best friend.

"Sunshine, I've done asked you to quit callin' me that. My name is Drake. You've known it since you were two." Drake kicked the dirt in the drive. "Momma sent me over here to apologize to you."

"Well, go on, let's hear what you gotta say." She motioned her small hands and threw them on her hips like she'd seen her Momma do when she was mad at Sunshine's Daddy. Sunshine watched Drake walk to the bottom of the steps, head hung low. Apologizing had to be eating him up.

"I'm sorry for putting that frog down your shirt yesterday," Drake mumbled reluctantly under his breath. Sunshine had gotten to where she didn't think some of the gross stuff Drake and his brother, Brice, came up with was funny. She was turning into more of a girly girl, and he didn't seem too fond of that. He had told her on more than one occasion that girls were weird.

"Thank you, Drake. I will tell your Momma you did a good job of apologizing. Now, I am spending time with my G-Daddy. Goodbye." Sunshine did her best to sound as grown up as possible. She turned back around to climb into G-Daddy's lap. Before she could walk two steps, she felt something plop against the back of her shirt.

"Drake!" Sunshine squealed loudly as she felt mud slide down her back. She ran down the steps and tackled him in the front yard.

"Quit being such a sissy all the time!" Drake yelled at her as they each wrestled to be on top. Punches were thrown for a few seconds. Sunshine managed to get him in a headlock for a brief moment and gave him a noogie.

"Does this feel like a sissy kicking your butt?" She jumped up and gave him a quick kick before he knocked her legs out from under her again.

"The necessity to stomp a mud hole in someone's ass and walk it dry if they deserve it was the last tidbit I was going to tell you, but you seem to have that one in the bag, Sunshine." G-Daddy laughed from the front porch as G-Momma came barreling down the steps to pull Sunshine and Drake apart, yelling at G-Daddy along the way.

"Damn it! Why the hell are you sittin' there laughing at them like a loon?"

"Because right now, Sunshine is giving Drake a hard life lesson. Never underestimate a woman or you'll get your ass kicked."

Sunshine should have known, from that moment sixteen years ago on, what a snake Drake could be. Even after all the years since he'd been gone, G-Daddy's voice continued to bang around in her head. She missed that crazy old coot.

She could hear the reruns of *Bonanza* on in the background. She didn't turn to look. It was an episode she had seen a blue million times. She bet one of the *Cartwrights'* best friends hadn't stolen their damn bull. Truth be told, that happened at least once, but that was beside the point. She had told herself she wouldn't think about last night's cattle thievery incident. That

3

line of thinking would cause her to shoot something. She had to get her mind off of the jackass behind her pissed-off mood.

She smoothed her hand over the leather of her couch as it engulfed her and made taking it easy simple. Hair thrown up in a messy bun, head draped over the arm, she glanced at the seventy-inch TV. She purchased it for the main reason of watching the Tide roll during football season. Her eyes roamed over to the barnwood-framed picture of Momma and Daddy at her college graduation. They were smiling and looking at her with complete adoration in their eyes. The Lord knew Momma didn't look at her that way anymore. Now Momma's eyes gleamed with predatory calculation that scared the bejesus out of her.

You'd think she'd have a good Southern man by now, according to Momma. After all, she was Lawrence County's Chicken and Egg Festival Queen three years running. That accolade had not been by her choice. And let us not forget to mention there were a few crazies in the family. The crazy gene drew in Southern men like flies to honey. Sunshine had a college degree, good birthing hips, and knew her way around a stove. In the South, a lady was supposed to have already married by her advanced age of twenty-six. She had shot that ideal to shit.

She could swear that woman tried to figure out how long Sunshine was still going to be fit and pretty. She hadn't aged significantly since high school. She had great genes in that regard. Her Momma was still as pretty as ever, and looked more akin to being her sister. Bless her Momma's heart, always trying to set her up with some man. Sunshine didn't know when her Momma was gonna figure out that she was as bullheaded as her. She had no need to be set up by the woman, as if that wasn't embarrassing in itself.

Sunshine needed food. She snagged some Oreos out of the pantry. She'd had to make a grocery run the other day to get some more, Lord have mercy on everyone if she ran out of Oreos or peanut butter. Momma had met up with her to tag along, and it'd seemed she'd been shopping for something a good deal different than what Sunshine was. She giggled over the *aisle eight fiasco*, named by her mother. That crazy woman stopped a good-looking man who'd been minding his own business right there in the middle of the store. Momma had started listing Sunshine's attributes, as if she were a cow at the stockyard. She could have crawled behind the Dale Earnhardt Jr. poster board display, she was so embarrassed. Sunshine laughed out loud remembering the look of shock on the guy's face when he heard the words pouring out of her own mouth. "I would be happy to go on a date, soon as I get permission from my probation officer to leave city limits." She had sighed for dramatic effect at that point, adding, "But that might be a while since last time I stole a car…again." He stood there slack-jawed and ran off. She got a smack in the head, but it was worth the look on her Momma's face.

Sunshine was hitting her prime, but she was happy being single. She'd never needed a man, and didn't intend to start now. She huffed out a breath of anger at her Momma. She still had many years of being a bachelorette left. She didn't need to toe to an old traditional line of being married just yet.

Sunshine's grip about crushed her Oreos when someone started beating on her new front door. She had it installed two weeks ago. It had some magnificent metal and woodworking details. Sunshine loved that door. It was rustic, almost medieval. It was the John Wayne of doors. In other words, it was a badass. That door was the finishing touch on her plantation-style home that sat back on two hundred and fifty some odd acres of beautiful pasture. One of Sunshine's most proud achievements. If she was being honest, she'd have to say that while she loved picking out all the details of her house, what she'd been working on the hardest was building up her herd of registered cattle. She had been raising them for the past three years over in the neighboring county, out from under the watchful eye of her loving, but nosy parents.

She had found out this past week that she had the chance to supply a new up-and-coming cattle farmer with his first herd of registered Brangus. She was striving to get her herd from Moonshine farms sold in full and start another. The payout of that alone would set her up pretty for a good while.

Sunshine stalked towards the front entrance. There had better not be a scratch on her new door or she would shove her size six boot up someone's ass. She seemed to be leaving a trail of manure, whether cow or horse was not determined, on the hardwood floors. She maybe should've wiped her feet better. Either way, she cringed at the fact that someone would see her house untidy. She may raise cattle and work long hours, but she still tried, on occasion, to resemble a Southern Lady, and hated for anyone to see her house out of order. Hope springs eternal and maybe it was her Daddy coming to tell her that some of the cows they owned together had calved. Even if it was Friday evening, sometimes you gotta go to the field. Hell, most times the field was where she would rather be.

Sunshine opened John Wayne to see a man who would stop most women dead in their tracks. Drake Augustus Caldwell. She gave herself a mental pat on the back for not being most women, and also for not slamming the door in the jackass's face. If she hadn't known him all her life, and he hadn't put that frog down her shirt when they were ten, and stolen the bull she wanted during last night's incident, she might find him good-looking.

Lord knew what other despicable, immature things he had done over the years that kept her from looking at him any other way than as a friend. Things being what they were, she saw the fourteen-year-old poopy head that stole her bathing suit top while they were swimming at the creek with some of their friends, which had included her crush at that time, Alan Peebles. Alan was a happily married man now. She was sure he had forgotten the flat chest of a twelve-year-old, or at least she hoped. Sunshine leaned on the doorframe, not in the least bit inclined to invite him in.

She took in all of Drake's six-foot-five muscled frame looming over her in her doorway. His messy black curly hair fell across his forehead, and his trademark shit-eating grin was plastered across his face. Those steel-blue eyes of his gazed down at her. She couldn't decide if she wanted to kick him in the shin, or berate him for daring to bang on John Wayne. Sunshine decided on the silent treatment. Let him squirm. He hated when she got quiet. Served the cattle thief right. Sunshine gave him the *aw you done stepped off in it now* stare. The one that made grown men cry, and animals tuck tail and run.

After her death glare, she made a quick turn and headed straight to get one of her guns. She had them under the stairs in

7

the safe room she had installed for tornadoes, and emergencies. She was going to teach him a thing or two. She decided not to kill him, because his parents and hers would have something to say about that. She didn't know why. He had been a pain since the day she was born. Everyone talked about how she screamed bloody murder the moment Drake got to hold her. Sunshine was certain it was probably because he pinched her and she was crying at the fact that she would have to deal with him for the rest of her life. Anyone would cry in those circumstances. But no, she wouldn't kill him. She could scar his nice ass for life, or make him piss his tight-fitting jeans. Either of those options held appeal.

Wait till she told Belle and Willow about his cattle thieving. Drake was going to wish he had never even looked at that bull. When they got done dragging him through the mud, there wouldn't be a woman in a hundred square miles who would even think about going near him.

Sunshine tossed her hair over her shoulder to get it out of her face while she fiddled with the lock. She kept a handgun beside her bed but didn't think the situation should go that far. She would get her shotgun out of the safe. She turned around and noticed that the cattle thief was still on her porch.

"Drake, dear," Sunshine said in her sweet as honey voice. He hesitated to look around, and rightly so, seeing as she was armed with her new Benelli MAX 4 SBE2 12 gauge. She had bought it for duck hunting. Which was perfect in this case, since she was fixing to shoot a Drake. Sunshine's smile turned evil. "Where's *my* bull?"

# CHAPTER 2

# Frenemies

Drake had suspected, when he knocked on Sunshine's door, that she might decide to take a swing, or a kick. Hell, at the very least yell at him, but this eerie gun-toting calm? That he did not expect. She hadn't been calm since the womb. Sunshine had come out screaming at birth. He knew since his parents had been best friends with hers from way back before he and Sunshine were even thought of. He had held her while he sat in his Momma's lap that first day at the hospital when they welcomed her to the world. Drake had thought she was sweet, soft, and innocent. Then she had let out a scream, and he had almost thrown her out of his lap. If his Momma hadn't grabbed Sunshine, he would have. That woman was born with a set of lungs on her that could rival a stuck hog's.

Damn it. Not only was he getting an eerie calm as he stared her down, he was getting her evil look while she held a gun in her hands. That look sent chills down his spine, because who knew what the crazy woman was gonna do? If those squinty hazel eyes could shoot death rays, he would've been dead a hundred times over by now. Lord help him if she decided to try and take him down without the gun. He'd have to fall and act as if she'd hurt him to not make it worse on her pride, or anything that was connected to his body. It was a good thing he knew how to deal with a lunatic. He had a lot of practice with this one type in particular. Drake decided the best course of action was to tell her the truth.

"Sunshine, come on now, don't be angry. It's only a bull. You can come over and look at him in the pasture anytime you want. Don't be mad. We've been friends our entire lives. Don't let cattle come between us." He tried his best to appear contrite.

As he waited for a response, he peered through the doorway over her head and tried to think of any way to get out of this pile of horseshit he had stepped in.

He had been at the stockyard last night, a usual occurrence, and saw a Brangus bull come in last minute. The bull shouldn't have been at their sale; he was worth more than the going price of beef due to his genetics. He and a few others had recognized the bull's brand. He was worth a pretty penny. The lady unloading him just wanted him gone. He had belonged to her husband, who'd passed away. Drake tried to tell her that she could get more at the registered sale in Tennessee, but she said she didn't need the money. He wasn't gonna look a gift horse in the mouth, or in this case a gift bull.

The bull came up for auction, and Drake bid high. A bidding war ensued with someone he couldn't see in the crowd. He shouted five thousand and won the bid. Unfortunately, his competition had turned out to be Sunshine. He hadn't seen her till all was said and done. Drake had sighed and shaken his head. That woman brought meaning to the phrase, *hell hath no fury like a woman scorned*.

The crowd had parted like the Red Sea, and all he saw on the other side was Sunshine's furious eyes, ready to kill. He'd tried his best to find her last night, to explain, but she hit the road like a bat out of hell as soon as it was over. All he'd seen were the taillights of her F250 by the time he reached the parking lot. He wanted to come explain this morning, but that seemed similar to a dead-end trail.

"Now, Sunshine, I wouldn't have outbid you had I known it was you." He was lying about that part, but he wasn't about to tell that to the woman in front of him. He'd be a Drake-skin rug on her wall if he did. His heart rate kicked up a notch. Shit. He watched her eyes turn to liquid lava. *Here she blows.*

"Drake Augustus Caldwell, don't you dare lie to me."

"Now, Sunshine, calm down…"

"Calm down? Are you serious right now? Get off my damn porch before I shoot off your favorite appendage."

Her head was fixing to turn around on her shoulders any minute, he was certain. He racked his brain, trying to find a fast way to defuse this situation or family ties with the Blackwells were gonna be shot to hell and back. They had supper planned for Sunday night with Sunshine and her parents, and he wasn't about to be the one to ruin it. His Momma and Daddy would of course blame it on him, because Lord knows everyone thought Sunshine was the perfect child. They all pretended she shot daisies out of her ass, but he knew better. Drake had smelled what came out of there, and there wasn't anything daisy about that. Yeah, she was beautiful and all, but everyone in town knew she was meaner than a two-headed rattler.

He loved Sunshine's parents. They were his godparents, and

he didn't want to upset them. There had to be a way to make sure he didn't get killed over a bull and ruin Sunday's plans.

Sunshine turned away from him and headed inside. He didn't know what the hell for, but he strode into the house behind her and stopped dead in his tracks. It was the first time he had seen her house since it had been finished two weeks earlier. He and his parents were—well, hopefully still were—invited to have supper at Sunshine's for the big reveal.

Sunshine had kept everyone out of the inside for a month, even her own parents. All of them had been dying to take a peek. What she didn't know was he had been driving by and sneaking a look when he knew she'd be off working cattle with her Daddy. If she had an inkling, Drake shook his head, he would be dead.

High coffered natural wood beam ceilings with a deer antler chandelier were constructed over his head. Native American paintings stood out on the walls with splashes of color. Big couches with saddle leather and thick wooden tables shades darker than the hardwood floor dominated the living room space. Country and Western elegance was displayed throughout what he had already seen of her home. And that wasn't to mention the kitchen—Lord that woman had always loved to cook, but she had outdone herself.

Granite countertops lay across the custom cabinets. A horseshoe wine rack stood against the far wall near the bar to the right. A huge island with chairs on one side took up center stage in the kitchen with a horseshoe pot rack hanging above. The details were innumerable. She even got herself some tiny belt buckle cabinet knobs and a refrigerator that blended in with the cabinets. Sunshine was living high on the hog. Drake found himself feeling something akin to pride over what she had built, and a little envious. He was going to build a legacy for himself too. He was making substantial progress in that area, and that new bull he got out from under her would be another step in the right direction.

He could hear Sunshine inventing new death threats under her breath as she rummaged through her pantry. He took stock of the house, and then spotted something even nicer than the house—her ass. Damn it was looking mighty fine in those jeans, and her long blond hair flowing down her back made a man want to wrap his hands in it and… Stunned, Drake's thoughts came to an abrupt stop.

Where in the ever-loving hell had that come from? She was Sunshine for crying out loud. She was the burr under his saddle blanket, the fly in his lemonade, the damn gnat that irritated him, and the hair in his biscuit. He had lost his ever loving mind. He threw his hat on the counter, running his fingers through his hair in disgust. He jumped back when she swung around towards him with the gun in her grasp, and a scoop of peanut butter in the other.

"Sunshine…don't do it. I know I wasn't supposed to see the inside, but I promise I won't say a word to anyone. I won't spoil the surprise." He grinned and backed away towards the door, his movements slow and calculated.

"Get the hell out of my house, or I may shoot you and hang you from one of my rafters."

"Sunshine Grace Blackwell, put the gun down. If you dare think you're gonna shoot me so help me God, I am gonna pick you up, bend you over my knee, and spank your ass. Then I will call our parents and explain what exactly happened before you go tattletale like the spoiled brat you're acting. Now put down the damned gun."

He was fuming. He didn't know if he was mad because bending her over and spanking her was right up his alley, or because he knew he would still be in trouble even if he did tell his parents first. He wasn't going to think on that too much. He didn't want to dwell on the probable answer. He needed to settle the hell down.

"Now we are gonna talk this out and resolve this issue. We gotta try and be the adults we are supposed to be. If not, our parents will kill us both for ruinin' everyone's plans." Drake stared Sunshine down. "Neither of us wants to upset them. Here's what I'm gonna do for you, being the sweet, lovin', amazing man that I am. If you need sperm from the bull, I will give you a few sperm vials at a discounted rate. That should wipe the slate clean." He held his hand over his heart in promise.

He watched as she continued to think, and eat her snack. He tried not to stare when she wrapped her mouth around the peanut butter filled spoon.

"Why'd you want a registered bull for anyway?" he asked her.

"I recognized the brand. I was going to flip him in the registered sale in Tennessee. Back to your offer—why would I need sperm from a registered bull? I don't deal in registered cattle." She rambled on. "But you have to pay for this bull's feed, and I could get some sperm vials for free to put some better genetics into our herd. This idea does have potential."

"You cannot have the sperm vials for free."

"Yes, I think I can. Why did you want the registered bull?"

She shot his question back at him.

"Same reason you did. Get a few sperm vials, and then flip him." He hated to lie to her.

"You're missin' something though, Duck," she told him.

"That evil grin you got going on is creepy, and don't call me that stupid nickname. If you were a man, I'd knock your damned teeth down your throat. What's missing?"

"Duck, you neglected to include payback in your proposal." She laid her shotgun against her shoulder.

"Screw payback. I came to apologize and offer the new bull's sperm for cheap, not free, but if you're gonna continue to be an ass about this, I'm gonna leave. I've got plans to get to."

"Go on and get out of my house then. I'm not listenin' to your threats. You and I will be fine this Sunday because our parents will be there to keep me from killin' you. To the important matter of your proposition, I agree to it, but there will still be payback of some sort. Now, please leave. You can head off to whatever plans are so important. Make sure I don't have to set eyes on your mangy hide till Sunday, and don't slam John Wayne on your way out," she commanded as she pointed him towards the door.

He narrowed his eyes at her. One of them was confused over the way this was going to end, and he believed it was her. "What are you talking about? Don't slam John Wayne? Have you lost what was left of your mind?" He ran his fingers through his hair as he tended to do when he was stressed. He seemed to do it a lot around Sunshine.

"My door is tough and rugged looking, therefore I named it John Wayne." She crossed her arms and gave him a look that said not to try her. He wasn't fazed by it.

15

"Who on God's green earth is crazy enough to name their damned door?" He stared down at her, bewildered. Damn woman had lost it.

"I am not crazy. I happen to be a little in love with my door."

"You're crazier than a loon. Who knew you could get so worked up over a big piece of wood?" Drake smirked, wiggling his eyebrows at her.

He watched as he got her in a tizzy all over again, and just as they had managed to defuse the situation before it got bloody. "Get out of my house before I call your Momma and tell her you're calling me names and making sexual innuendos," Sunshine shouted at him.

"Real mature. Guess what, sugar? I'm a grown ass man, and that threat doesn't scare me anymore." Drake stared her down. However, he panicked when he saw her pick up her iPhone and dial in some numbers. He ran towards her and jerked the phone out of her hand before tackling her to the floor. He did his best to soften their fall with his forearms.

"I thought that threat didn't work anymore, Duck."

He felt her small hands grab his face and make him do fishy lips. He answered her laughter with a chuckle of his own.

"I didn't want Momma to be mad. I'm not scared, but respectful." He attempted to sound serious. Which was ridiculous given their current position. He pulled her hands up above her head, pinning them there, and stopped her from squeezing his face.

"You are so full of it. Get off me." He let her wiggle her hands free and felt them on his shoulders as she shoved at him to move.

"I will move when I'm good and ready." He tried his damnedest to not grind into her. He was enjoying right where he was at, but he was going to have to run before she saw, or felt, anything that would cause her to get even madder. A cold shower was in his near future. Damn it. This entire run-in with her was weird. How could he all of a sudden be attracted to a woman he'd known his entire life? Not that he hadn't noticed her before, or had a fantasy here and there, but their families and work were intertwined. This was a fluke, tensions running high. It would pass. His dick would notice someone else and be on its merry way.

He got up and headed straight for his Stetson, admiring the exposed beams, swooping staircase, and monstrous kitchen as he did. She'd done a great job with the design. It was a house a man and woman would both be comfortable in. He wondered if she was seeing someone. Nah, he would know it if she was. She would have told him herself, or his Momma would have.

He heard Sunshine's phone ringing. "How 'bout them cowgirls?" By none other than George Strait. He watched as she snatched up her phone. "Hey, Willow… Um uh… Yeah… Sure thing… I'll be ready by nine… Okay, can't wait. Love you too. Bye."

Drake had only heard one part of the conversation, but he was aware of trouble when he heard it, and Sunshine and the girls getting together meant Trouble. As in the past, having stolen the metal hog that was out front of the local gathering place, the Swine and Dine. They mostly had beef on the menu, but they also served barbecue, and bacon, of course. He wasn't quite certain why they had named it Swine and Dine. He reckoned the owners enjoyed the way it sounded.

"Sunshine, what are y'all gettin' into tonight?" He crossed

his arms across his chest. He tried to appear stern, but he let his grin sneak out.

"Not that it's any of your business, but we're heading out dancin'."

"I might swing by later." He'd want to be present to witness their shenanigans firsthand. She looked damn good in those jeans, and red Case IH top. He wiped a hand over his face and tried his best to erase the images that came along with that train of thought. He needed to head out to finish up some business with Bishop, and he needed to end his whatever he had going on with Raegan.

"Cowboy, it's time for you to head on out. I may see you later, but remember, payback is comin'. If you do decide to come by tonight you have to buy me a drink and compete on Bodacious."

He nodded his head as he walked through her foyer and noticed that there was a picture of them arm-in-arm sitting on the table. First thing Sunshine saw when she opened the door, and the last thing before she left. They were holding up a catfish that they had pulled in together at his Daddy's pond. He remembered that day as if it were yesterday. Right after his Momma took that picture, he put a frog down Sunshine's shirt. Drake laughed to himself at what a fit she'd pitched. Then, him being who he was, he opened John Wayne and slammed it as hard as he could.

He ran to the truck like a bat outta hell, slinging gravel on his way out. He looked into the rearview mirror and saw Sunshine waving her gun again. He loved to get her worked up.

# CHAPTER 3

## Treat Friends like Family

Sunshine stifled a laugh as she watched Drake speed out of the driveway. He didn't need to know the reasons behind her wanting that bull. She figured she had done a good job of throwing him off any thoughts of her breeding registered cattle.

When she had decided to call his bluff and dialed his mother, she hadn't expected him to go overboard. His boots had vibrated across the floor. But before she could brace herself, she had been knocked down by what had felt akin to getting hit by a Mack truck. Of course, it had been Drake jerking the phone out of her hand and hanging it up before it could connect. She roared out a laugh recalling his over-the-top reaction.

She had to admit, he had looked mighty fine in a rant, and when he'd mentioned spanking? Well, she would have taken her chances. She had wanted to poke the bear, and see the fireworks, and not in a good way.

What in the hell was wrong with her? She shook her head. Dear heavens to Betsy. He was her buddy, pal, amigo. That is, until he'd stolen her bull. She had gone insane, not that she had far to go in the first place. She thought she had recognized some heat within his gaze as he lay on top of her, but sure, that had to have only been his temper.

Sunshine ran her hands down her jeans and top, making sure her clothes were in place as she ran into her office for a quick overview of her finances before it was time to leave. She hadn't made it out to the Moonshine herd that day, and she would need to make sure she went by tomorrow to check the cattle over. She insisted on being present and altogether invested in making her registered herd profitable. Her drive back and forth between neighboring counties was getting old. She wouldn't have to keep Moonshine's existence private anymore within a year, sooner if she was able. She would be able to tell her family and friends about Moonshine before long and be able to shake off the nagging deceit.

Sunshine gazed at the bull on her laptop screen. She hoped Drake did end up coming to their favorite bar, the Badmoon, tonight. If he did, she might have some competition on Bodacious, the mechanical bull. Sunshine figured he wouldn't be able to resist a challenge from her. Plus she could bet on the outcome and win a little money. Part of her was glad she hadn't won the bid on the Brangus bull. She needed to keep as much money as she could.

Her phone chirped an alarm that it was time to head out the door. Sunshine pulled into the parking lot of the Badmoon twenty minutes later.

"Snap out of it, sister, and let's get this party started," Willow called to her as she stepped out of the truck. Willow bounced over to Sunshine, her long dark brown hair swinging down her back. That girl was always ready and up to something. She was the crazy friend you wanted at your back who would go to jail with you. Everyone needed a friend like that.

"Will, let the woman think. She's got that constipated look. What has you lost in thought?" Her friend Belle twisted her honey-blond hair through her fingers.

Sunshine knew she wasn't acting like her normal rambunctious self. They probably thought she had some hare-brained scheme she was fixing to pull out of her ass. Poor Belle, she always tried to ensure that she and Willow didn't get into too much trouble. Although Belle did help her and Willow move the Swine and Dine's hog that one time, but neither of them had ever told anyone she assisted. Belle was supposed to be the sane one of the bunch. She and Willow tried to keep Belle's occasional craziness under cover, and keep her out of jail, so she could be the one to bail them out. Not that Sunshine and Willow made a habit of going to jail. It was usually a wrong time, wrong place thing. Usually.

"Nope. I was lost in thought, thinking about work. Nothing to worry over," she told them. It wasn't a complete fabrication. She had been running Moonshine's herd through her head, considering the cost profit margin before she'd pulled up. "Will, honey, we are going to have us a night to remember. And Belle? Relax. No one is planning on going to jail tonight. What do you say we raise a little hell?"

Sunshine swung an arm around each of them, herding them towards the neon sign that promised a heck of a time. Willow's holler of excitement echoed off the cars in the parking lot. Sunshine and Belle laughed at Willow and walked with confidence towards the night's adventures that lay in wait. The road to hell was always paved with good intentions.

She hit the door open, paid the five-dollar cover, and waltzed over to the back bar near Bodacious, the mechanical bull. It was a spacious place, same as a barn on the inside for the most part. It had a big dance floor, one big bar, and one smaller side bar. There was a smoking area out back, nice bathrooms, and hardwood floors. There was cowboy memorabilia on the walls, and a small enclosed stage area for the live bands. All the locals enjoyed it since most of them felt right at home in a barn. Hell, most of them were raised in one.

Sunshine started scoping out the crowd. It was early yet, only nine thirty. She had wanted to arrive early to make sure they had a table and didn't have to stand the entire night. There was always a wide variety at the Badmoon. People ranged from twenty-one to seventy, and sometimes older than that. She could have sworn she saw an old lady check a walker and an oxygen tank once. Majority of people there were in their cowboy boots and jeans. The usual crowd of goodhearted, hardworking people. They were done with the week and wanted to blow off some steam, maybe dance a little.

Belle and Willow headed to the bar while Sunshine sat back and watched an older couple dance across the floor. You always saw people you knew at the Badmoon. And didn't Georgia Renee happen to walk up to their table on that thought. Another one of Sunshine's good girlfriends, Georgia had recently got married to Sunshine's cousin, Bubba. Sunshine wouldn't have been shocked if Georgia hadn't made it tonight. She was still in the lovey-dovey stage of newlywed bliss.

Sunshine hollered at her. "Georgia Renee, you look shiny as a new penny. Married life seems to agree with you." Sunshine smiled, figuring she was going to get chewed out for using her middle name. Georgia hated it, but she thought it was a pretty Southern name. Lord knew it made more sense than Sunshine. Made people think she had a glowing personality. What Momma had been thinking, she did not know. She must've hoped the name would work magic and make her a sweet child. Sunshine snorted. That shit backfired.

"Sunshine Grace, I should hit you for using my middle name, but I will let you slide this once," Georgia said, leaning down to hug her.

"Yeah, you keep on remembering how much you love me, I'll keep bein' awesome."

"Sunshine, if I hadn't known you all my life, I would swear you were a few posts short of a fence."

She pulled out a chair for Georgia and propped her feet up on the next chair over. She noticed her new boots and felt entranced. They were a deep brown, worn leather with studs in an intricate pattern on the heel and light brown stitching on the front. Gorgeous. Cowgirl couture was written all over those works of art.

She continued to stare. "Where did you get those boots? I've got to have them." She knew her eyes were bugging out of her head, and there was drool running down her chin, but she didn't care. She wanted those boots. They looked like walking billboards for cowgirl extravagance.

"Preston's, honey. These boots are flying off the shelves, they said. Better call and have them order you some before you waste a trip. Forget that—a trip to Preston's is never wasted. If you want a pair of these boots though, you really had better call."

Georgia grinned.

Sunshine snorted at her. "Heifer, you had to have known I would love them, you hobag."

Georgia laughed at her insults.

Willow and Belle slid down in the chairs beside them, infatuated with Georgia's boots too. She relaxed as her friends discussed current fashion trends and caught up on some gossip for a while before heading out on the dance floor. It was nice to let her more feminine side out instead of always talking business. Thank goodness for girlfriends.

"Cotton Eye Joe" came on and their boots ate up the floor. Sunshine and her gal pals danced and laughed and scooted along to the music till they were all giggling and out of breath. The song ended and on came a slow one—"My Best Friend" by Tim McGraw. Sunshine was surprised when a hand came out and grabbed her arm. Then she was spun straight into that someone's arms. She peered up to see a handsome, blond, brown-eyed cowboy. She had seen him in here a time or two before.

"Ma'am, I would be much obliged if you'd dance with me." The handsome cowboy's voice was deep and smoother than silk. He was something nice to look at indeed.

"Well, sir. I don't know your name, and it seems to me that we are dancin'." Didn't want him to think she was excited about dancing with him. He was going to have to work harder than that.

"Touché. I wanted to catch you before you got away again. Every time I've seen you in here, I've wanted to ask you to dance, but I hadn't worked up the courage yet. You are a beautiful woman, and I figured I'd have to wait in a long line. My name is Brody." He flashed a charming smile at her.

This one was a ladies' man. "Brody, my name is Sunshine, but there ain't a thing sunny about me. If a man wants a woman bad enough, he better have the balls to walk up to her and tell her that." She felt someone behind her and turned to look up, and up, until she saw Drake's pissed-off face staring down at her. Men shouldn't be that beautiful when mad, and a good many women would melt for him. Bless their hearts. They didn't know him for what he was. An asshole.

"May I cut in?" He glared at the cowboy. Brody backed away in haste and stepped off the dance floor, not bothering to glance back at her. What a chicken shit. She would make sure not to give him the time of day. Drake grabbed her and pulled her closer than she was comfortable with. He gazed down at her, his eyebrows furrowed, his mouth a straight line.

"Why were you dancing with that ass? Everyone knows he's a buck in rut. I can't believe you would let him touch you. I'm gonna talk to your Daddy…"

Sunshine jerked her hand from his and cut him off right there.

"I was telling him he didn't have any balls and was about to pull away to go sit with the girls when you showed up and pulled your macho act. I'll have you know I had the situation handled, and if he'd gotten grabby, he wouldn't have had any balls after I got done with him." She glared up at him when he took her hand back and led them along the dance floor. "You know if anything bad goes down, I have Bertha tucked away in my bra."

Her statement turned his frown to a grin.

"You beat all I've ever seen. The man that gets saddled with you better be knife and bullet proof or he won't make it out alive."

Bertha was a knife she kept on her person for those just-in-case scenarios. Daddy didn't raise no fool. Her friends got the biggest kick out of Bertha always being with them, but it made them feel more secure, as it did her. No one messed with her or her friends. She usually carried her gun, but she couldn't take it with her in the bar, it being illegal and all.

Sunshine glared up at Drake and considered pulling away. His arms circled around her tighter, and she decided she was enjoying dancing with him. She laid her head on his chest and listened to "My Best Friend" by Tim McGraw as it played. She felt a weird sensation—maybe comfort, contentment, or happiness—come over her. Wait, what? This was Drake who held her, and that was heartburn. She felt him pull her closer.

Sunshine screamed in her head. *This was strange, but a good kinda strange? Maybe? I dunno. Hell is freezing over.* Her body tightened and her pulse sped up. She started noticing how hard his chest was, and how nice it felt for him to hold her… She was losing her damn mind.

She broke apart from Drake and caught him staring at her with a strange expression. She had felt her world shift, and it didn't make a damn bit of sense. She could see that he wasn't happy about whatever he was feeling either. Oh hell no. This was a fluke and she would ignore it, but it seemed fate was trying to tell her something in that honky-tonk. Something neither she, or Drake she'd bet, would intend on heeding.

Sunshine did the only thing she could think to break the weirdness. She gave him a quick smile smack-full of snark. "Come on, cowboy. Let's see if you can beat me on Bodacious." That seemed to shake the confused look out of his eyes and bring back the Drake she was comfortable with.

"Give me your best shot, short stuff."

Sunshine noticed his smile made its way all the way up to his mischievous eyes. He had been a handsome guy since he was a teen, but as he matured, he'd only gotten hotter. Of course, his Daddy had always been a nice-looking older man. Claire, Drake's Momma, had told her on more than one occasion about how she looked at Ben and knew that big bear of a man was hers. His parents were more in love now than ever. Same as her parents, but Momma and Daddy on the other hand? Their love hadn't been so easy. How could it be with her mother involved? Daddy had to chase her, catch her, and wear her down. Momma told her she had to make sure he was a keeper, but that she loved him from date one. Momma was a mess, but she did love her family till she turned you blue with her love.

Sunshine walked over to her girls and noticed their matching smirks. "What is it? Why are y'all lookin' at me with those goofy faces?"

Willow started, "You and Drake looked…"

"Awful cozy on the dance floor," Belle finished.

Georgia smiled and wiggled her eyebrows. "Yeah, he pulled you up close and personal."

"Whoa, damn it. Drake is my friend, and also my own personal pain in the ass. Y'all know how we are. There wasn't nothin' to that. He was tryin' to protect me from that ruttin' bull of a cowboy over there. Not that I needed it," Sunshine defended herself, not making eye contact as her gaze roamed the bar taking in the people that were there.

"Yeah, okay," Belle said. She turned back to see Willow and Georgia rolling their eyes at her.

"Well, y'all don't know what y'all are talking about. Now get your butts up. Me and Drake are fixin' to compete on Bodacious." Sunshine turned towards the bull and noticed that Brice was standing by Drake.

Brice and Drake had a few differences in their appearances, but still favored one another enough that you would easily figure they were brothers. Brice was three years younger than Drake, and one year younger than Sunshine. He was the irritating little brother nobody asked for, but as it turned out, she wouldn't know what to do without him. She loved him to pieces. She jumped into his arms and climbed him like a spider monkey. "Brice, my love, how have you been? I haven't seen you much in the last few months."

Brice caught her in his arms and gave her a big bear hug. "Sunshine, my shining star. I've been busy trying to get over my unrequited love for you. Alas, I have failed at my mission and have come back to ask you to run away with me."

Sunshine leaned back into his arms. "Oh, I thought you would neva ask!"

"Alright, knock it off, you two," Drake snapped at them. Drake's hands slipped around her waist and set her feet back on the ground. "Brother, you're an idiot. Now, let's all go over to the damn bull."

Will and Georgia jumped to their feet while Belle stayed back a bit. She seemed to be avoiding getting too close to Brice. Sunshine watched a moment longer as her friend eyed the man with hesitation. That would be a conversation for another time. She strode away from the group, confident in a win. She had an ace up her sleeve.

Sunshine gave Drake a serene smile. "How much?"

"Two beers," Drake told her. Confidence laced his arrogant attitude too.

"You have a deal," Sunshine said with a wink.

Her eyes followed him as he walked over to the bull. She watched as the cocky ass took a bow towards her and grinned his panty-dropping smile that showed all his Hollywood-straight white teeth. His grin went to the left, making it crooked. He was dangerous with that grin, and he used it on her and everyone else to his advantage. He jumped up on Bodacious's black and red back, grabbed the rope, pulled his Stetson down tight, threw his hand up, and nodded his head. He had beaten her on this bull more times than Sunshine cared to admit, but tonight would be different.

# CHAPTER 4

## Loose Women

Drake caught movement out of the corner of his eye and was stunned to see Sunshine taking her damn pants off. What in the hell did she think she was doing? Right then, Bodacious took a mean spin, and Drake went flying. The clock stopped at ten point four seconds. He got up, spitting fire, and looked around for the culprit.

"Sunshine!" he bellowed. "What in the hell!?"

He watched as her head jerked towards him, her eyes wide. She smiled. Everyone turned to see what the commotion was all about, and the crowd parted as he stepped in her direction. He spotted her behind a group of people, wearing a microscopic pair of spandex shorts that must have been under her jeans. Damn it all. The woman was going to give him a heart attack. She had done lost her mind, more so than normal. Thank the good Lord above she hadn't stripped down in front of everyone. He would have gone to jail. Not that he was jealous. It's that his Daddy would have wanted him to defend her honor and all.

After Drake gave her a swift appraisal, he decided she looked damn fine in her cowboy boots, shorts, tight T-shirt, and that long blond hair pulled back to show off her beautiful face. He scowled at her. Shit fire that woman needed to go put on some more clothes. She was causing him to become…uncomfortable. Shit, who was he kidding? He was hard as a damn rock. As was every other red-blooded male in the room. Aw hell, his brother was even looking at her.

Sunshine gave him an innocent, "Whatever are you talkin' about, Duck? I was changin' and gettin' ready to ride the bull."

He swallowed back a hateful retort as he watched Sunshine walk away, self-assurance in her step, her hips swaying. She jumped up on Bodacious, looked Drake straight in the eye, and winked. "Now, cowboy, this is how it's done."

Did she ever show him how it was done. Sunshine rode that bull, moving with every twist, turn, and buck. Her back bowed, her body swayed, and she tightened with every movement. Drake thought he was going to cum on the spot. That could have been the most downright erotic thing he'd ever seen outside the bedroom in his life. The way her purple shirt clung and those shorts rode up… He swallowed the drool that wanted to escape. He took off his hat and ran his fingers through his hair. He was going to have to talk to her Daddy about her riding that bull. Men were looking at her in a way that he didn't want them to. If she could cause him to not have friend thoughts, then she didn't need to be doing it. He was protecting her. The green-eyed monster hadn't reached up and bit him on the ass.

Sunshine leaned into her hand a tad too much and was caught off balance by a quick left turn and got thrown. His heart stuttered a bit when she hit the mat, but she jumped up, yelling and grinning. "How about that, cowboy? How ya like me now?" Sunshine pretended to throw her imaginary cowgirl hat and took a victory bow. She laughed and high-fived people as she walked through the crowd towards him. She had ridden for eleven seconds. A victory she would rub in his face until their next battle. He could see it now, every Sunday supper, she would bring it up, and then again during the week whenever she ran into him. He would be a good sport and let her have her moment.

"You did good. You wouldn't have beaten me if it wasn't for your dirty tricks, but a win is a win." He reached his arm out towards her, taking her small hand in a handshake.

"If you ain't cheatin' you don't want to win bad enough is what you've told me through the years."

"That's in Monopoly." Drake grinned at her and pulled her in for a side arm hug.

"It has a blanket meanin'." Sunshine giggled when he goosed her on the ribs.

"Come on. Let's hit the bar and I'll buy you one of those beers I owe you." He placed his hand to the small of her back and they maneuvered themselves to two bar stools.

"How'd you figure out wearing shorts would give you an advantage?" he asked as he signaled the bartender for two Bud Lights.

"Interestin' story. So, you know Becky who works at the Subway?"

"Yep, I do. She gives me free cookies."

"Well, she told me once that skin adheres better to plastic than fabric does. That you don't get as much slippage. She knows this because Becky has a fetish. A fetish that she decided to tell me about one rainy afternoon."

"At this point I'm afraid to ask, but what's her fetish?" Drake watched as her whole face lit with a smile and laughter.

"Becky is Mistress Bitchin' Becky on the weekends. When she isn't handlin' the meat for your sandwich, she is handlin' someone else's footlong in her toy room. That's what she calls her bedroom. She probably gives you cookies because she wants your man meat."

Drake spit beer out of his nose when Sunshine made a BJ movement with her tongue and hands.

"Damn you. Don't do, or say, that shit when I have a full mouth."

"Oh, Mistress Bitchin' Becky wants to give you a mouth full of…"

Drake slapped his hand over her lips. "Don't you dare finish that sentence."

"What is it? You scared Becky's cat is gonna get your tongue?"

Drake slammed his head down on the bar. He tried to erase the mental image that came along with Sunshine's words, but it wouldn't leave. He was going to have to scrub his mind with Ajax.

"I'll never look at our Subway lady the same. Hell, I'm never eating there again. All those cookies she gave me? And I thought she was being nice." He shuddered, then took a sip of beer.

He glanced over to where their friends were and around the bar. "Damn it." Drake whooshed out the words. Raegan was across the room, staring holes through the both of them. He hadn't done anything to warrant that amount of rage. He'd texted her earlier to let her know he wasn't coming by tonight, but that he would swing by tomorrow. Breaking up with her was going to be a pain in his ass any day he did it. He had wanted to enjoy his night out with Sunshine and the gang. Not that he had told Raegan they were even exclusive, but it seemed she had other notions about that than he did.

"What? Didn't expect a beer to cost you that much?"

"No. Raegan is here. She appears to be trying to murder me with her eyes." Drake swiveled back around to face Sunshine. Seeing her smile and hearing her deep belly laughs was worth Raegan's wrath.

"Raegan? Already? I've not even heard this one's name. What's wrong with her?"

"Nothing."

"Out with it, cowboy. She can't sit the saddle well? She doesn't care for your dog?"

He laughed as Sunshine gasped and slapped her hand to her face with a look of horror. "Is she allergic to cows and horses?"

He rolled his eyes at her. "No, fart wad. It was time for her to go. She has become a clinger. As you can see from her showing up here."

Hands wrapped around Drake's forearm and tugged at him to face their owner.

"I see who you cancelled our plans for. I shouldn't be surprised," Raegan spat out.

"How the hell did you know where to find me?" he asked her. Her mouth worked to push out an answer. Sunshine reached over and snatched his iPhone out of his back pocket. He didn't bother telling her the passcode.

Sunshine made quick work of the mystery for him. "That's what I figured. She had your location turned on in your text messages to her. She can check up on you wherever you have a cell signal."

"Thank you, Sunshine. I will buy your beers all night for that. Hell, maybe all week."

"Rookie move." Sunshine clucked her tongue at him.

He looked back at Raegan, who didn't appear the least bit concerned by her stalker actions. Instead, she stomped her foot and caught her wind. "The way you act around her tells me I was right this whole time about her not being just a friend. Just a friend, my ass. You've been sexing her up with your eyes this entire time."

What the hell had he been thinking dating this woman? She'd been a wildcat in the sack, but she was a damn psycho. He needed to start making women fill out a mental health sheet after this fiasco. "She's my friend, and always has been. I was not _sexing her up_ with my eyes.

Whatever the hell that even means. We can finish this conversation at your house tomorrow. There isn't any need to air dirty laundry in public."

"We will talk about this now, Drake. You screwed me over, sleeping with other women. Sunshine here, probably being number one."

"Do you hear yourself? Not once have I slept with anyone else these past couple of weeks. It's over, Raegan. It was never anything official between us, and certainly not enough for me to have to be dealing with this. I told you up front what I was offering, and you're the one who decided you wanted more. This isn't on me. I made you no false promises and gave you no expectations. Now let's leave it at that and call it a wash."

"Screw you, Drake Caldwell," Raegan spat at him.

Drake felt Sunshine tense beside him. It was going to get

rowdy. He would have to anticipate Sunshine's moves if he was going to keep her and Raegan apart.

Raegan had a good five inches on Sunshine. It would be a hell of a fight. Taking bets might be in his best interest instead of ensuring it didn't happen. There would be money to be won. Sunshine's Daddy had taught her to fight, and not many people here had seen her in action. She didn't hold well with people insulting her God, family, friends, or herself. Over the years he had witnessed her involvement in a few scuffles. She was quick, mean, and she fought dirty. He knew firsthand how dirty. He winced thinking of more than one incident involving his balls when they were teenagers and he had pissed her off.

Sunshine gave Raegan a pitying look. "Drake and I have been friends since the day I was born. He broke up with you. So what? There are more bulls in the pasture. Truth be told, there's more attractive and bigger ones out there."

Drake tried to contain his snort of disagreement. Now would not be the time for him to speak up and defend himself.

"Listen here, home wrecker, this isn't any of your affair. Why don't you go jump on that mechanical bull again and give all these men a show?" Raegan's mouth curved viciously. There wasn't any doubt Raegan was a beautiful woman, but her attitude ruined it for him.

Sunshine laughed and put her arm around Drake's waist. Damn, the woman was trying to get Raegan mad enough to hit her first. "I don't know what you're trying to say about me, but you oughta take time to consider what you say next."

"Shut up, slut. I told you this isn't any of your business. Go on and steal someone else's man."

Drake winced. That statement would be the straw that broke Sunshine's back. He tried to grab Sunshine's arm, but she stepped a few feet away from him, out of arm's reach. Raegan didn't know when to shut up. They could have settled this at her house, without Sunshine in the vicinity, if she hadn't decided to go all stalker mode on him. That was creepy as hell.

"Excuse me, but you may want to take back that statement, because if there is anyone here that stays on her back more than her feet, it's you. You shouldn't talk about yourself that way, sweetie." Sunshine threw the barb with accuracy. Raegan reached out and slapped Sunshine across the face before Drake could pull Sunshine out of harm's way. He didn't think Raegan would take the chance, but he was wrong. Again.

"That was your one," he heard Sunshine say as she lunged at Raegan and punched her in the nose. Raegan crumpled to the ground, and Sunshine jumped on top of her. He heard her grunting with the effort to make every punch count. He saw that she got in a few good shots before Clint, the local cop he hadn't seen come in, came over to help him pull her off. She was small, but getting her off Raegan without hurting either of them was harder than he thought it would be.

He saw Raegan holding her nose as she ran out of the Badmoon with her head hung in embarrassment. The cop hadn't seen Raegan take the first swing, or hightail it out of there. Good thing she had ran out or Drake would be pushing the point with Clint to arrest Raegan instead. He hadn't wanted this scenario to happen, had tried to prevent it, but Raegan kept pushing at someone who wouldn't back down. He couldn't save her from her own mistake. Maybe Clint would go track her down later for leaving the scene.

"Crap, Clint," Sunshine griped at the cop. "You didn't let me get enough punches in for it to be worth any jail time."

"I told you the next time I caught you in a fight, I'd have to take you in. It isn't my choice. With this many witnesses, it's something I have to do." Clint frowned at her.

Drake watched as Clint tried to be gentle as he cuffed her wrists. He was an outstanding police officer and a good guy. Drake didn't have to worry about Sunshine in his custody.

"Can one of the girls ride with me in the back? I need someone to talk to." Sunshine batted her eyelashes at Clint, trying her best to appear innocent.

"Yeah, sure. Why not?" Clint conceded. "Y'all are used to going to jail together by now."

"Hey! This is only the third time, maybe fourth. Anyway who's counting?" Sunshine smiled with a demented twinkle in her eye.

Clint walked Sunshine to the exit and Drake fell in beside them. Brice and the girls were right behind. Sunshine got a standing ovation from all the women as she walked out.

Drake shook his head. He would have to tell Clint that Raegan took the first swing, because he knew Sunshine wasn't going to. She didn't give a rat's ass if she got in trouble or not, but he did, and her parents would.

"Alright, which of you are going in with her this time?" Clint questioned.

"It's my turn to go with her. Willow went last time." Belle shrugged.

"Willow and I are going to ride home with Bubba. He's coming to pick us up," Georgia said as she hugged Sunshine, and went back inside to wait for her husband.

Drake followed Clint to the car. "Sunshine, I'll follow y'all there and bail you out quick fast, and in a hurry. I can take y'all home afterwards."

"You better seeing as how I defended your honor as well as mine." Sunshine scowled at him from the back of the car.

"I can follow y'all and take Belle home. That way, y'all won't have to make an extra stop," Brice volunteered.

"No, no, that's okay, Brice. I'll ride with Sunshine and Drake. My house is on the way."

Drake glanced over to his brother. A scowl crossed Brice's face at being shot down for a ride. He thought it was a mite bit strange himself that Belle had declined a separate ride. Not that he minded taking her home.

"I'll talk to you tomorrow, Will. Love you. Thanks for the fun night," Sunshine yelled to Willow from the back of the car.

"It's always an adventure! Love you." Willow waved and walked back inside to wait with Georgia.

"We will talk later," Drake heard Sunshine murmur to Brice when he reached down and into the back of the cop car to give her a hug.

"I'll be lookin' forward to it," Brice answered with a smile, and walked to his truck.

Clint shut the door on Sunshine and Belle and turned to face Drake. "Why didn't you stop her from hitting that woman? You aren't the type to sit idle and let a woman get hit."

"Raegan slapped Sunshine first. I wasn't going to deny Sunshine the right to defend herself. You might've heard what was going on, but I don't think you saw that critical moment

40

that started the thing. Sunshine wouldn't have told you."

Clint nodded. "You're right, I didn't. Yep, she wouldn't have said anything. Never has been one for tattling unless it was on you."

"Damn, you're right. I shouldn't have told you that. She deserves multiple nights in jail for all the shit she's gotten me in trouble for over the years." Drake laughed.

"Follow me on to the jail, and you can pick her up there. No booking this time. I'll give her an official warning."

"Thanks, Clint. I appreciate it." He shook Clint's hand before the cop got into his car.

Drake patted the top of the trunk before they pulled off. That little slip of a woman was crazier than anyone he knew, and twice as fun. He walked over to his truck, his big boots echoing, and climbed up inside to follow them to the station. Hopefully it wouldn't take too long since they both had work in the morning. But what in the hell was he going to do about Sunshine?

# CHAPTER 5

# Conspiracies

From the back of the cop car, Belle and Sunshine carried on with Clint, catching up on Clint's family, and some of the gossip going around town. Sunshine and Belle had graduated a year behind Clint in high school. He was a good-looking man—six feet of muscle with dark caramel skin and light brown eyes. Clint was one of the finest men in town, but he only had eyes for his wife, even back in high school.

"How are the kids and wife?" Belle asked him.

"Growing like weeds and Trisha is doing good. She starts a job at the new OB/GYN office in town within a week. She is going to be the clinic's nurse practitioner."

"I had been wonderin' who the new doctor would hire. I'll make sure to switch my health records there." Sunshine was due to have her annual Pap smear.

"Me too. I don't care for my doctor, or her staff," Belle chimed in.

"Yeah, she would love that. It took her about a year longer to get out of school than most on account of havin' the kids. Now that she has a job lined up close to home, the kids and I are enjoying having her around more."

"I bet y'all do. Trisha worked hard to get to where she can

have more time with y'all. Tell her to call me. We need to catch up," Sunshine said.

The gravel crunched beneath the tires as they pulled into the parkin' lot of the county jail, and Clint opened the back door of the car for them. Sunshine rubbed her wrist as he took off the handcuffs.

"Freedom!" she yelled across the parking lot and pretended to make a break for it.

"Sunshine, get your ass back over here. I am not going to book you. Drake told me Raegan hit you first. It was self-defense, and given what that woman said, I don't blame you for hitting her. Everyone here knows you aren't…well, you know that word she called you," Clint said, anger lacing his voice. "I don't know what the hell Drake saw in that woman."

"Same thing all the men do," Sunshine said point-blank. "An open vagina and easy lay." She wasn't about to beat around the proverbial bush. One of the many reasons people either loved or couldn't stand her. Though truth be told, it bothered her that Drake had picked a woman akin to Raegan to spend his time with. He could do better.

"Guys, give him a break. He's male and y'all tend to think with one appendage," Belle said.

Drake's truck turned in, lights shining on the redbrick building behind them. His truck was something she allowed herself to lust after. He had bought himself a new steel-colored Dodge 3500 Laramie Longhorn edition, all blacked out. It was a badass truck. Drake got out, lumbering up to them as if he had all the time in the world, and smiled, same as the bird that got the worm.

"Speak of the devil, there he is," Sunshine snapped. Took

44

him long enough. She took in his rugged handsome looks. A cowboy devil underneath the shadows of the security lights is what he appeared to be. His bedroom eyes and rock-hard body tempted her in ways that were new and frightened her resolve. The cocky asshole.

"Hey, I came to get you. And why were y'all just talking about me? My greatness perhaps? My devastating good looks and how they cause women to fight?" Drake asked with a look that failed to resemble anything akin to humble.

"Clint, go ahead and book me. I'm gonna hit him," Sunshine pushed out through clenched teeth. Her eyes went squinty, her surefire look of danger.

"No, Drake, we were talkin' about the floozy that caused Sunshine to stomp a mud hole in her. I let her in on the fact you told me Raegan hit her first," Clint answered and stepped between them.

"Yeah, didn't your Momma tell you that if it's glowed green, don't touch it?" Sunshine asked, pointing her finger in Drake's direction.

"Hey, you watch it, miss priss. You were flirting with someone who glowed green."

"I was not flirtin' with him. He was flirtin' with me. I was about to tell him to back off when you showed up. Let's not forget that fact, you ass wipe." He had another thing comin' if he thought he was going to compare a quarter of a dance with some douche-canoe to him dating someone who needed a canoe full of douche.

"You need to get your ass in the truck so I can take y'all home. I will drop Belle off, and then me and you are going to have a nice, long talk about your manners or lack thereof," Drake told her while he gestured to Belle to get ready to run to the truck.

"Try and make me, big shot, and remember what happened last time you tried to make me do somethin' I didn't want to," Sunshine taunted him, sticking out her tongue. Drake reached out and grabbed her before she could react. He threw her over his shoulder, clamped down hard on her legs so she couldn't kick him, and bolted.

"Sorry, man. I gotta get her out of here before she gets violent," Drake yelled over his shoulder at Clint as he ran.

Sunshine's head bounced as he carried her across the parking lot. Son of a bitch. They were out of the station parkin' lot before Sunshine stopped sputtering. Damn it. They'd conspired against her. She was wedged in between them and couldn't reach the doors. She did what she could in a dire situation of mutiny. She tickled them both. First, she went after Belle. She'd let Drake dread what was coming. She stopped when she thought Belle had had enough. She didn't want either of them to have to sit in pee the rest of the way home.

"Don't do it, Sunshine. Let the good part of you win. Don't surrender to the dark forces," Drake told her with a solemn face. His curls were everywhere, making him look somewhat sweet and adorable. She cut him no slack. He horse-laughed, and about swerved off the road when she dug her tiny fingers between his ribs. After he swerved, she showed mercy and stopped. By then they were all laughing about their antics that night. She took in the fact that Hank Williams Jr. was on the radio, singing about all his rowdy friends. A perfect song after their night. God she couldn't imagine a more insane group of friends to have, but she loved them.

"I'm sorry, Sunshine. You would argue all night and take a swing at him if we didn't get you out of there," Belle announced with a slight smile.

"I'll forgive you on one condition. I want a peanut butter milkshake, and one of you has to make it for me." Sunshine waited for one of them to concede. She thought it sounded excellent. She pouted as they expected her to, but she wasn't mad. She was as amused as they were, but figured she should get something out of the deal.

"I'll make you a milkshake at your house, because I don't have a blender, and because you had a near encounter with jail. That unfortunate situation was something you shouldn't have been involved in," Drake said and patted her head as if she were a good dog.

Sunshine did what came natural: she bit him. Drake yelled out in surprise. She scowled at him with his pinky in her mouth. Belle doubled over in her seat laughing.

"You know she does that. Why did you pat her on the head?" Belle laughed harder at the astonished look on Drake's face.

If you had been around her long enough, you'd probably been bit. She had a set of jaws akin to a pit bull, and she made sure she used them to her advantage. Her parents tried breakin' her of it by biting her back, but she would only bite harder. She figured that they should have gathered then what type of stubborn woman would lie ahead.

"I'm sorry, Drake. In my defense you know better than to leave yourself open to attack. It's instinct." Sunshine tried to appear contrite. She hoped her slight pout and puppy-dog eyes would keep him from being too mad. She didn't want him to back out on that peanut butter milkshake.

"There will be repercussions for that. I'll still make you a milkshake, but later you will pay," Drake said with a mischievous glint in his steel-blue eyes.

"Okay, I gotcha." She tried to figure out why she felt a slight tingle at his words.

Sunshine admitted that she didn't want to get him worked up, or herself for that matter. She had to bite her tongue to keep from reminding him that she'd beaten him tonight. He might throw her out of the truck if she did that, and she didn't feel like walking home. She started twisting her hair, a habit she'd had since she was in diapers. It was the same as having a security blanket, except it was attached to your head.

"Y'all are worse than two bucks going at it butting heads. I don't understand how you have managed to stay friends this long without killing one another." Belle sounded exasperated.

Sunshine looked over to see Belle giving her a peculiar look. She realized then that she'd been lying all over Drake. It was a comfortable position, and she didn't give a rat's ass. She was exhausted. Drake wouldn't care; he was used to her mood swings. She'd have to grill Belle later about actin' strange when Brice showed up tonight. She wouldn't forget that detail.

"Alright, Belle, I'm going to slow down. Jump out, tuck, and roll." Drake chuckled at her non-amused look. "Kiddin'." He pulled in Belle's driveway and let her out at her door. As she was stepping out, Sunshine uncurled enough to say, "Night! Love you! Talk to you tomorrow!"

"Night, Sunshine. Love you too! I will call you sometime

tomorrow. Do not call and wake me up at the butt crack of dawn, no matter how many times I ask. I mean it," Belle warned, walking to her cute cottage of a house.

Belle's house looked akin to something in a fairy tale set back in the perfect backdrop of the woods. It was fitting because Belle reminded her of a fairy sometimes. Her home was sturdy but appeared delicate. Being situated in the middle of nowhere, it gave Belle the space she needed. Sunshine thought Belle was more aloof than her or Willow at times, but her looks could be deceiving.

Sunshine had enough sense to sound exasperated. "I call when I have a stroke of genius, thank you."

"Yeah. I remember the time you called to tell me about your dream about wolves raising you and you being a cannibal," Belle shouted over her shoulder as she unlocked her front door.

"That was an extreme circumstance. I needed consolin'," Sunshine yelled back before pouting. Sunshine had the curse of being an early riser, and therefore her friends were often cursed by it too. She thought everyone else should be up when she was.

"Night, Sunshine. Night, Drake. Thanks for busting us out of the slammer—well the parking lot of the slammer," Belle yelled as she went inside. Sunshine reached over and shut her door, then snuggled back up against Drake's side. Before they even pulled out of the driveway, she was dozing off.

Sunshine woke up when she heard the familiar crunch of gravel as they turned into her driveway. Leaning up, she stretched. She cast a defiant look at Drake. "I'm ready for my milkshake now." A grin spread from ear to ear. Her dark purple shirt had ridden up her stomach to show off a small stretch of

49

skin. Sunshine noticed that Drake noticed as she tugged it back in place.

"Drake, it's a stomach. You have seen it before. Now come inside and fix my milkshake. You promised." She hopped out of the truck and went crunching across the gravel.

She left the door open for him and swatted him on the butt as he walked through. Damn that was a firm ass. "Get in there, cowboy, and fix my milkshake. I want extra peanut butter!" She followed him to the kitchen and got down the blender for him. She left him to ramble around while she went to lie on the couch. She could hear him opening and shutting cabinet doors while he muttered and fussed about something. She got to thinking, which was dangerous, and started talking, which was worse.

"Why would you want to date Raegan?" Sunshine inquired. "She is pretty on the outside, but her attitude is shit." She heard him pause and looked up over the couch. Drake was staring at her with the strangest look on his face, and then he shrugged.

"I'm a man. I look at the outside first. It was what attracted me, but I found out quick she had a shitty personality. I care about the inside too, it just takes a bit longer to find out about that part."

The couch beckoned her back as she waited on him to finish the milkshake. She cracked open an eye and extended her hand to grab her treat. That first sip was heaven. Creamy peanut butter flowed over her tongue, her taste buds basking in the delicious delicacy. Drake sat and she plopped her feet in his lap, wiggling her toes. With luck, he might get the hint. He hadn't tickled her feet in years. She hoped he remembered what she wanted…

"Oh, yes! Thank you!" She groaned when he touched her feet.

50

She loved for her feet to be tickled. It felt delightful after being in boots all day. It didn't actually tickle her, but rather felt relaxing.

"Don't say it like that." Drake's voice sounded deeper than normal as he spoke to her.

"Okay, movin' on."

Sunshine snuggled back into her pillow and sipped on her milkshake. "This is the life. I got a man ticklin' my feet and a peanut butter milkshake in my hand. It doesn't get better than this." Sunshine sighed with contentment. She pulled her hair out from behind her neck and dropped it over the pillow.

Drake had sunk back into her couch. He sipped his own milkshake with one hand and tickled her feet with the other. He sure was pleasant to look at. She could admit that to herself. Those looks he was blessed with had been damning to an abundance of women over the years.

"Why don't you ever date?" Drake asked. Sunshine peeked open an eye and for once, thought about what to say before she spoke. She didn't know how much she wanted to reveal to him. "I do date. I try not to date around our neck of the woods. I know all the guys and grew up with them. I want someone who doesn't know everything about me; that way I might have a chance." She took a deep breath, deciding to reveal the ugliness she thought sometimes. "It's hard when no one wants to date you because they know you're a pain in the ass. No guy around here wants that challenge. I work a lot and am cow and horse mad. I still haven't forgiven you, by the way, for stealin' my bull." Sunshine shrugged. "I don't let people know when I date. I don't want them tellin' the guy all my sordid escapades. I'm not ashamed of who I am, and I love myself, but men have a hard time puttin' up with a big personality like mine."

"There isn't a thing wrong with you. It's the men, they aren't man enough for you."

She grinned at him. "Thank you. That's what I say too."

She had been told on many occasions she was too much. They'd say too much sass, too much personality, too much work, but to her, the men had too little patience. It often wasn't that she was too much, but that they weren't enough of any one thing. Screw the dating world.

"You know what?" he asked.

"What? Chicken squat?" she asked with a chuckle, pulling her hair around to play with it.

"Your feet smell rancid," he answered her, holding his nose. "Don't you ever get a pedicure? Hoofs belong on horses, not women." He pulled at her toes, popping them.

She shrieked. She hated for her toes to be pulled, so damn if he didn't have to pull them. She put her milkshake down for safety, jumped up as fast as a cat under a rocking chair, and came at him. She was on him like white on rice. She had him in a choke hold and was attached to his back before he could squirm away. He threw his hat off and rolled over onto the floor with her on his back, squishing her. Oh shit.

"Get off me, you big donkey ass, before you smother me to death." Sunshine started to panic. She hated being held down. One time one of her uncles held her down under the covers and farted on her when she was little. Ever since that day, being pinned terrified her.

"Shit, Sunshine, I'm sorry."

She laughed it off, trying her best not to sound terrified. Stupid irrational fear making her seem weak. "You can't help it, I am a chicken shit about it. Don't let word get out or I will smother you in your sleep. Come on, Drake." Sunshine nudged him with her arm. "I have got to go get into bed. Either you can crash in the guest room or go home. I am going to be dead in the morning as it is." Sunshine yawned. Drake got up and pulled her to her feet. She walked and got her milkshake off the coffee table and chugged, before heading back to lay on the couch.

"Alright, I'll see myself out." Drake walked through her foyer. The rustle of paper reached her ears.

"I heard you steal that candy, and don't you dare slam John Wayne. I'll see you later." She couldn't help but bark out a few orders from where she laid. The front door shut and his truck cranked as she listened to him head out.

Sunshine didn't think she could make it up the stairs. She twirled her hair as she drifted off. She hoped Momma didn't find out anytime soon about the bar brawl incident or her ears would be ringing for a week on the ideals of being a Southern Lady. Dread filled Sunshine's stomach at the thought. She'd only have to explain, then Momma would understand. It was getting Momma to calm down and listen that might be the hard part.

Her thoughts drifted to Drake and she smiled. He was such a good guy past all the goofiness, stubbornness, and craziness. She kinda wished she hadn't known him her entire life. She drifted off to sleep and dreamed of tall dark-headed cowboys with a Hollywood smile that made her weak in the knees.

# CHAPTER 6

## Hell in a Hand Basket

The night had seemed promising when he'd first walked through the Badmoon doors. He should've had an inkling that his intuition was wrong when he got pissed seeing Sunshine dance with another man, especially after he'd pulled her out of that other dick's grasp. He hadn't known what to think when Sunshine had laid her head on his chest and hadn't argued with him. That wasn't normal behavior for her. Maybe she was mellowing out as she was getting older. He didn't always realize how little of a thing she was, but man, tonight she had felt good in his arms.

He couldn't, and shouldn't, be thinking these thoughts about her. It seemed all kinds of wrong. They were best friends, practically kinfolk, given how close their parents were. But damn it if it hadn't felt right. Hell, she felt a lot more than right, and if she wasn't who she was, he wouldn't be going to bed alone. Conceited as that was, he could lay the charm on the opposite sex when he needed to.

The truck ride home with her hadn't helped matters. They'd rode around together innumerable times throughout the years. Tonight had been a different matter; she had him in knots. There'd been a touch of intimacy to the way her head leaned on his shoulder as she snuggled up to his arm. He could feel her curves up against him, and that had played havoc with his desires. She was beautiful, all that blond hair and an innocent look about her while she had slept.

He'd recognized her as a woman who was hot as hell, and that made him uncomfortable. Her shirt had rode up in the truck, exposing a hint of her stomach, and even though it was Sunshine's stomach, it'd turned him on. What in the hell was wrong with him? Why had this all of a sudden happened? What if he'd acted on his urges? His mind was as skittish as a jackrabbit as he tried not to dwell on the situation too much.

Drake walked around the side of the truck and headed up to his loft apartment in his parents' barn. He had paid to have the loft added when his Dad had decided to build a larger barn after a tornado had done enough damage to the old one for them to tear it down and start new. It had an open floor plan of around thirteen hundred square feet with the master suite being separate from the rest. He considered it a necessity to his happiness, being out of his parents' house, but still close enough to help them and their cattle business.

Drake wasn't shocked to see that Brice sat on the couch watching ESPN. "Hey, B. What are you doin' up here? I figured you'd be out reacquaintin' yourself with the female population of Moulton since our night came to an abrupt end." Drake walked by and ruffled his little brother's hair. Drake ignored the fact that he and his little brother were now only separated by two inches of height and twenty pounds of weight.

Brice shook his hair back into place. "Nah, thought I would hang out with my big brother for a while to remind myself of why I don't want to turn into an asshole."

Drake tossed his brother the bird as he headed to the bathroom to wash off the stale bar smell.

He glanced over at his brother still sprawled on the couch as he walked back into the living room after his shower. "You want somethin' to drink?"

"Bottle of water, if you have it."

He handed Brice a bottle as he kicked back in the recliner. "Did you stop in at Mom and Dad's to let them know you were coming over?"

"Yeah, I watched TV with them for a minute. When I couldn't go to sleep, I thought I would come out here and see if you were back."

"I stayed at Sunshine's for a bit. She wanted a peanut butter milkshake to soothe her problems."

Brice rolled his head over at him. "And you made her one. She's spoiled rotten as it is."

"Yep, that she is."

He hadn't minded the milkshake, but he had minded her thoughts about herself. He was a little pissed about the fact she had been keeping her dating life from him, but not surprised. They talked a good bit, and saw each other at least once a week, but they didn't talk about anything deep. Neither of them were the type to pour their soul out to another person, no matter how long they'd known them. The fact that she didn't want to date anyone that she had known a long time didn't sit well, but now wasn't the time to dwell on that shit. She had been open with him in the past about guys when he'd come out and asked her in a direct way, but tonight she looked a mix of forlorn and pissed as she sat there and told him about her dating woes. Hell, he knew half the guys in town wanted Sunshine. They were intimidated by her was all, but a man that was intimidated by Sunshine would never be good enough for her. She needed a challenge. A man that couldn't stand his ground and give her what she dished out wouldn't survive.

"Belle shot you down tonight." Drake watched his brother's shoulders tighten.

"Yes, she did. What of it?" Brice cut his eyes towards him.

"Nothing, just wondered if something had happened there."

"Nope. Night, Drake."

"Night, B." Drake pushed up from his recliner and went to catch a couple minutes of work and a few hours of shut-eye before having to get up earlier than the chickens to go check on his cattle. He suspected his Dad may know he was dabbling in registered cattle, but was letting him keep it to himself. Whatever the answer was, he was glad to know his Dad was respecting his privacy.

He had started out hoping to start his own herd, separate from his Dad's. It had been nothing to keep quiet, but then he started talking to Brice's best friend, Bishop. Bishop's family owned three registered stockyards in Mississippi and one in Tennessee. Bishop showed him the solid figures on registered cattle, and the possibilities of running a registered cattle sale.

A good line of genetics on paper made a significant difference in price point. He had thought about dabbling in registered stock off and on. His Dad had even mentioned it, but with them running the stockyard for beef cattle only, it didn't leave room for venturing out. He wanted to broach the subject of running a registered sale night at the stockyard, but he knew his Dad would be resistant to another iron in the fire.

He took a seat at his desk in the master bedroom. After staring at the computer screen for ten minutes, he decided he wouldn't be getting a damn bit of work done between cattle and Sunshine running rampant through his mind. He would get it done tomorrow.

After a restless night, Drake woke up Saturday morning two minutes before his alarm at 4:30. Today would be a struggle with only four and a half hours of sleep under his belt. He got dressed and kept his footsteps quiet as he passed by Brice asleep on the couch in the living room. He didn't want his brother tagging along for this morning's activities. He trusted Brice, but he didn't want him to feel torn about keeping a future business idea from their Dad.

The stairs creaked as he headed down them to check on his new bull. The one that he'd bought out from under Sunshine. It was out in the catch lot beside the barn. He wouldn't move him out to the bull's new home until after Drake found out if his herd had been chosen by a buyer Bishop had lined up. No sense in making his Dad any more suspicious than he already was about his expensive purchase. Hell, he had wondered what Sunshine wanted with a bull that expensive himself, but if she'd found out he was coming up for sale, she would have read up on his genetics. Flipping him for a better price at the registered sale across the state line in Tennessee would have been a quick and tidy profit for her.

He strode out to the catch lot to look over the bull that caused Sunshine to want to put his head on her wall. The security light shined against his black coat. He was a fine piece of lean beef. Drake watched as he walked at a leisurely pace around the catch pen towards him. No sign of a pot gut on him, had a wide ass, and muscles gleamed across his frame. His future offspring would be dandies.

If the future heifers he produced had asses like that, he would be sitting pretty. He preferred to have a bull that shot more female sperm than male. He didn't want to have to steer as many. Took some of the work off him if there were more heifers.

The bull stood in front of him as a soft snort echoed against the light buzz that filled the air. He pulled out his phone to see that Bishop had texted him and asked to meet for breakfast at the Swine and Dine. He rubbed his hand along the bull's back before heading towards his truck. The bull remained calm as a cucumber. Wild ass genes belonged in wild asses, not bulls.

Wouldn't take him long to drive, maybe ten minutes. He would have preferred the Waffle House, but the closest one would have been Muscle Shoals or Decatur. He had too much to do that day to drive twenty to thirty minutes down the road. He loved the Swine and Dine's food, but he wanted something different on occasion.

Drake walked through the doors a few minutes later and was greeted by the smell of bacon grease. His mouth watered. He was hungrier than he'd thought. The usual crowd of older gentlemen sat at the long table in the back corner. His Dad would be joining those older gentlemen within an hour. He gave them a cordial wave and headed to the opposite end of the restaurant, taking a corner booth. It was best if he and Bishop were gone before his Dad got there and started questioning. Luck was on his side. Bishop walked in and sat down in front of him not a minute later.

"How's it hanging?" Bishop asked as he shook his hand across the table.

"Long and strong." Drake grabbed his hand and shook harder than necessary.

"Dickhead." Bishop pulled his hand back and flipped him the bird.

"Takes one to know one." Drake shot one back at him. He waved at the waitress to let her know they were ready. She was one of his favorites.

"Hey, Mrs. Margret. I'll have my usual. And might I say you look beautiful this morning? You tell Dale I'll take you off his hands any day." He smiled at her. The gray-haired granny swatted his arm at his flirting.

"And for you?" Mrs. Margret turned to Bishop.

"I'll have whatever he is having, and may I say I would treat you much better than Drake here ever would."

"The two of you need to behave," she scolded them, her cheeks flushing as she rushed off to send their order back to the cooks.

"Now that the pleasantries are aside, how's business looking?" Drake leaned back against the booth as he waited for Bishop to answer. Bishop's carefree attitude changed before Drake's eyes. The smartass cut up was replaced by the businessman.

"There is your herd, and one other that Mr. Alexander is looking at. Both herds are in luck because he doesn't want quantity as much as he wants excellent genetics, and his cattle coming with papers. You do have an edge for having a greater quantity than the other."

"A fifty-fifty chance or better. I like those odds."

"You talk to your Dad about adding a registered sale night?"

"No, Brice coming back is a big change as it is. If I start talking about adding another night now, he may have a heart attack."

"If you want registered buyers coming to y'all's stockyard, you are gonna have to grow your registered herd's numbers by one hundred or better, two hundred and fifty head of cattle within the next two to three years. You are also gonna have to have a marketing strategy."

"Shit fire. Bishop, are you trying your best to make me go broke so you can take over my job at the stockyard? Because it sounds as if you want me to go ass up." Drake scowled at his friend. He'd spent a pretty penny as it was. Damn, he made good money, but buying that many cattle at once was out of the question.

"Hell no. I'd go with some good breeder cows, and then you could buy the embryos to have them artificially inseminated. They'd just be carrying the calves, and you would have the genetics you wanted without having the high cost up front. You've got some damn good quality, but that would be a cheaper alternative to buying the amount of registered head you would need."

"For the amount of money I've been putting into these cattle, they need to be shitting gold turds. The idea to do artificial insemination has some merit, and one I've considered before. I'd be able to do that with the unregistered herd I have now and have the numbers sooner rather than later. This was in part your idea. If it doesn't work out, I'm movin' in with you." Drake ran numbers through his head and tried to continue to listen to Bishop.

"I heard about your recent purchase. That will go a long way towards helping your chances of selling semen, and his offspring. You got a hell of a steal on that bull. I'd have paid four times that for his genetics, so be glad no one around here knows his true value. If I'd have been there, I'd have driven the price up on you for the hell of it," Bishop told him as he shoveled in more eggs.

"Sunshine tried to buy him, but I beat her to him." Drake gave Bishop a grin. He hated to break her heart, but business was business.

"Oh, did she?" Bishop mumbled as he shoved his bacon into his mouth.

"Hey, did you find a house here yet?"

"Hell no. I can't find shit with the land that I want. I don't have the time to build, but that may be what it comes down to." Bishop frowned at his phone and took a swig of tea.

"You need to talk to my friend Willow Sullivan. She is one hell of a real estate agent. She'll find what you want and for a good price."

"Good price, and what I want? Sounds excellent to me. Shoot me her information." Bishop glanced back up at him and put his phone away. Drake had a hard time remembering Bishop wasn't as dumb as he tried to make some folks think.

"Why you want to move here of all places, and not to Mississippi, closer to your family, I don't understand, but it'll be good for the stockyard having you consult. The female population may take a hit with heartbreaks, but I'll enjoy having your ugly-ass kisser around." Drake pointed over his shoulder at a new waitress he noticed had been eyeing them both. He wasn't interested, but maybe Bishop was. He watched as Bishop saw who he had gestured towards and shot her a wink.

"Keep it in your pants till I leave. I don't want to see your pathetic excuse for flirting."

"You don't have to flirt when you look this good, and mini Bishop ain't a mini. Word of his greatness tends to transcend state lines." Bishop gestured to his face and body before pointing to his crotch with the last of his sentence.

"And with that exaggerated pile of bullshit, I believe I'll leave." Drake threw his money down on the table, enough for his breakfast plus a tip for Mrs. Margret.

"Hey, Drake," Bishop called before he went out the door.

Drake walked back to the table. "Did I forget something?"

"Business is business. You and the other person will not get any preferential treatment or be chosen based on friendship."

Drake nodded his head at him. "I'd expect nothing more or less. I'm the same way, Bishop. You forget I help run a thriving business. We may be friends, but don't let this handsome face make you forget I can be cut throat." Before Drake could turn away, Bishop had a final caution for him.

"I can't tell you who's up against you for the contract, but I will say be careful who you talk to about this. I'd keep it to myself."

# CHAPTER 7

# The Shirt Off Your Back

Sunshine woke up on her couch the following morning as her alarm clock blared Tracy Byrd's, "Too much fun."

"Ugh, no, not yet," Sunshine groaned. She rolled over and discovered she was still in last night's clothes and makeup, and it tasted like a cat had shit in her mouth. She managed her way up the stairs without incident.

"Damn it!" Her yell echoed around the room. There was an ornate mahogany bed with a cream linen duvet taking up the center of the room, and damned if she didn't stumble into it and stomp her toe on the big, beautiful bastard of a bed's post. She sat down on the chest at the end of the bed as she held her toe, cussin'. She took a deep breath and got up. She took care to put the slightest amount of pressure she could on her toe as she walked on through to the door that led to the bathroom.

The heated tile floor felt great on her sore toe. Her huge bathtub, big enough to fit four people, beckoned to her. She passed it up for the walk-in shower stall with multiple jets. She took a seat on the shower bench and showered off. The hot water eased her aches.

She gazed over at her vanity. It was void of most anything. She didn't want her stuff all over the counters. Everything had a place in the cabinets, tucked away nice and neat. She had decided to put two separate vanities, one shorter and one taller, for the extreme, remote possibility of marriage. She had fine-detailed her home for the past two and half years, but it was worth every minute and every cent.

After her quick shower, the drawers to her dresser were pulled open and shoved closed with haste. She threw her clothes on in record time and was out the door. She stepped out onto her wraparound porch and looked out at her pasture and the scattered trees. As far as she was concerned, she lived in paradise, but it didn't run on looks. She headed to her other home.

The barn was a large structure that was made, in part, from old barn wood she and her Dad had salvaged. Its big red doors opened up into an eight-stall interior, a birthing stall, a tack room to the left with a fridge, and a loft up top. Big wooden beams jutted overhead with lights for those late nights. The work in this haven was relaxed, pleasurable, and fun.

Bo jumped up on her leg as soon as she opened the big wooden doors. "There's my stud muffin." She hugged the sweet dog and petted his slick brown coat for a short while. Bo continued to wag his nub of a tail all around her feet as she walked over to her love, Deacon. He was a beautiful Carmella quarter horse gelding—sixteen hands high, solid muscle, and the most loving temperament there was.

Sunshine ran her hand across his nose. "Not today, boy. I need to take Sugar Baby out for some exercise." He whinnied at her as if he understood and licked her hand in forgiveness. "I wish there were men that were as easy to please as you two are," she murmured to her boys.

She pulled her ponytail holder off her arm and pulled back her hair. It was time to get to work, with a slight smile on her face, she started mucking the stalls and putting out hay. She fed Deacon, and then headed out to her truck and horse trailer. The trailer and truck were hitched up and ready to go.

Daddy and Momma must have come over last night and done that for her. It was hard for Sunshine to back up and get the goose neck in line. For some odd reason Sunshine had never quite got the hang of backing up. Her Momma said it was because she was too busy barreling ahead in life to worry about going backwards. Sunshine chose to take that as a compliment.

She would have ridden to her parents' place, but she might need her tools in the back of the truck. Never knew when you would need extra barbwire or fence post. She was also going out to Moonshine at her first opportunity and she might need the supplies for then.

Her phone vibrated. It was a funny meme from Drake. She rolled her eyes, but had to laugh. His sense of humor got to her funny bone. He could be such a dork sometimes.

Drake had looked damned good yesterday, causing her to have an inkling of something she shouldn't with one of her best friends. Sunshine, on occasion, had a sighting of those emotions for him here and there, but they had never hit her with the yearning they had during recent events. They didn't let each other get under the other's skin often. Maybe it was from all the pent-up anger of him getting that dang bull she wanted? Maybe she was stressed from keeping the secret about Moonshine?

She patted her horse as she walked. "Sugar, it's gonna be a

long mornin' of workin'." She had to come home and get out to Moonshine this afternoon. She wouldn't take Sugar for that.

She jumped in the truck and headed towards her parents' place. As she turned out on the road, she noticed it was only 6:15 a.m., according to her clock. That meant she would be right on time. They lived down the same road, but she still had to get the horse unloaded and saddled.

Sunshine pulled up in her parents' driveway, passing over the metal bars in the ground at the start of the drive and between the fences on each side that lined the driveway, keeping the cattle in. She saw her parents' house come into view, a two-story white farmhouse that had been filled with love and laughter, and on occasion, yelling between her and her Momma. She pulled up to the side of the house by the barn and hopped down onto the gravel. She sluggishly went up the porch and walked through the door into the kitchen.

Sunshine screamed and slapped a hand over her eyes. "What in the hell!? Can't you two keep your hands off one another and keep it in your pants? It shouldn't be a surprise that I was goin' to be comin' over this mornin'. Remember me? Your only child? I came here to help, but now I can't because I'm blind. Gag a maggot." Disgust crawled up into her belly. They broke apart being the guilty culprits they were. Her Mom's hair was disheveled and out of place and she still had on her pajamas. Oh hell no. She was not going down that thought road. She never had gotten use to their displays of affection. They grossed her out. She got here by the stork and that's what she wanted everyone to let her believe.

"Sunshine," her Momma said disapprovingly, with one hand

on her hip as the other scrambled eggs in a skillet. "When are you gonna quit actin' like a baby about your Daddy and me kissin'? You are twenty-six years old. Act like it!"

"That's right, Sunshine. You should be happy your Momma and I still got it," Sunshine's Daddy pronounced with a chuckle. Sunshine gave a delicate sniff. "Well, y'all caught me off guard. All I came in here for was some coffee and breakfast, not a show."

"Here is your scrambled egg, mushroom, cheese, and bacon wrap. You can eat while you ride." Her Momma threw her breakfast over the table. Thank goodness she had wrapped it in tin foil. Sunshine snagged it out of the air and walked over to the counter to fill up a travel mug of coffee.

"Um, smells better than angel farts." Bliss went through her system as she stood over the coffeepot, sniffing the aroma. She poured her some up and added more creamer than one cow put out. She got her cup ready and turned to her captive audience. "Come on, old man, let's get started so we can get'er done."

"You got you a hot date tonight, darlin'?" her Daddy asked as he kissed her Momma on the cheek and followed her out the screen door.

Sunshine shrugged with a smile on her face as they walked out. She thought she would let her mother stew on that bit of information for a while. The only plan she had was to go to Moonshine and have the girls over. Sunshine felt a twinge of guilt and regret at not telling her parents about her business venture. She quieted that emotion.

She and her Daddy stepped off the porch and headed to unhook the trailer from the truck. They would take Sunshine's truck with them since it was already loaded up with tools. "You know she's in there callin' Claire right now?" Sunshine asked her Dad, exasperated.

"Yeah, I'm sure she is. They tell each other everything."

She glanced around for a second and smiled up at him. "She is gonna be pissed when she finds out I misled her." Her Dad's chuckle reached her ears.

Sunshine went and saddled up Sugar, while her Daddy got a few things together. He had worked hard all his life. Raising cattle and owning his own construction company. One of his crews had helped build her home, but she had tried her best to keep him out of the house for the past month.

Sunshine led Sugar Baby through the gate. Sugar Baby had all the pastures memorized by heart, so Sunshine let her take the lead while she sat back and rode. She surveyed the land as they went. Scattered trees, cows and calves, a pond: things she had always seen around her, but she'd never lost her awe of them. She loved being out, working with her Dad. Sunshine was glad she also made a good living out of it. She was praying her investment in Moonshine would pay off sooner rather than later, otherwise she may have to go to her parents and ask for a loan. Damn that to hell. She couldn't and wouldn't think that way.

The absence of the sound of her Dad's engine pulled her out of her sleepy daze. Her Daddy had pulled a good way in front. "Let's go, Sugar." Sunshine clicked to her. Sugar Baby took off at a slow gallop. Sunshine urged her into a faster pace. She knew her Daddy's horse, Cartwright, which was tied on to her horse, wouldn't have a problem keeping up.

They both got to the corner of the fence at about the same time. "You in la-la land, cowgirl? You fell a ways behind there for a minute." Sunshine climbed down off Sugar. Feeling the guilt pull at her heart.

"Yeah, I guess I am. Stayed out too late last night is all."

"Well, let's get started on this fence. Looks as if there are at least two strands of barbwire broken, and we need to replace twelve or more of these fence posts in this section alone." There was no more talk, just the occasional curse or grunt. Sunshine enjoyed the peace and time alone with her Dad and her thoughts.

Sunshine's Daddy got through pulling a piece of barbwire tight, while she nailed it into a post. She turned and looked up to see someone galloping through the pasture. She could tell he was big, brawny, tan, and looked fine in the saddle. He had an amazing horse beneath him that carried him across the pasture as if he wasn't there. Which was a feat since he was six foot five inches tall and weighed at least two hundred and forty pounds.

Drake pulled Chief's reins to a quick stop in front of Sunshine. She didn't blink an eye, walked up, gave Chief a pat on the nose and then a kiss. She turned to Drake and growled her words at him. "You could have ran me over, numb nuts."

Drake rolled his eyes. "You would have moved if you thought that. Chief worships the ground you walk on for some reason no one knows. He would never hurt a hair on your head."

"That may be true, but that's not the point. He might have not stopped," she argued for the sake of arguing.

"My my, didn't you wake up on the wrong side of the saddle this morning," Drake drawled out.

"Shut your pie hole. What did you ride out here for anyway?" She wondered if maybe he came to hang out with her. She fancied that idea more than she would care to admit.

71

"Mom called and told me y'all may need some help," Drake said as he was climbing off his saddle. Sunshine watched as his jeans tightened on his butt. Whew, was it getting hotter out here? You could fry an egg on that ass. She meant the ground—yeah, the ground. Sunshine fanned herself. Her slowed mental process caught back up to what he said, and her bubble popped like a fart out of a tight ass.

"Thanks, Drake, another hand is always appreciated. How about you and Sunshine finish this up, and I'll go ride the rest of the fence to make sure there isn't anywhere else to patch?"

"That's fine, Mac. You go on. Me and Sunshine will be done with this in no time, so long as she doesn't murder me with the mood she's in." Drake cast a quick grin over at her.

Sunshine crossed her arms, glared at both of them, and stalked over to start stringing more barbwire.

"We really should have beat her more as a child." Mac sighed, saying it loud enough for her to hear.

Drake laughed. "You honestly think that would have helped?"

"Maybe, she might not have turned out as ornery as an old mule. You think it's too late?"

"Yes, sir. I would have to say it is. There is no hope for her, I'm afraid." Drake shook his head.

"Would one of you go to the house and get my waders?" Sunshine sneered. "The shit out here is gettin' deep." They rolled their eyes at her but their grins stayed in place.

"Alright, you old jacks, let's get to work and quit shootin' the shit," she demanded, shooing them with her hands. Mac waved bye and got up on his horse to go on his way.

Drake pulled on his gloves. "What do you need me to do?"

72

"That list is too long to even begin to discuss, but for right now, hand me that hammer and pliers," she said as he watched her pull the wire tight to the post.

Sunshine got the barbwire strung up on one row while Drake held the wire tight. When they got through with that strand, she sashayed to the truck and stripped her tank top off. She had her sports bra on underneath. She considered herself decent enough. Whew, she should have put her shorts on. The Alabama humidity was smothering her. Either that or Drake's presence. His white tee was plastered to him already from the sweat. It was a shame to keep that all covered up.

Drake scowled at her. "Put your shirt back on."

"I have always worked without a shirt out here, and there ain't anyone in sight but you." Sunshine continued pulling barbwire while he nailed it in place to a post. She saw the way his eyes raked over her body. She wasn't fooling herself either. She enjoyed the way he looked at her. He had made things go tingle that shouldn't. Her heart stuttered when he stripped his own shirt off and threw it near the truck.

Sunshine tried looking at what she was doing, but behind her glasses, she was eating up the sight of his chest and back. Damn but that was Grade A prime meat right there. Drake was muscled everywhere. She really could lick…um no. No, she couldn't and wouldn't go there. *Daisies, horses, cows,* she thought over and over. Trying not to imagine the things she could be doing with a shirtless Drake. She wanted to shove him on his back and have her way with him in this moment of lunacy. Tension and confusion rushed through her system, warring with one another. Sanity won when she remembered her Daddy was still somewhere in the pasture.

"Did your Momma and Daddy ask you anything about last night?" Drake grunted as he pulled at a rotten post.

"Naw, they haven't said anything yet, but it's too much to hope that they won't find out at all." Sunshine pulled at a stubborn strand. "I know once they know what she said they won't care, but I hate gettin' lectured on the finer points of bein' a Southern Lady. Then they will want to know if I won, after the fact."

"Yep, you bet they will, cause your Momma is a tad bloodthirsty."

"Momma does tend to be."

The conversation came to a stall, except for when she asked for a tool, or Drake spat out a curse when he hit his finger, or she gave a yelp when she stabbed herself on a barb.

"Let's go ride around and look over the herd," she said, breaking the silence as she jumped on Sugar Baby's back and headed off.

"That heifer is about ready to be thrown out there with the big boys."

She followed Drake's outstretched finger to the heifer in question. "Yeah, it's about time to put her out there to be breed, but Daddy's worried about her since she was a preemie. He said we might hold her out for a little longer than usual.

"If you don't mind helpin' me get these calves separated, I'd appreciate it." She glanced in Drake's direction. The sooner she got done here, the sooner she could get on her way to Moonshine.

"Hell no, this is the fun part of what we do." He grinned and clucked at Chief.

Her Dad rode up when she had shut the gate on the last calf.

"All the other fences look good. If y'all already got all of them sorted that need to go to Drake and to the sale, then I am going to head to the house."

"Okay, Daddy, we will be there in a bit. We have to go back to the truck and bring in the horses."

"Sunshine, you get on and ride with Drake. I'll take Sugar to the house and rub her down. Y'all can bring back the truck and won't have to worry about two horses," Mac directed them.

Sunshine looked over at Drake and he shrugged.

"Okay, don't feed her too much sweet feed."

"I would never do that," Mac said.

Drake didn't slow Chief when he passed the truck. She called out to him. "Where we headed?" Butterflies went crazy in her stomach when she saw that devilish smile and the mischievous look in those eyes when he turned to look at her. Damn she was in trouble.

"The blue hole."

# CHAPTER 8

# Hard Work Pays Off

He slowed Chief to a walk while they rode the woody trail down to the swimming hole. The trees were thick and green and the squirrels were going crazy at being disturbed, jumping from limb to limb above their heads. They passed big oak trees and pines as they made their way further through the woods. Drake felt Sunshine snuggle up to him, and his dick came to attention. There went his peaceful state of mind.

Her breasts were pushed up against him, and her arms were around his stomach. It was a sweet torture. If he could only move her hands down a little lower and maybe get some relief. Hell yeah, he would settle for a hand job, as if he was back in high school again. He had condemned Sunshine. He thought there was a flicker of interest in her eyes, be damned the consequences of knowing for sure. This chemistry he felt for her was gonna explode, and he had every intention of taking her down with him.

He pulled Chief to a stop at the swimming hole a few moments later. It was a quiet place back in the woods. The water was a blue so pigmented, it appeared fake. A few rocks jutted up around it, perfect for jumping, and a large willow tree hung out over the water a little piece. It used to be someone's home way back when, but now the rock chimney was the only structure left standing over about fifty yards from it.

Tension began to build in Drake's gut. Something was simmering beneath the surface of their friendship. He wouldn't be able to step back from what it was, or forget, once he got a taste of it. That he knew for sure. He could feel her hands slide over his muscles when Chief took a step. He restrained himself from moving her around to sit in front of him.

He felt her slide off the side of his horse and followed her. She walked over to the hole and stripped off her boots. He swallowed his tongue when she bent over and took her socks off and shimmied out of her pants. As she dropped them to the ground, he was sad to find she hadn't taken off her panties. They were red with polka dots. He was happy to see that they didn't cover much. She turned and caught him looking. He didn't give a damn if she saw him appreciating her.

He threw his hat up on the saddle horn and went to undo his own pants. He stopped before pulling them down. "Sunshine, you want to continue to look, or are you going to turn around?"

"Duck, are you getting shy on me? I remember not too many years back hearing some talk about you gettin' on the rock over there and shakin' your white ass all around for everyone to see."

"That was more than a few years ago, about thirteen if I do recall. Jealous that you didn't get to see this fine ass that day? Even back then, you know I looked sexy. And hell no, I'm not shy. I wanted to give you a chance to look away, but please continue."

He took her heated look as approval. He slipped his boots off and pulled down his pants. He tried to turn away from her enough that she didn't get a full-frontal view of the Duke in all his glory. He found it ironic that she named her wooden door John Wayne, and well, he named something else that stayed wooden the Duke. She would be pissed off if she ever found that out. He slipped his pants off the rest of the way and took a running go at Sunshine.

"Drake! Don't!" Sunshine yelled as he scooped her up and jumped into the pond. She screamed death and appendage threats all the way till he pulled her under.

"Why? I was gonna jump in. I didn't need you to throw me in." Sunshine was shooting spears at him with her eyes. She treaded water a few feet from him. Still within his reach.

"I thought it would bring back old memories." Drake grinned from ear to ear. He wanted to touch her, had since she'd stripped her shirt off that morning. When she had been crouched down there working earlier, sweat had glistened on her chest and ran between her breasts. All he could think about was where it was headed, and that he'd wanted to follow it with his tongue.

"Thank you, your selflessness knows no bounds. I had forgotten what an ass you are in the last thirty minutes." She rolled on her back, ignoring him, and floated around in the water.

Drake had other plans in store. He pounced on Sunshine and wrestled and rolled around with her. He continued to joke around till he thought she may be getting tired, and he was getting turned on. A graze against a thigh, a caress between the legs, and a small grope here and there. He felt himself slipping and called a truce to get things in check.

Drake watched her as she went back to floating. She looked peaceful and at ease. Neither of those he wanted her to be feeling.

He debated whether to swim over pick her up and kiss her or dunk her under and let her attack him again. Either one was a win for him. A slight movement on the bank caught his eye. Drake's body went cold. A copperhead glided into the water's edge towards her.

"Sunshine, do not move quickly, but make slow gentle movements and head this way." He tried to speak in a calm manner, not wanting to spook her. His body vibrated with tension as he made his way towards her.

"Drake, what are you talking about? I am enjoying this moment right now." She sounded exasperated.

"If you want to enjoy any more of these moments, you need to do as I say right now." He'd be damned if any snake but the one between his legs was gonna ruin her.

"Drake, what is it?" Sunshine sounded worried as she started paddling towards him. She turned and looked behind her to see the snake making its way towards them. Her eyes were as big as saucers when she turned to look at him.

"Oh Lord. Oh Lord. Don't let me die. I don't want to die in my underwear. Momma and Daddy will be embarrassed if the EMS have to pick me up half-naked."

"Relax, stay relaxed. I have the gun over there strapped to the saddle. Once we get to it, I will kill it, okay? We have to swim back to shore and try not to aggravate it," Drake told her as he pulled her up close to swim beside him. He swam backwards on the way to the bank, keeping an eye on it. Once his feet could reach bottom, he pulled her out of the water.

Drake ran up to Chief, grabbed the gun, went back to the edge, and blew the snake clear out of the water. After he went over and made sure it was dead, he looked over at Sunshine. "You alright?"

"Yeah, I'm fine, give me a minute. I'll work up the nerve to get back in." She turned her back towards him and faced the water.

Drake took in the sight she presented: an ass that was made for him to grab, hair dripping wet. She looked like every man's fantasy come true sanding there on the bank. Hell, she looked like his fantasies come to life. He wanted her, no sense in denying it.

"Come over here," Drake demanded as he pulled her into his arms. He picked her up and toted her out into the water. He had been wanting her in his arms, but hell, he didn't want such drastic circumstances. He pulled her closer as he waded out deeper. He couldn't believe the little spitfire was allowing him to hold her. She wasn't scared of anything—except spiders. She was terrified of those. He guessed a snake would bother anyone when it was venomous.

He was chest to chest, face to face, with Sunshine, her legs around his waist. Drake was in shock, but not so much that he didn't know what to do with her if he had the chance.

"Thank you for handling the situation."

He had never seen this softer, sexy side of her. She was always rough and tough, softness was not her cup of tea. Drake enjoyed this side. He looked into her eyes and noticed they'd turned green since they'd been at the pond.

"Your eyes have changed colors."

"They do that when I'm outside for long periods of time or feeling strong emotions."

He nodded his head. He surmised he was experiencing same emotions at the moment.

When Sunshine moved her arms, Drake figured she would pull away. He was relieved when she moved them up around his neck, and then things down below decided to get even harder. She laid her head on his chest as he held her. The touching her and having her be quiet was nice. He chuckled.

"What are you laughing at?"

He looked down at her, and she looked adorable with her eyebrows crinkled in the middle and her lips pouty. He couldn't restrain himself any longer. He leaned down and caught her lips with his. She opened in welcome and Drake took control. He kissed her in a way that let her know what he wanted to do with her. He devoured her mouth, tasting a heaven with her that he knew was going to damn them to hell. He wouldn't mind the burn for the chance to taste more of the sweetest honey he'd ever had his tongue in.

Sunshine moaned into his mouth as he stroked his tongue against hers. He grinded against her as she wrapped her legs tighter around his waist and squirmed to get closer. Her body was letting him know how much she wanted what he was giving.

Drake pulled back before he got any more carried away and ripped those thin panties off to get what he wanted. He was more turned on than he'd ever been and was ready to say the hell with it and take her in the damn swimming hole. That little moan of hers about put him over the edge. Damn woman was going to give him blue balls from hell.

She looked up at him and demanded, "Why did you stop? I'm surprised to say I was enjoying that."

"Cause if I didn't, there would have been other parts of your body I would have been kissing before too much longer." He smirked down at her. He'd bet she was demanding in bed and worth every minute of it. He hoped to find out before long, but now he'd have to sit back and wait till all this sunk in for a few days. Let her simmer over, think about the possibilities of what he could do to her. Then he would be ready to start laying the groundwork for getting her into his bed. He and Sunshine had been friends forever. He reasoned they could survive having sex.

"The heck you would have. I wouldn't have let it go that far," Sunshine snarled at him. She tried to wiggle down out of his grasp, but ran into his dick in the process. He watched as she sat still for a minute after she'd figured out what she was up against. Her shock showed across her face. He moved her off his body and set her feet down on the bottom. He watched as she sloshed towards the bank.

"Get your butt out and let's go. I've wasted enough time out here screwin' around with you." She jerked her clothes on as she was yelling at him from the shore.

"Darlin', unless you want to get acquainted with a part of my anatomy that wants to be acquainted with you, I am going to sit here and cool off." He shot her a big smile.

"It ain't nothing I haven't seen before—or felt all too recently. I think I'll survive the shock." He kept in shape and knew most women appreciated the way he looked both in and out of clothes. Drake felt even more cocky than normal as he saw Sunshine trying not to look at him but failing. He walked over to Chief and dropped his drawers; he threw them at her feet.

Drake figured she had enough of a look as he pulled his pants up. Commando wasn't going to be comfortable, but it was a damn sight better than riding in wet underwear. He pulled his boots on and swung up on the back of his horse. Sunshine came over and climbed up behind him. He maneuvered Chief up the trail, back towards the truck, carrying a shitload of sexual tension with him.

"We have supper together tomorrow. Please act normal and don't be mooning after me," she said as she wrapped her arms around his waist tighter as Chief climbed an embankment.

"What in the hell? Moon after you? Act normal?" Drake turned his head to see if she was serious.

"Yes, all those things. I know I am a fabulous kisser, but I don't want you gettin' the wrong impression. You saved me from a snake and that kiss was a thank-you."

"You enjoyed that kiss as much as I did. Don't feed me that line of bullshit," he snapped at her. He turned halfway in his saddle and pulled her to sit across his lap.

"I've kissed a lot of guys, it isn't a big deal. I don't want you gettin' your hopes up." Sunshine patted his chest in a patronizing manner and shook her head at him. He wanted to throw her off the horse.

"Getting my hopes up? You're crazy as hell. You're the one whose hopes are getting up about me. I'm a damn stud, woman. Who all have you been kissing?" Drake drew Chief to a stop.

"Are you jealous, Drake? Can't handle the thought of me kissin' another man? That's too bad. I have a hot date tonight. You're a stud, alright. Whew. Oh Drake, hold me back, I can't keep my hands off you." He grinned as she threw her arm to her forehead and pretended to be in pain.

"Why you little piece of work." He jerked her up closer to him. Running his fingers through her hair, he pulled her head up to get a better angle and kissed her—well more so ravished her mouth. This kiss was even better than the last one. It was hot and fiery. There was no give, only a battle of wills and want. He gave and she took and then gave just as much. There was no finesse, but the wild passion that had been pent up for years.

When she started leaning against him and his hands started wandering, Drake knew it was time to stop. He needed to regain control of the situation. They were on the back of his horse; poor Chief was gonna be scarred for life.

"Don't tell me that was any other kiss. You remember that tonight whenever you're out."

"It was nice, Drake, but don't pat yourself on the back too much. It wasn't the best I've ever had."

He didn't bother responding as he picked her up and sat her in a more comfortable position in front of him. He clicked at Chief and they started back towards the house. Her riding in front of him was painful, but in a good way. He had to make sure he didn't rub up against her on purpose. Hell, who was he kidding, he was going to take full advantage of the situation. He would dry hump her ass like the horny man he was if she would let him.

"You have anything planned for tonight?" she asked.

"Yep." Drake sat behind her stone-faced, unwilling to give anything away.

"What kind of plans? Maybe bow fishing, snipe hunting, or rolling yards? All of the above, or none of the above?"

"No, we ain't in high school anymore." Drake tried to keep a straight face. "I am more mature now. I'm going to the titty bar."

Sunshine's face was priceless. Her mouth dropped open, and

she looked akin to a largemouth bass gulping for air.

"I'm kidding. I have some lady company comin' by to watch the Alabama game tonight." Drake tried to get a rise out of her. He was lying through his teeth. He planned on staying at home and watching the game with Brice.

"Oh okay, maybe we can all go on a double date sometime."

"What you cookin' for supper tomorrow?" He changed the subject. It would be a cold day in hell before he went on a double date and watched Sunshine be all over another man.

"Pot roast, mashed potatoes, corn on the cob, and sweet corn bread."

"You're talkin' my language, sweetheart." He patted her belly since he couldn't get to his. He left his hand there, enjoying the way they felt together.

"Anything to do with food is talking your language. I'm surprised you're not as big as a cow."

"Yeah, not everyone gets to look this good. It is hard being as sexy as me." He sighed and pulled Chief to a stop by the truck. Sunshine tried to get down, but he held her in place. He put his head at the base of her neck and leaned up to nip at her earlobe.

He felt her shiver as his hand grazed her abdomen. She was feeling the fire between them as much as he was. He whispered in her ear as he ran his hands back down. "That kiss wasn't just any kiss. You think on that, because come a few days from now, we will have to decide what we're going to do about it."

# CHAPTER 9

# Gather 'Round

Sunshine didn't trust herself to turn or lean into his mouth. Did he want sex or to date?

She never could figure men out. She wished they would come out and say what they wanted. Drake did in normal circumstances; that was why they'd been friends their entire lives. This was new territory for them, and she wasn't sure what the rules were gonna be.

He was walking away from her towards his horse when she pulled him back to the truck and pushed him up against it. "You think of this when you have your woman company tonight." Sunshine ran her fingers through the back of his hair and pulled him close for her to kiss. In turn he picked her up, turned her around till she was against the truck, and they could reach one another better. She moved her legs around his back and pulled him closer. Her body as close to his as she could get with clothes on.

"We have to head back. Momma will have lunch ready by now." She ended the kiss abruptly, climbed down off of him and jumped in the truck.

Drake shook his head. "You are going to be the death of me."

"No one ever died from blue balls. You'll live. You coming to the house for lunch?" When he nodded yes, she headed towards the house. She bet his lady friend wouldn't be able to hold a candle to that. *Get you some of that, Drake Augustus Caldwell. You ain't the only one who can play the game.* Sunshine gave herself a mental high five. Score one for Sunshine.

She marched up the front steps to her parents' kitchen with Drake on her heels, hoping there was not gonna be a replay of this morning with her parents.

"I caught Mom and Dad makin' out hot and heavy in the kitchen this mornin'. You want to talk about ruinin' your appetite?" Sunshine said as they walked up to the porch. She kneeled down to scratch Tonto and Lone Ranger behind the ears. Her old mutts had been around for many years, eleven to be exact. She had noticed the gray around their muzzles this past year.

"That had to be a disgusting moment for you. I would have vomited on the spot if I had seen that shit first thing in the morning."

Sunshine watched as Drake ambled through the front door to her parents' home. That man had a scrumptious ass. She took a moment to try and calm herself while breathing deep to get her bearings. Drake was gonna to be one hell of a man to deal with if she decided to go there. She had Moonshine to keep up, and she wasn't quite sure she could add him to the list of things taking up her time. She wasn't ignorant enough to think either of them would have their fill after one roll in the hay. But she knew she wouldn't solve the problem of him standing outside her parents' house.

"The prodigal child has returned from workin', makin a

hard-earned livin' for her family. Please, no one get up and applaud. It is what I do," Sunshine announced, as she walked through the door, and bowed her head in a humble gesture. She looked up to see her parents fighting back grins and shaking their heads. They were both already sitting down at the table, waiting for her to stop messing around. Drake snorted from where he stood standing at the sink washing his hands.

"Be careful not to fall over while you're patting yourself on the back," her mother, Sophia, told her.

"If anyone needs a standing ovation in this house it's me and your mother," Mac told his daughter as he leaned back in his chair to grin at her. "After all, we created you."

"You answered my question," Sophia said aloud, patting her husband on the hand.

"What question?" Mac looked at his wife, perplexed.

"Where our daughter got her attitude from. Sunshine, what took y'all so long to get back with the truck? We were beginning to wonder about you both, but I see you may have taken a dip." Sunshine turned towards Drake and saw that he was staring straight ahead. Well, he'd be of no help.

"Sorry, Momma. We didn't mean to keep you both waitin'. You should have eaten without us. Drake and I decided to go take a quick swim at the blue hole to cool off." Sunshine sat and reached for the bowl of butter beans and scooped some onto her plate to keep herself occupied. Her momma raised a brow at her, and she sat the food back down.

"Drake did kill a copperhead that tried to make me its lunch," Sunshine told her mother as she tried to keep a blush from spreading up her face. She didn't want her parents to suspect anything, or her mother and Claire would have her and Drake married off by tonight.

Drake nodded as Sunshine spoke. "Yeah, I don't think it had you in mind for a noon meal, but it could have ruined a good afternoon if we had to spend it in the hospital." She heard him grunt when she kicked him under the table. "I killed it and didn't see any more around the pond when I looked," Drake told her Dad.

"I'm glad you had a gun, Drake." Mac said.

"I would have had a heart attack. What did you do?" Sophia asked in horror. The one thing Sunshine knew her Momma was scared of, snakes.

"What do you think I did? I swam back to shore and ran, of course."

"What did you do, Drake?" Sophia asked.

"Oh, he's the one who first spotted it. He swam out to meet me, and we swam backwards, keeping an eye on it. He pulled me out of the water and went to grab the gun and blew the snake out of the water." Sunshine spoke for Drake, telling the story in her animated fashion. She had a habit of talking with her hands.

"Good thing you were there, Drake, or our prodigal child might have been hurt," Mac said in all seriousness. "Never go out there without a gun. Understand?" He looked back at Sunshine.

"Yes, sir, I won't," she answered. Daddy meant business; he used the tone. When he used the tone everyone listened, including her Momma.

"Alright now, Sunshine, be quite for a moment so we can start eatin'." Sophia placed her hands in front of her and waited for Mac to speak.

Mac prayed before they ate. "Thank you, Lord, for protectin' Sunshine and Drake today. We thank you for your Son who died on the cross and for all the blessin's you have placed on this family. Thank you for the season of fall, and all the glories of huntin' and football season that come with it. Bless those servin' our country in the military. In Jesus name, Amen."

"Let's dig into this meal your Momma made for all us hard-workin' people."

Momma passed around the fried pork chops, mac and cheese, corn bread, and butter beans. There wasn't anything better than good ole Southern comfort food.

"Did you hear about Elizabeth Smith?" her Momma asked between bites.

Sunshine rolled her eyes. "Naw, what's goin' on now?" Always was something with that woman.

"She's suspended from her job down at the bank. Rumor is she got caught giving the banker some extra services under his desk. If you know what I mean," her Momma told her, appalled.

"Elizabeth was always loose with her favors in high school. I'm not all that shocked. I figured it would have happened sooner rather than later. She did lose her job at the grocery store." Sunshine giggled and snorted. "I never have been able to look that guy she got caught using the banana on in the eye."

"I can't look half the guys we went to school with in the eye. Most of the football team was with her at one time or the other," Drake said between bites of food.

"Bless her heart, she ain't right, and neither are the men that mess with her either," Sophia stated.

Her Momma cleaned up the table while her Daddy started

doing the dishes. Sunshine admired how her Daddy helped her Momma with chores. She hoped she could find a man that she could have that kind of partnership with. Drake and her worked well together, but he wasn't the settling down type, and at the moment, neither was she. She was content with the way her life was. She was working hard to build something that was hers. She looked over at Drake and he was giving her a smirk. Now was not the time for a smooth-talking cowboy to screw everything up.

Sunshine excused herself and headed upstairs to her childhood bedroom. She needed a breather from him, and her parents. She sat on her old bed and looked in the mirror across from her. Things were different since the last time she slept here a few weeks ago. She had her own home. She was working at Moonshine more often. Then up and comes Drake, morphing to take on a different role in her life, a role she wasn't sure about at this time. Her independence and freedom had been something she was growing into in the last month.

Sunshine's parents hadn't been smothering when she had lived here, and yet, she had only just moved into her home close to a month ago. There didn't seem to be room on her plate for one more thing, or someone else, needing her attention. Emotion churned inside her. She wasn't one to waffle back and forth between decisions. Once she made the choice to pursue something with him, she wouldn't be changing her mind.

Sunshine lay back onto her bed for a second, closing her eyes to shut off the self-examination for a moment. She tensed when she heard him on the stairs. It was for sure him and not her Daddy. She knew the footsteps of the people who had lived in her childhood home by heart.

Sunshine glanced from beneath her eyelashes and studied Drake for a moment as he leaned against her doorframe. He looked handsome with his long eyelashes and dark steel-blue eyes staring at her, chiseled cheekbones, and square chin. His curly hair was all over his head and made her think of his playful side. He looked as if he stepped off the cover of Cowboy *GQ*. He reminded her somewhat of Eric Decker, except a more rugged and less refined version. Eric was her number one on the hot guy list. She gazed at Drake's full lips and she had never wanted to kiss a man more in her life. She had the knowledge of what lay behind those perfect lips, and what feelings his lips could awaken in her.

She'd had some steamy kisses in the past, but Drake had shot them all to hell. She wanted to crawl all over him and kiss him till the stars came out. Not that she would let him know that. His big ego didn't need any feeding, nor did his dick from what she'd felt of it. She wanted to explore more with him. Her decision wasn't far from being made.

"I've got to head out. I've got some business to attend to this evenin'," Drake said from the doorway. She was glad he didn't come into the room. She would rather not be tempted while her parents were downstairs. There wasn't any sense in waving their attraction for one another around in front of the them. Mac would strangle the life out of him while Sophia kicked him in the balls if they thought he was getting frisky with her. Her parents were a bloodthirsty lot.

"Same here. I've got people to do and things to see," Sunshine claimed as she heaved herself off the bed to follow him downstairs.

It wasn't a hardship to watch him walk from behind. You could serve breakfast off his ass. It was muscled and what she saw earlier had been tan. Apparently thanks to Drake, she was an ass woman now. Great. She had to admit she was jealous of his ass. It had always been perky and bubbly, made you want to smack it or take a bite out of it. She'd also noticed earlier that he was a boxer briefs guy. Her favorite, at least it was on the packs she had seen in the store. She had seen her share of real-life men in their underwear, but they'd all been boxer guys.

She reached out to pinch the ass on display when he hit the bottom step. She saw him jerk but not miss a beat.

"We gotta go, y'all, love you," Sunshine said, traipsing down the last couple of stairs. She hugged her Momma's neck. "I love you too, Daddy," she told Mac as she hugged him. She walked out, waving as she went. Not inclined to give them a chance to question her or Drake. Sunshine saw that Sugar Baby had been loaded, and she was ready to hit the road.

"I love y'all too." Drake hugged both her parents.

"We love you too, baby," Sophia said.

Mac grunted in what may or may not have been agreement with her Momma. Her parents went back inside, leaving her and Drake alone to say bye.

He walked Chief up to her truck window and had to lean down a bit to see in the window. "We *will* talk more later."

"Yeah, I guess we'll have to." She was busy shielding her eyes from the sun.

He nodded at her and rode off down the driveway headed towards his parents' place.

She pulled out of her parents' driveway and pulled into hers not five minutes later. Sugar Baby whinnied in her trailer and she moved along to put her out in the pasture to graze. Sunshine rushed into the barn to load Deacon. She needed to change into some clean and cooler work clothes. The girls would be here before long to help her finish up decorating, and she needed to spend a couple hours at Moonshine and talk to Bishop.

She swung open John Wayne and laid her back against the cool door for a second. Drake had run her behind schedule. Damn it, he could kiss. She about forgot who they each were while he moved that magic tongue of his. Sunshine giggled. She couldn't help it. She had kissed Drake Caldwell and it was hotter than hell.

# CHAPTER 10

# Duck and Cover

Drake clucked Chief up to a slow gallop. He and Chief had about a fifteen-minute ride home. Long enough for him to clear his mind. He heard the crunch of gravel behind him and turned to see Sunshine pull out towards her house. It would take him about twenty to get to her house on horseback. Not that he'd thought about sneaking over there, at least not in the last thirty seconds. Potential alone time was more accessible now that she was living in her own house.

He had noticed her room at her parents' hadn't changed. He'd been in there on more than one occasion. Sunshine, Brice, and Drake had a good many sleepovers throughout their early years. Their parents had called a halt to those when they hit their teenage years. The boys could still sleep over at Sunshine's, but she had to sleep in her parents' room. Belle and Willow were often there spending the night as well.

Snips of their past together ran through his mind, but he recognized that she wasn't the same person she was when they were kids. He thought he knew who she was at her core, but she'd hidden her dating life from him for years given what she'd told him the other night. How much more of herself was she holding back?

After the heat that sparked between them, he wasn't so sure he knew all he wanted to about her. She had kept her eyes guarded from him during their heated exchanges today. That was the woman he didn't know, the one that didn't tell him everything with her eyes, or words.

It had felt different for him earlier as he'd stood in her doorway and gazed at her as she lay on her bed. Her pants had been dirty, and so was the shirt she'd slipped back on before they'd come in the house. It didn't seem to matter to him. Now that he'd noticed her as a woman, all he could think was how beautiful she was. Her hair had been pulled back, and she radiated peace in that rare moment. The way her plump lips were relaxed had him yearning to kiss them. Her lips were often pouting at him for something he had done or said. The pout was meant to fool. She'd follow it up with a sucker punch when he got out of line.

A horn blew behind him, shaking his thoughts loose. He'd be pissed if Chief was spooked easy, but he was a solid horse. He patted Chief for staying calm. "Good boy." He murmured. He recognized the truck and camper and threw up his hand in greeting.

Drake pulled his phone out and called Sunshine. "Mr. Ivey and Mrs. Ivey just passed by and blew the horn. Does Belle know they're back in town?"

"Shit fire, no. I don't think so, at least."

"How long did they stay gone this time?" Drake asked. Belle's parents tended to forget their only child existed while they traveled and lived their life.

"A good six months this go-around." Sunshine's sigh reached

his ear through the phone. "Maybe they will be gone again before long. Belle is better off when they aren't around. You can't help but enjoy their personalities, but they've been shit parents."

"Your parents and Willow's made up for their lack. They love her like their own," Drake reassured her. He glanced at the pasture beside him, where a bull happened to be mounting a cow. It was where his parents' land line started, and the cattle in question were part of their herd.

"Umh," was all Sunshine said.

"There's a bull hammerin' it to a cow beside me and Chief. I'd give him an A for effort, but his overall performance appears subpar." Drake heard her chuckle.

"Poor girl, she probably won't get to finish before he does."

"Have you ever heard a heifer have an orgasm?" Drake asked her.

"No, have you?"

"Not yet, but I will the first time I make you cum." Drake grinned at her gasp and sputter of laughter.

"Drake, you somehow, some way, manage to make me laugh by saying the stupidest shit." She continued to giggle. "Dream on, Drake. You comin' anywhere near my lady bits isn't a sure thing."

"I beg to differ. It's a sure thing that I'll be cumin' if I'm allowed anywhere near your lady bits." Her braying laugh made him laugh harder. Sunshine's laugh was funnier than the joke nine times out of ten.

"Stop, stop. You win the wordplay of the day. I've got to get off the phone and get some shit done." Sunshine's voice was still laced with laughter.

"Okay, I'll let you know what I figure out about this cow. I'll sit here and watch till they finish to be sure of the findings. Also, I need you to google cow orgasms."

"Clear my search history ASAP if I die after this conversation."

"Same here," Drake replied before hanging up. Contrary to their conversation, Drake didn't wait to watch his cows have sex. That wasn't on his to-do list for the day.

Drake gave Chief a quick brush down and put him up in the barn before jumping in his truck. He headed out to edge of Morgan and Lawrence County where he had rented some property to keep his Duck and Cover registered herd separate from his and his Dad's non-registered cattle. He hadn't been wanting to keep Duck and Cover a secret from his Dad so much as he just didn't want to discuss it with him. His Dad could be high-handed, and interfere, or offer advice when it wasn't asked for. He worked with him every day, and Drake needed something separate from his family to keep the peace. A business where he made all the decisions.

Bishop had been feeding Drake the numbers and stats for years, but Bishop could be cut throat when it came to cattle. If he told you something was silver, it was gold, and he was keeping the best part to himself. Drake didn't mind his way with business. If you asked outright, Bishop would tell you what he planned. Otherwise, most smart businesspeople kept their plans to themselves, and both he and Bishop were smart businessmen. You didn't share your plans until you were sure of success.

He eased up to the pasture and through the gate. He had lucked out and been able to rent three hundred and sixty acres from a guy that was retiring. He'd found Mr. Mitchell through the stockyard. He'd come in and had been talking to Drake about selling his cattle off in large lots at the sale barn. It had worked out for the both of them. He found property to rent, and he also found Mr. Mitchell a few buyers to split his herd between. Drake's Dad kept his ear to the ground when it came to property coming available, but Drake had asked Mr. Mitchell to keep who was renting his pasture between them.

Drake unlocked the small barn on the property and got out the ATV he stored there. He drove around the pasture, checking the Duck and Cover herd. He looked at the notes in his phone on which cows were dropping their calves next. Seemed numbers fifty through seventy-five should be dropping that week, based on the dates he'd put them with the bull. He walked around where some of the herd was gathered in the far back corner to get a better look at number fifty-two. Her vulva was swollen and she appeared to be stringing fluid. Her bag was swollen out too. She'd be dropping her calf within the next day or two. The others' bags were swollen, but they hadn't started stringing out yet.

Drake felt sorry for number fifty-two as he watched her waddle off. Bless her, that would be her third calf. The cow had a handle on how to give birth by that point. Drake didn't keep many heifers. They had a harder time birthing. He preferred to get a cow that had a couple of births and had the experience of raising a healthy calf. It cut down on the losses of calves and cows for him.

An image of Sunshine pregnant and waddling flashed across his mind. He shuddered. She would be beautiful pregnant, but whew, that was heart-attack inducing. Those boobs of hers filling out more, and her ass gaining weight wouldn't make him mad. He could imagine she would be a tyrant to deal with. What in the hell? Sunshine being pregnant wasn't a concern of his. That was a situation for another man to deal with.

He finished up, riding around checking on things and headed back home. He was anxious to get on the couch and watch the game. He ducked his head into the catch lot beside the barn to check that his new bull had enough water and feed. Once that was ensured, he headed up the stairs.

Drake eased his front door open. He could see that Brice had made himself at home by sitting in his recliner, his back to the door. The Alabama vs. Texas A&M game was blaring. Not one to waste an opportune moment, he snuck up behind his brother and pushed the recliner forward, dumping Brice out.

"You dick, you gave me a heart attack." Brice shot him the bird as he leveraged himself out of the floor. "And you missed a hell of a good series. Alabama scored on the second play of their first possession."

"I have the game set to record. I'll go back and watch it." He had to shower off the day's dirt and sweat. He considered rubbing one out in the shower using the blazing hot image of Sunshine's ass hanging out of her panties, and the memory of her legs clenched around his waist as inspiration. He refrained from fulfilling his baser instincts while his brother was out there. That seemed weirder than he was comfortable with.

Hunger gnawed at his stomach. He opened the fridge and pulled out some bacon and eggs. He glanced over at his brother, still sprawled on the couch, hollering out the play-by-play. Like Drake couldn't hear the damn TV himself.

"You want some breakfast for supper?"

"Yep," Brice answered as he continued to stare the TV down.

"Touchdown Alabama!"

Drake went to cooking one of his and Brice's favorite meals: pancakes, scrambled eggs with cheese, and bacon. He would brag about being able to throw down in the kitchen, but no sense in making his brother feel inferior today. Drake went about flipping the pancakes, bacon, and mixing the eggs. He glanced back and forth between the TV and what he was doing. Keeping up with the game as best he could.

Drake sat down and dug into his meal. Brice noticed him shoveling his food in. He paused the game and peeled himself up off the couch to join him.

"You ready to get to work on Monday? It's been playtime for you for the past few years." Drake shoved some more pancake into his mouth while he waited for Brice to answer. Brice put his fork down and picked up a piece of bacon, pointing it at Drake.

"The last two years of school I only partied every other weekend, and kept my dick to myself, but yes I am. It'll be nice to start a new challenge. Getting Dad to let me help will be the problem." Drake had gone to UNA, and stayed closer to home, but Brice had gone off to Miss. State to study Agri-Business. He'd gone on to get his master's and do an internship.

Drake nodded his head. "Yep, he wants to remain in control. That isn't a problem, but you and I both need to learn everything we can from him before he retires. We want that to be a seamless transition when it does happen. And I understand wanting a challenge more than you know."

He reckoned his challenger would be getting ready for her date right about now. Bullshit, if he ever heard it. She never even said who she was going out with. Drake's phone rang and

Bishop's name popped up. He hit the shut-up button and sent him to voice mail. He would call him back later when he was alone. Drake huffed as his phone rang again, but this time he saw that it was his Momma.

"Hey, Momma, whatcha need?" Drake picked up his plate and carried it to the sink. Brice could do the dishes later.

"Hey, baby. I was wondering if you could run by Sunshine's tonight and check in to see if she needs anything? She probably won't let you in since the house is supposed to be a surprise, but you know if we call or text, she'll just say not to bring anything to supper tomorrow." Drake would have fussed and sent Brice to run the errand, but he thought that might be the ticket to interrupt her date night. He wanted her thinking of him, not some other dickhead. He found himself answering, "Sure, Momma. I'll head over there at halftime."

"Ask your brother if he will be stayin' the night at your place, or comin' home."

"B, you gonna go home to Mom and Dad's tonight or stay here?"

"Stay here."

Drake ended the call with an I love you and sat back down at the table. "Momma wants me to ride over to Sunshine's tonight. Seems I need to ask her if we need to bring anything to the Sunday supper."

"Why not text her?" Brice asked.

"I was gonna suggest Mom do that, but she vetoed that idea by heading me off. She said Sunshine would just say no. Hell she is gonna say no even if I go over there, but it isn't far out of the way. Women can be weird creatures." Drake watched as Brice rolled his eyes and shook his head.

"I don't know why Momma didn't go over there herself. You aren't known for your impressive culinary skills."

"Did you say cunnilingus? Because I do happen to be known for my impressive skills in that area." Drake leaned across the table and jerked the plate out from under his fork while Brice processed his words.

"And what was that about my cooking?" He wasn't a chef, but he could cook breakfast.

And grill. Asshole was sitting there eating his food not gagging.

Brice grinned. "You can somewhat cook, you dickhead. However, what the female population says about your skills, or lack thereof, isn't something I want to know about. Give me my plate back."

Drake slid the plate back towards his brother and went to put on a shirt. He needed to go screw up some shit for Sunshine at halftime. If that thought didn't bring a demented grin to his face, he didn't know what would. Irritating her was one of his favorite pastimes.

"You coming with me?" he asked his brother as the ball game went to halftime.

"Might as well. Sunshine will have the game on at her house if we decide to stay."

"Okay, get in the truck and let's go."

Drake and Brice headed out the drive. "Sunshine may have company tonight. If she does, we will ask her to please give Momma something to bring to Sunday supper tomorrow and leave."

"Company? Like a man?" Brice raised an eyebrow at Drake. His brother saw through his bullshit. "Is that why you told Mom you'd go to Sunshine's? So you could see who was at her house?"

# CHAPTER 11

## Moonshine

After Sunshine had disconnected the call with Drake, she pushed harder on the accelerator as she hurried towards Moonshine. He was such a goober. Cow orgasms. He came up with the most random shit to ask her. She had time to reflect on the way to the adjoining county, but she didn't want to think about him, cow orgasms, or the news he had delivered anymore. He'd been on her mind enough as of late.

She hated keeping a secret from her parents, and her friends. But there wasn't any getting around it. Her Momma and Daddy had given her more than a leg up in life and she wanted to be able to accomplish something that was her own. Her Dad had helped build her home, granted she paid for it, but still she got a discount on materials and labor thanks to him.

She had sworn the USDA office employees to secrecy when she went and applied for her loan for Moonshine. They were required by law to keep it a secret, but just in case, she had made them promise. She hated to borrow money, but it was what it was. She needed to do this on her own, separate from their monetary backing. No one would take her serious if she kept relying on her parents.

It wasn't that her parents would take the credit for the things she had accomplished in her life, or the fact that they didn't deserve thanks and praise for what they had done for her. It was more along the lines of her need to succeed, separate from her family. She craved the knowledge that she was building a business for herself. Moonshine hadn't become what she had envisioned yet. She was gonna bust her ass to make sure it would. She couldn't go to her parents for money if she went belly-up on a loan. Their disappointment in her would be too much. Her disappointment in herself would be too much.

She and Bishop had become fast friends when she'd met him through Brice. He was slicker than green grass through a goose, but he had been raised in the cattle industry. His knowledge and guidance could help her in the long run, but right now she may have gotten ahead of herself. She may have tried to grow too fast instead of doing it at a slower pace and staying within a more conservative loan.

She had paid half the loan off, but if she could get in with the buyer Bishop had lined up, she would be able to sit easy and not guess if she was going to make a profit this year from her cattle. She wouldn't have to wonder if she was going to clear enough to pay the loan back or herself for her time. She loved the cattle business, but it was getting harder make a living with cattle due to the rising cost of land, feed, and hay.

Sunshine was blessed in the fact that Atticus Chapman was a tight-lipped man. He was the owner and landlord of the pasture she rented, as well as the adjoining trailer park. He helped her round up cattle on occasion. It had been three years of keeping her side work hidden from her parents and friends. She wasn't sure how she had succeeded this far into it without them finding out but she was damn proud of how far she had made it in such a short time.

Sunshine pulled into the pasture behind the Mountaintop mobile home park. She had rented this specific pasture due to it being behind such a large trailer park, surrounded by trees. The trees had tended to be a pain in her butt over the course of the past few years. On occasion, they would fall on her fences here and there, causing her more work, but this particular pasture offered her the privacy she needed. The ever-revolving tenants helped Atticus keep an eye on things, and he had her number in case anyone happened to see any cows out.

Atticus was her secret weapon. He had a good hand with cattle and was seventy-four years young. He was tall and rangy looking as the day was long with a slow drawling voice that tended to make you lean closer to hear what he had to say. He worked more, and harder, than most twenty-year-olds. His mobile home park was spiffed up and taken care of. Atticus made sure the tenants stayed out of the pasture and kept their trash tidy so it wouldn't blow out for the cows to get a hold and eat it. He wouldn't want to be told, but without him looking out for things, Sunshine wasn't sure she could sleep well at night.

She parked the truck in the middle of the pasture and walked towards the herd. Her top dollar Brahman bull, Armor Up—his sire was Maddox Manso—was standing towards the back, watching over the lovely ladies he serviced. Well, Armor Up thought he serviced them all. He didn't realize that she used his semen for artificial insemination. He was gentle, thank goodness. She wasn't going to have a wild ass bull running up and down the pasture and passing that on to his calves. Speaking of the calves, there were more bull calves this year. She would be spending a good amount of time having to steer them, but some buyers preferred their beef cattle to be steers.

Her cows weren't anything to shake a stick at either. They were F1 cows meant to be the best milkers, and mommas, on the market. While they were also known for throwing off a low birth weight calf with a quick grow off rate. Most of the calves took on their mommas' tiger-stripe appearance. This was another selling factor that put her cattle at the forefront of the registered sales. She hadn't been taking any of her cattle to the Caldwells' stockyard. She didn't want Drake, or any of the others, to know about her herd quite yet. Drake and his Dad, Ben, would never be able to keep that from her Momma and Daddy.

Drake. She had done better than she had anticipated on not thinking about him. He was already something else on her already heaping plate to deal with, but that inner fire she felt burning wasn't something she wanted to quench. She hadn't found herself attracted to many men throughout the years, and never the way she was to him. Her body betraying her mind was a new experience, and one she didn't care for. She could feel her fingertips tingle with the memory of gliding them over his chest and abs. Sunshine shook her hands and rubbed them through her hair and then on her jeans, trying to wipe them clean of his memory.

Men were difficult, and Drake would be more than most. She did know most of his dirty secrets and habits. That knowledge would give her more of a hold on his moods and what he was thinking. Maybe, possibly, probably. Hell. Who was she kidding?

Drake had her mind spinning and questioning his motives. He would be a nice break in the drought she had been in with the men.

The cattle didn't seem to mind her preoccupied presence. They were used to seeing her multiple times a week when she fed them and came to inspect. Sunshine took her mind back to where it should be and took the time to count the cows, one hundred and twenty-two not including the bull. There were already ninety-eight calves on the ground. She had a lucky year with the calving thus far. Only five calves had been lost to date to differing and unfortunate circumstances.

Sunshine walked back over to the catch lot behind the landlord's trailer at the far end of the trailer park abutting the fence row. She checked the salt buckets and feed troughs. Sunshine was ever thankful for the natural spring that kept a small pond filled year-round in the center of the pasture. She ran her cross fence straight through the middle of it. That spring saved her a ton of time and work with not having to haul water back and forth.

A cough behind Sunshine jerked her out of her thoughts. She turned to see Atticus leaning up on a fence post.

"Evenin'." His voice soft, Atticus had the weathered face of an outdoorsman, kind brown eyes, and a thick shock of white hair that he kept under a hat.

Sunshine had to restrain herself from giving him a big hug. He wasn't much on affection. "Evenin', Atticus. Anyone I should be keeping an eye on?" She turned towards the herd, her back towards him as she eyed all of the cattle.

"Number thirty-four has been limpin' some. I watched her, but she seems to be fine. Probably stepped in a hole an' twisted it. Number twenty-two seems to have dropped some weight. You may want to shoot her with an extra dose of wormer and LA-200."

Sunshine looked at both of the cows he mentioned and pulled out her phone to get into her notepad. She went to each cow's number and typed the observations in.

"I missed that on number thirty-four. She hasn't walked around much since I've been out here. I will need to keep a closer watch over her to make sure she doesn't have anything else going on. Thank you for keepin' an eye out." Sunshine turned back to him and grinned.

Atticus nodded at her. "You're welcome. I am going to go back inside." Sunshine watched as the sweet man with few words walked back into his mobile home. Atticus was a dying breed of man that she would forever be thankful she knew a few of.

Sunshine's phone rang. She smiled to see Bishop's name on the screen. "Hey, handsome. You got a package for me?"

Bishop laughed into the phone. "Yeah, I've got one alright. How 'bout I drop it by for you to inspect later tonight?" Sunshine rested against the railing of the catch pen.

"That would be a mighty tempting offer if I didn't have some other packages coming by tonight that I plan on having fun with."

"Sunshine, you wound me. And multiple packages? Even in all my conceit, I don't think I could keep up with you. However, I did want to call you and check to see if you'd gotten any statistics back from the vet on your bull's semen? I remember you saying you were concerned about his numbers being low." Sunshine could hear the faint tapping of Bishop at his computer coming in through the background.

"Yeah, he's fine. Vet said his sperm were still good swimmers. You want to meet up later this week for a business lunch, mixed with the pleasure of my company?"

"Sure thing, babe. I never turn down a meal with a pretty lady. I'll see you later." Sunshine ended the call and headed to her truck. She needed to hurry home before Willow and Belle got there to watch the Alabama football game. She had also invited Georgia, but she didn't think she'd be able to get off work in time.

Sunshine was pulling on her jeans when she heard one of the girls pull in. She walked out through the French doors onto the balcony and saw that it was Belle. She yelled down at her, waving, "Hey, sister, come on up."

"Be up in a second. Gotta get my snacks out," Belle hollered back.

She walked back into her room and pulled on an old T-shirt over her sports bra. Some people might think it was strange to walk out on their balcony with no shirt, but out here in the country, you could barely even see Sunshine's house. There were trees she had left in parts of the pasture and down the driveway for the specific reason of privacy. She recalled that there had even been a few times she had run out to her truck butt naked. If that didn't scream country living, she didn't know what did.

Since Sunshine had spoken to Bishop earlier, her mind had been running between the cattle business and the Drake business. It was time to turn it all off for a bit. She had her hair blow-dried and slapped on some makeup. She headed downstairs to see Belle unpacking some of her health snacks. She was a freak of nature; Belle actually wanted to eat that kinda crap.

"You're granola, my dear. I don't even know why I bother to

be friends with a weirdo such as yourself."

"Alas, it is my burden in life to make you a better person by bringing health food into your house. If you don't eat it, at least I will have something here to snack on next time." Belle started putting some real-deal granola bars in her cabinet. Sunshine would continue to eat her Oreos and drink her peanut butter milkshakes.

"Have your Momma and Daddy found out about your escapade at the Badmoon yet?" Belle turned to look at her and propped against the bar.

"They didn't mention it earlier today at lunch. I'm surprised they didn't know. Truth be told, I'm disappointed in the gossip vine around here, but my parents are sneaky. They could be letting me stew."

They both jumped when John Wayne suddenly opened and Willow hollered, "I'm here, bitches. Let's watch this game! Roll Tide! I got beer, candy, and I'm ready." She did an awkward dance as she walked in that looked like a cross between the Texas Two Step and the Cupid Shuffle. Belle and Sunshine busted out laughing. Willow always brought the party with her. She was high on life and had energy like a rat on crack.

"I can always count on you for junk." Sunshine mock-bowed down to Willow. She jerked her head towards Belle and fake whispered, "That skank over by the bar brought us freakin' granola bars. Can you believe her?"

"You're welcome, I'm awesome."

She gave them a quick tour of the finished house, and headed back to the kitchen. She needed to get the game on. The sound system came alive with the announcer's voice, as she poured a glass of tea.

"How was work today, Sunshine? What all did you have to do?" Willow inquired as she poured herself some sweet tea vodka in to her glass of sweet tea. Looked like someone needed something to take the edge off.

Sunshine tried to be nonchalant as they sat down on the couch to watch the game. "Oh, you know, the usual stuff. I fixed the fence and worked cattle, and then Drake stopped by to help. After work we went swimmin' in the blue hole. There was a copperhead and he ended up savin' me from it."

"What the mess? You're only now deciding to tell us this. Are you okay?" Belle asked.

"Why are you acting weird? You're twisting your hair into a knot. You're not telling us something. What happened that has you looking like that?" Willow gave her the inquisition. Her dark brown hair in a messy bun on top of her head, and her eyebrows arched towards Sunshine.

"I'm fine. Belle, please stop hoverin'. I didn't tell y'all yet because I knew y'all would get in a tizzy. I'm not hidin' anything." Sunshine got up to fix herself a sweet tea vodka. She would need a glass of it to have this conversation.

"You are lying through your teeth. Get your butt over here and spill the flipping beans, missy!" Belle demanded.

"Oh fine. Y'all are nosier than a raccoon on garbage day," Sunshine snapped and threw her hands up at Belle and Willow. "Drake and I made out. There, okay? Are y'all happy?"

"Oh, my Lord. Are you for serious right now? How was it? Was it good? Did he initiate it? Was there more than one episode of hotness?" Willow was on the edge of her seat.

"I never imagined it would take this long to happen." Belle bounced up and down.

"Hold up. What do you mean you didn't imagine it would take this long? Drake and I have never even had a hint of this in our friendship." Sunshine was puzzled by her friend's statement.

"Y'all may not have noticed, but everyone else sees the sparks when y'all are together." Belle told her with sympathy.

Sunshine snorted. "Both of you have lost your minds. You're imaginin' things. To answer your other questions, it was damn hot. Ain't nothin' like a good-lookin' cowboy almost naked. Yes, there was more than one episode."

"Please further explain the almost-naked part." Willow motioned for her to go on with her story.

"We went partial skinny-dipping. I had on my sports bra and panties, and all he had on was his boxer briefs."

"Belle, you owe me five bucks. Pay up." Willow held her hand out to Belle. "I knew he would be a boxer guy."

Belle shook her head in disgust and handed her money over to Willow.

"Y'all bet on his underwear selection?" Sunshine asked, amused at the two.

"Yeah, we didn't let you in because that wouldn't be fair to us. You would find out and then bet," Belle explained.

"How make-outty was this session?" Willow asked.

"We were close as you could get with what little clothes we had on. He had me wrapped around him, and I can't even explain how hot it was." Sunshine put her head on the bar as she answered. Her face felt flushed from the memory.

"Okay, we get it was hot, but exactly how many episodes of

this were there?" Willow wanted to know.

"Three steamy episodes: one in the water, one on the back of Chief, and one up against my truck." Sunshine shivered from the memory his touch.

"Holy guacamole, this is big. This is bigger than big. This is ginormous. Drake will be eating out…of your hand before you know it," Willow said with devilish delight, wiggling her eyebrows up and down suggestively.

"Will, I ain't about to go there with Drake. He ain't the type to mess with." Sunshine gave her a stern look. She didn't want them piddling in her situation with him. It was confusing enough as it was without these two and their harebrained ideas.

Belle pointed at her. "You don't know if you don't try."

"I ain't tryin'." She sat in silence while they chatted.

"It's halftime, not that either of you have been payin' any mind to the game. What do y'all want to do?" Sunshine asked as she tried to keep their attention off of her.

"Let's dance." Willow got up, pulling at her hands when she groaned.

Hell, she wasn't fooling them. She loved to dance. Sunshine went over and turned on the house's sound system, put her iPhone on the dock, and set up an assorted playlist with country and classic rock to dance to. "Shake It for Me" by Luke Bryan came on and she laughed as they broke it down all over the house.

Belle danced on top of the coffee table, and Willow was on the floor, trying to do what appeared to be the worm. The song changed and they both pointed to Sunshine.

"It's go-time, sister. Put on a show!" They dragged her to the bar.

"Guys, are y'all ever goin' to make me stop doing this?" She never should have let them see her dance to that song. Alas, many years ago during some fun times in Panama City, her inner stripper was revealed, and they were the ones to be witness to it.

"Never! At least not till you get so old that your hips can't move anymore," Willow told her.

She was on top of the bar singing "Pour Some Sugar on Me" by Def Leppard. She grabbed a spoon and sung her heart out to it. She was in the middle of an air guitar solo when she saw someone out of the corner of her eye at the fridge. Belle and Willow were situated where they could see the intruder, and they weren't ringing the alarm. She figured it was Georgia, off work in time to join them.

She shimmied up off the bar and broke out into moves that ensured her hips would be sore in the morning. She never danced like this in public, but at home, she let loose. The song ended and Sunshine bowed to her audience. She turned to bow in the newcomer's direction and stopped in her tracks.

"Oh, shit a monkey."

# CHAPTER 12

# Sugar Ain't just for Sweet Tea

Drake leaned against the fridge and gave her a slow clap. Those moves should be illegal in any state Sunshine was in. He noticed Sunshine's speech still hadn't returned. He had the urge to cover his brother's eyes. He turned to Brice, his brother's face was red as a beet. He did believe Brice was embarrassed.

"Hey, Drake, glad you and Brice caught the show. Y'all are now some of the few people who know about Sunshine's secret stripper side," Willow told him with a smirk.

Drake shrugged. "What are you talking about? Everyone knows she can dance."

Belle rolled her eyes and shook her head in exasperation. "Yes, people know she can dance a two-step, but no one knows she can dance like that." She nodded to the bar. "Sunshine keeps it close to her chest. She doesn't want anyone in town, or her parents, to know."

"She's afraid they might think she's a stripper. Or loose." Willow snorted at that. "Anyone who knows her would know that couldn't be further from the truth, but you know our rumor mill around here."

"Okay, that's enough telling Drake and Brice about my inner

ho." Sunshine regained the ability to speak and glared daggers at all of them. Drake could see that she was firing on all cylinders and was fixing to pitch a hissy fit.

"Y'all couldn't have let me know these two walked in before they saw the whole show." She jumped down and pointed to Willow and Belle.

The girls laughed. Willow went up and gave Sunshine a hug. "I'm sorry, I love you and good night. I'm bustin' outta this joint."

"What? You're leaving? Belle, are you leaving too? But the game is fixing to come back on."

"Yes, darling, I am. I'll watch the rest of the game at home. Night. Love you." She hugged her and headed to John Wayne, where Willow was waiting.

"Bye, Brice. Byeeeee, Drake," both of them said at the same time, giggling after they stretched out Drake's goodbye. They turned and waved with mischievous grins and shut the door.

"I believe I'll go catch a ride with Belle. Night. Love you." Brice gave Sunshine a quick hug and ran out the door.

"Well hellfire and brimstone," Sunshine said to the door as it shut. "What was that all about?"

Drake stared her down, waiting for her to face him. "I thought you had a date tonight?"

"I did, and they left me." Sunshine told him with a defiant look, putting her hands on her hips.

"They are not dates. They are your best friends." He pulled off his baseball hat and laid it on the bar. He went to the fridge and got himself a beer.

"You didn't ask what kind of date, or with whom."

He turned to look at her and gave her a droll stare. "You

thought I'd be jealous." He walked over to the bar and sat on one of the stools.

Even sitting on a stool, he was taller than her. She pointed her finger at him as she walked his way. "I will have you know that is not true. I didn't want you to know what I was doing. Plus, I thought you had a date tonight?"

"My Momma sent me over here to see if she needs to bring anything tomorrow night for supper. I also brought your bandana. You left it in Chief's saddle bag. Brice rode along since it was halftime and I would be gone." Drake pulled her bandana out of his back pocket and tossed it to her. "I did have a date, but it got canceled." He didn't mention that his date was hanging out with his brother, who'd also run out her front door. He was glad his brother was smarter than the average bear in this instance. He was glad to get some alone time in the house with Sunshine.

"Thank you, and tell your Mom no, but I appreciate her askin'. Brice didn't even say he liked the house." She turned and walked to the laundry room and threw her bandana in the clothes basket. She came back with a frown.

"It was an oversight on his part. I think your dancing blew apart some of his brain cells."

"What?" Sunshine demanded, throwing her hands up, exasperated. She walked up to him and poked him in the chest. He didn't give her time to finish her sentence, just reached out and pulled her in between his thighs and put his lips to hers.

He kissed her as if he'd missed it all day, then picked her up and carried her to the couch. He laid her down then followed suit, trying to keep his weight on his arms, but she wasn't having any of that. Sunshine pulled him as close as she could get him.

He loved the feel of her, the smell, the taste. Hell, he was crazy about the whole package as long as she kept on kissing him this way and didn't speak.

She had pulled up his shirt and was running her hands up and down the bare skin of his back. She was driving him crazy with each graze. He needed her to stop that. He was acting like a man that hadn't ever gotten any before as he tried not to grind into her. She was squirming under him and trying to pull him closer and he wanted to get a lot closer.

She slipped her hands in his hair and tugged him down for an even deeper kiss. She pulled back and nipped at his bottom lip and then slid her tongue along his in a slow tantalizing way. One of his hands wandered up her shirt while the other started heading south. His hand slid along her skin making a trail to her breasts. He couldn't take much more temptation. He leaned away from the kiss, not wanting to, but knowing things could go a lot further than she was ready for if he didn't.

He was losing control of himself and he didn't care for that one bit. Drake looked down into her hazel eyes. She had to be one of the most beautiful women he had ever seen. He couldn't believe he'd never allowed himself to notice her. Hell, he could have been in this very situation right here a lot sooner.

"I would say I'm sorry, but that'd be a lie. I'm sorry if I'm moving things too fast for you, but not for what I did," Drake said but didn't make an effort to move. He enjoyed where he was at.

She pushed his hair off his brow. "I understand. All of this is confusin' for me right now. This attraction for you has flared up in the last couple of days and I don't understand it."

"I know how you're feeling." Drake sighed and rolled over

on his side. He scooted her around till she was lying on top of his chest. He pulled her hair to the side, out of his face and wrapped her up in his arms.

"This is weird," Sunshine said as she looked up from his chest at him. "We have hugged our entire lives, but the kissing and holding thing is different."

Drake sat there for a minute, looking at her. She was waiting for him to tell her the answer to whatever this was. He didn't have one for her.

"We will figure out something." Drake pulled her back down on his chest and held her there, rubbing her back.

"Where's the remote at?" he asked. "The game is back on by now, and I'd like to finish watching it."

"Shoot, you're right." He watched as she ran to the kitchen and hurried back to lie down with him. She enjoyed watching football as much as he did. But he'd been more interested in her tonight than he had the game.

"I may have forgotten the game for a few minutes."

"My hands and tongue are magic. I can make you forget your name, but you won't forget mine. You'll be screaming it." Drake chuckled when she slapped his arm. She curled up beside him on the couch, allowing him to be the big spoon.

"You are a conceited ass."

"It isn't conceit. It's truth, and admit it, you want to know how I can make you feel." Drake rubbed his hand along her hip and felt her breath quicken. She was turned on, maybe almost as much as he was.

She gave him the side eye. "Drake. I am sure in your mind that you can make all sorts of magic happen, but turnin' a friendship into somethin' more ain't anything to jump into."

Drake saw the confusion in her eyes and the fear. The confusion he understood, but not the fear. She knew he would never set out to hurt her, didn't she? He would make sure it was what they both wanted and were comfortable with where they stood.

"You're right." He'd made up his mind; he would have to wait on her to make up hers.

He turned his attention back to the ball game, and felt Sunshine playing with and twisting his hair. Her breathing evened out. She had put herself to sleep. He remembered her doing that when they were small and he would sit beside her at different events. She would reach over where ever they were, grab a twig of his hair and twist till she fell asleep on his shoulder. Some things never changed.

Drake was going to get up and leave, but decided it felt too good where he was. He wrapped his arms around Sunshine and positioned her so he could carry her upstairs without waking her. He stood up slow and hooked his heel with his boot toe and slid off his boots. Drake carried Sunshine up the stairs, pulled the covers back, and laid her on her side.

He slipped off his shirt, jeans, and her jeans too, because nobody liked sleeping in jeans, and lay down beside her. He would take her bra off for her, but it looked like she had one of those sports bra things on. He figured it might be comfortable enough to sleep in. He didn't want her to think he took advantage of her while she slept and coped a feel, so best to leave that on.

He would have looked for some pajama pants, but he knew she would have nothing his size. Heck she had seen him in his underwear earlier today anyway. He couldn't count the number of sleepovers they'd had when they were little, but he was aware this was different.

She might not be too pleased to find him in her bed in the morning. Her bed was comfy as all get out. It was a monster for such a small person. He rolled over and pulled Sunshine against his chest, relaxing as she snuggled up against him, then threw her butt so hard into his stomach, it about knocked the breath out of him. He let her position herself and then held her close.

Drake looked around at her room. It was feminine, but not over the top. She had picked out dark, heavy furniture. That had to be a pain for the movers to get up here. It dawned on him that Sunshine had built this house for whenever she had a family of her own. She may not have realized it, but that was what she'd done. Any man would be comfortable living here. She built a house for a man and children that didn't even exist in her life yet.

Damn, that meant she was ready to settle down, and hell, he wasn't there. Drake started panicking; he didn't know what to do about her. Drake had been hoping she would be up to having a fling. She knew the score with him though, he told himself. She would understand once they talked things out.

"Damn it, Drake. I about shot your ass!" Drake woke to the startling sound and sight of an irate woman. Sunshine had busted into his slumber, literally. He should have remembered to pull those curtains to. He raked his eyes over her and noticed she was in last night's shirt, with a raging temper and no pants. After he got through lingering over the finer parts of her anatomy, he registered that she had a gun in her hand. Damn, she looked sexy. The gun made her all the more exciting. He liked a woman who knew her way around a gun. If he hadn't already made up his mind, this would have. He had to have her.

"Darlin', how 'bout you put the gun down and come on and get back to bed?" He gave her a patronizing look and patted the open space beside him. He raised the covers for her to climb on in.

Drake saw the look of consideration on Sunshine's face as she thought hard about what to do. He hoped she would make the decision he wanted her to. She looked beautiful even with her hair messed up and makeup smeared on her face. Yes, Sunshine was a sight to behold in the mornings. The sun was highlighting her, making her hair even more gold. He watched her and her eyes popped open wide. Well there goes that idea of his.

"Drake, you have got to leave." Sunshine rushed to the bathroom, away from him. "People will be getting out and about soon. Get your truck outta my driveway. I don't want talk goin' around—what in the ever-loving hell do you think you're doing!?" Drake watched as Sunshine about fell off the toilet and flailed around trying to cover herself. He'd snuck up on her peeing. She had been sitting with her legs crossed, with one elbow propped on her knee brushing her teeth. Leave it to her to find a way to multitask while peeing.

"Men think we have it made because we can stand up and pee, but after seeing the way you do it, I have changed my mind. You looked to be pretty comfortable." Drake chuckled at the daggers Sunshine was shooting at him with her eyes. Her face was as red as a firecracker. She looked like a cat trying to do aerobics on the toilet to make sure she was covered.

"Get out now." She emphasized each word. "You have seen most of the show. Now I have to wipe, you sicko."

"We have been to the bathroom multiple times together in our life. You ain't got to act embarrassed now. It ain't nothing I ain't ever seen anyway." He laughed and leaned against the doorframe.

"We were five at the oldest. That doesn't count anymore, and I'm sure there ain't much left of a woman you haven't seen," Sunshine spat at him. She glared till he gave in and turned his back.

"Did you really have to do that?" He rubbed his head where she had snuck up behind him to slap the back of his head. "Good grief you were only peeing. It ain't like you were dropping a load of cattle off at the watering hole."

Sunshine gave him a confused look and threw up her hands. "You are insane."

He chuckled as she stomped out of the bathroom. He snatched her toothbrush off the sink and put some toothpaste on it.

"Get out of my house, it's already nine o'clock." Sunshine ran into the bathroom, jerking him by the arm away from the toothbrush and paste. "Were you going to use my toothbrush?" she demanded, shaking his arm.

She looked cute mad. She thought she was scary and truth be told, she kinda was, but she didn't need to know that. "I wasn't going to, I already did. I couldn't kiss you bye with morning breath now could I, darlin'?" Drake drawled as he grabbed her around the waist and tugged her to him. He looked down into her eyes and waited on the okay. Sunshine wrapped her arms around his neck and that was all the encouragement he needed.

He ran his hands down to Sunshine's scantily clad ass and

gave it a good, firm feeling, pulling her up against him. "Damn it," Drake moaned. But if that wasn't the finest feeling ass this side of the Tennessee River. This could get heated in a hurry if he didn't back off.

Sunshine must have read his mind. She pulled back from him, smiling. "Alright, cowboy, time to get along."

Drake stared down at her. Her eyes were heavy with a desire that he was sure matched his. She switched moods faster than a twister, he couldn't keep up. He turned and grabbed his shirt, pulled it on over his head, and slipped his jeans on. Drake walked back towards Sunshine's bathroom door and hollered out at her, "I'll see you tonight, Sunshine. I'll show myself out."

"Okay, see you tonight," Sunshine yelled to him over the sound of her running bath water.

He moseyed on downstairs and slipped on his boots where he'd left them in the living room. He looked back up at Sunshine's door. Right about now that woman was probably getting out of her clothes. If that wasn't a thought that made him want to charge back up those steps, he didn't know what was. Drake ran his fingers through his hair and down over his eyes in frustration. He had to get his self in check. He was going to be sitting at the table with his parents and the person he desired. That'll throw a cold blanket over you in a hurry. Drake got up and headed towards the door. His feet felt like they were being dragged through molasses. He wasn't a saint by any means.

He opened up John Wayne and stepped out to greet a beautiful Sunday morning. There were birds singing and the sun was streaming through the trees. Hell, he wasn't one to usually notice that kind of stuff. He was beginning to think that he was becoming a damn Disney princess. He slammed the door to spite Sunshine and jumped in his truck. He looked back to see her standing out on her balcony in her towel, waving her shotgun at him. Drake chuckled and shook his head. She sure did love that door, and where the hell had she been hiding that gun? He pulled out of the drive and headed to his house. Drake needed to get away from her for a bit and regain some control.

# CHAPTER 13

# Nobody's Perfect

Sunshine stomped back into her room, putting her gun away. She loved to yank his chain, but that infuriating man was going to be the death of her. When she had woken up in bed and realized she was snuggling up to a person in her bed, she about jumped out of her skin. She had recognized who it was as soon as she'd gotten out of bed and taken a better look, and he'd looked yummy curled in her bed. Better than a peanut butter milkshake. She had wanted to crawl back in bed and curl up next to that body. Sunshine could wash clothes on that stomach of his. She wanted to trace his abs with her tongue. The morning scruff on his face had called to her.

She shook her head at the thought of him putting her to bed. She was sure he enjoyed the undressing her part. She hadn't had the pleasure of being awake for that stimulating portion of the evening. She blamed these thoughts on her vagina. She couldn't control it around him, damn thing had its own agenda.

She needed to start getting ready. She took stock as she stared in the mirror. Her hair was all over. There were dark circles around her eyes from her makeup, and there were crusties at their corners. She was a frightful sight. Sunshine hit the radio on the vanity and heard the country twang of Waylon Jennings. She moaned aloud, "Ugh, I could scare a fainting goat with one look."

She took it easy for most of the day and left her house just in time to pull up to the Swine and Dine before the crowd. She needed to get a dessert, and there wasn't anything better than the chocolate pie at the Swine and Dine. Although the strawberry pretzel salad over at Pages gave it a run for its money in her book. She skidded to a halt when she ran into Drake's back. Mac, Sophia, Claire, Ben, Brice, and Drake stared at her. Damn it they all had the same idea.

"I told y'all I had everything covered."

"We know, dear. We just wanted to bring something." Sophia said.

"Well did one of us at least get a whole pie?" She gave them a hopeful look.

"Yeah, we got one!" Claire crowed with delight.

"Thank goodness. I was banking on that pie, or I would have had to fall on Emerson's mercy at Pages to make me a strawberry pretzel salad last minute." Damn pie was hard to get, and they only baked it at certain times. You had to be first in line and put your name down just to get a slice somedays much less a whole pie.

She took a seat by the bar, and everyone else did the same, with Drake plopping down beside her. She sat with eager anticipation as they waited for the pie.

"Mom jumped out while the truck was still rolling to beat me and dad to claim the prize," Drake told her.

The door to the Swine and Dine swung open, and Belle and

Willow waltzed in. They both had cute smiles on their faces. Was there any way to escape this situation? She didn't even get a chance before they were on her.

"What are you two doing here?" she asked them.

"Thought we'd stop in for an early supper and some pie." Willow said.

"What are you doing here? Belle asked. "Thought y'all were eating at your house so you could give them the tour tonight." She looked sharp in her black skirt and bright red blouse. Simple yet beautiful at the same time. That was Belle's style and she pulled it off well.

"Needed a dessert. Was gonna take someone down for the pie, but I didn't have to. All of them had the same idea." She pointed over her shoulder to everyone behind her.

"Sun, did you do anything interesting last night?" Belle asked.

Sunshine would make her pay for that, but at the moment she could only stand there, staring her down.

"Yeah, what did you do after we left last night?" Willow's gray eyes sparkled with mischief. Her long black hair was pulled up into a stylish ponytail that morning instead of her normal style of wearing it down and flowing over her bohemian maxi dress. Willow didn't have to try to be beautiful, she just was.

Brice grinned along with them. "Yeah, Sunshine, what did you do last night? I thought we were running away together?"

Everyone's head at the bar snapped around at lightning speed. Sunshine expected that she did a wonderful impression of a largemouth bass for a while. Momma looked as if she didn't know if she needed to shout, cry, or scream. Daddy looked likely to bust a gut. Claire smiled, and Ben looked oblivious.

The most interesting bit was when she glanced over at Drake and he looked ready to wring their necks, but instead turned his glare towards Sunshine.

"What did you do last night, Sunshine?" Drake gave Belle, Willow, and Brice a hard stare as he spoke. It was obvious he didn't want the parents to know either. Maybe this was her opportunity to get her Momma off her back somewhat.

"Momma, now don't go getting your panties in a wad. The girls came over last night to watch the game, and then I went to bed. They were trying to get a rise outta you. Trust me, nothing of interest happened last night, and I'm sorry, Brice. I have more important things to do than run away with you, but maybe next week." Sunshine made sure to put emphasis on that nothing of interest part.

"Sunshine, you wound me, but I will take you up on your offer of next week. Mom and Dad, I will meet y'all at the house to catch a ride." Brice jumped in his truck and left. He must have already been in town.

Sunshine noticed Belle watched him as he left, and she seemed to be much more relaxed with him gone.

"Nothing interesting happened at all, Sunshine?" Drake turned from his parents to look at her.

Wounded his ego, did it? Sunshine felt triumphant. She batted her eyelashes. "Not anything worth remarking on or remembering."

Drake walked over to Sunshine. "I think I will drive Sunshine to her house to help with the food. See y'all in a bit." He dragged her by the arm to her truck, glaring at her the entire way. Easing her keys out of her hands as she tried to swat him away.

"Who do you think you are? It's my truck!" Sunshine sputtered at Drake wide-eyed and angry as he tossed her through the driver's-side door, and then eased her on into the middle seat. "What the crap, you shit head? You probably have the whole of the Swine and Dine talking about us now."

Drake gave her a droll look. "They talk about us all the time anyway. It ain't like it will be anything new. They enjoy our shenanigans. It keeps them happy, and gives them gossip fodder." As he finished talking Drake pulled her across the bench seat over into his lap sideways. Forget the seat belts he'd take the back roads, and drive slow. She gave him stubborn look as she sat there with her back against the door panel and her arms crossed.

She could feel the tension building between them as soon as he dragged her across his lap. She thought about fighting to get back to her seat, but the truth was she enjoyed sitting in his lap. Something she hated right now and loved all at the same time. Since they had about a ten-minute ride to her house, she relaxed against the window. She sat there in his lap and wondered why her traitorous vagina all of a sudden decided to want him.

Sunshine gazed at him through her eyelashes. Honestly his handsome features made her resolve against him weaken. He looked as if he had a five o'clock shadow and had a small scar just above his right eyebrow. His body was amazing, with well-defined abs that made you want to lick them, all muscle and no fat that promised a good time. Sunshine knew this man could put a hurt on her in more ways than one.

She grinned at him as he leaned in to give her a swift peck on the lips, but her grin faded when she decided she needed more and deepened the kiss. She wiggled around to get closer to his lips that were working some magic on her. It was either her, or this truck, but it was getting hot. She felt her truck come to a halt.

Sunshine let Drake move her to a more comfortable position. He maneuvered their bodies so he could glance at the rearview mirror, and what seemed most important at that moment in time, kiss her. Drake continued to check his mirror and kiss her all the way up until a horn blared at them. She heard Drake breathe a muffled curse and slid her back over. She buckled up as he got them back to her house quick fast and in a hurry.

His lips dived for hers when he put the truck in park in the drive. She felt the strength in his arms as he picked her up, and carried out of her truck, and into the house. As her luck would have it, the door was unlocked. Drake got her inside and had her backed up against the wall before John Wayne was shut.

"Drake," Sunshine moaned against his mouth.

"Yeah, baby, what is it?" Drake groaned as he pushed against her, getting them as close as possible. His hands were sliding under her butt holding her in place for him to be nestled right where she wanted him the most. If her damn tights weren't in the way he could really be giving her a good time. He ground his pelvis against hers, and she could feel him straining against his pants. It set her inner flame roaring even hotter. Sunshine moaned again and squirmed. That seemed to encourage him even more.

"We need to stop," Sunshine told him after she pulled her mouth away. That was not what she wanted to say, but without a doubt, it was what needed to be done.

Drake dropped his forehead against hers. "You're right. You're right. The parents are going to be here soon, and you still gotta cook." He groaned. "I lose my mind whenever we start this." Drake moved his pelvis against hers, proving his point.

Sunshine gave him a soft kiss. She could see why the women fell at his feet. He had some serious sexual game going on. She looked back up into his eyes again and it clicked. This was going to happen between them; it was only a matter of time before they'd be going down in a blaze of glory. Maybe the flames would keep her warm long after the crash. She glanced down before he could see the turmoil and want in her eyes. He had been able to tell what she was thinking most of their lives. She slid off him and checked her dress.

"Alright, let's get to cookin' and quit jackin' around," Sunshine ordered as she turned and walked into the kitchen.

Drake leered at her, his eyebrows raised. "You can jack me around anytime you want."

"You pervert. Go jack yourself," Sunshine shot back over her shoulder. She tried not to let her thoughts wander over the way he'd look jacking himself off, but failed miserably. Thank goodness her back was towards him.

"What do you need me to do?" he asked as he leaned back against the fridge.

Sunshine turned to look at the beefcake of a man in front of her. She could imagine all kinds of things she needed him to do to her. Her body demanded she say it, but sanity won and she instead asked, "Why don't you set the table and get everyone a glass?"

Drake rubbed his hands together and rolled his sleeves up his muscular forearms. "Prepare to be amazed." He winked and turned to do as she asked.

Sunshine smiled and couldn't resist slapping his butt when he turned around. She rushed back over to the stove to put on the mac and cheese and get herself back under control. She watched him out of the corner of her eye, and he looked good any which way he turned. *Sunshine, focus*, she snapped at herself. Her parents and his would be there any time now, but she couldn't seem to help herself where he was concerned. She was having a terrible time keeping her mind off the things he could do to her. Her cheeks were flushed, but he would think it was from the heat of the stove, maybe.

"How about we…" Sunshine stopped short as she heard their parents and Brice barrel through John Wayne. She straightened her posture and headed to the door to meet her family.

"This place is breathtaking. I knew it would be. You do have my excellent taste in, well, everything," Sophia exclaimed as she walked in.

"Aww, now I don't know about all that. She got a lot of her ability from me. I picked you out after all, didn't I?" Mac grunted as Sophia smacked him in the stomach.

"As of right now, I am responsible for all the genes that inspired this gloriousness that my daughter has worked hard to bring to fruition," Sophia stated as she hugged Sunshine till she thought her spleen would rupture.

She patted her Momma's back. "Momma, let me go now so I can hug Daddy before someone has to read me my last rites due to blood loss to the brain." She mumbled the last part on a huff. She had run out of oxygen.

Mac pulled her out of her Momma's arms, picked her up, and whispered in her ear,

"Honey, I am so proud of you and what you have built for yourself."

"Lord Daddy, between you and Momma, I most certainly am going to pass out."

"Come here and give us some loving, Sun," Claire said once Mac set her back on the floor. Sunshine walked over to Claire and Ben and hugged them both as they told her how beautiful the house was and how proud they were of her.

Brice grabbed her up in a hug too. "It's official, Sunshine, we are going to get married. I want to live in your house, or how 'bout I just move in? We don't get married and can date other people? That sounds better."

"Hey, I'm hungry. Can we get started eating so I don't pass out from starvation as y'all fawn over Sunshine?" Drake asked.

She rolled her eyes at his lack of patience but went ahead and led them to the dining room to do as he asked.

Food was passed from hand to hand as she watched her wonderful family laugh and argue in her home. The pie was last to be eaten and savored. Gosh it was good. She was glad they were able to get one.

Family, love, fun, happiness, and surprises where what homes were made of. She turned and caught Drake staring at her. Some surprises, as it turned out, seemed inevitable.

"Alright, let's get this show on the road." She guided everyone from the table to show them the house. An hour later, after she had walked them from room to room, giving them all the details she could think of, Mac and Sophia announced they were going to head out.

"Darlin', you want me to help you with these dishes before

I leave?" Sophia pushed at Mac's arm as he was dragging her towards John Wayne.

"No, thanks though, Momma. I've got it handled. I have the rest of the night to get everything cleaned up and back in place."

Claire turned towards Drake as she and Ben paused by John Wayne. "We are gonna head out too. Drake, baby, you goin' to ride home with us?"

"Yeah, Drake, aren't you coming home with us?" Brice asked.

She saw Drake raise his head up off the couch, where he had plopped down five minutes earlier. "Naw, I'll get Sunshine to carry me home later. I'm feeling pretty good right where I am." Drake threw his arm over his eyes and rested his head back against the armrest.

Sunshine rolled her eyes as she turned towards John Wayne to say her goodbyes. "I guess I'll be bringin' him home later. Bye, I love all y'all!" Sunshine shut the door and walked back into the kitchen, glancing over in Drake's direction. He had a blanket pulled up to his chin and was rolled onto his side. She didn't mind his napping and turned away to start cleaning up.

Her thoughts sounded loud enough to her that she was surprised they didn't wake him. There were too many things at stake if they let this go further than they should. Or if this thing, whatever it was, caused problems, it would be a shit show. There was a lifetime of friendship at stake with a wonderful man. Sunshine looked over at Drake again as he slept on through her mental onslaught over everything she was feeling towards him. She wanted him, but she didn't want to want him. Maybe she'd let him sleep over again.

When she felt a hand on her hip, she jumped up and slammed

her head back against a solid chest.

"Good grief, Drake, you scared the hell out of me," Sunshine huffed as she relaxed into his touch. "I didn't hear you get up." Drake turned her around in his arms.

"You should have waited on me to help you. I had hoped you would come get comfy with me on the couch." Sunshine felt his hand caress her face as he pushed the hair out of her eyes and leaned down to catch her lips with his. He walked her backwards and laid her onto the couch. His lips met hers as she explored what he liked and he did the same.

Drake stopped the kiss and turned over so she was lying on him.

"Why don't you sit down and relax. We will watch a movie, rest for a while, and then I will help you do the rest of the cleanup?" She let him rub her back for a moment and decided she liked this charming side of him.

Sunshine leaned in for a quick kiss. "I think that sounds perfect."

"I get to pick the movie." Drake shoved her off the couch to beat her to the TV stand.

"Right when I think you might have a sweet side, you go and pull some shit." Sunshine pushed herself up off the floor and curled back up on the couch under her favorite blanket. She couldn't find it in her to be upset, but she wouldn't let his stunt go unpunished. She slung a pillow and hit Drake square in the head for good measure. He continued on, looking as if he never even noticed.

She lay back and closed her eyes, listening as Drake fiddled with the DVD player, getting the movie ready. She felt him over her and scooted up to the front of the couch so he could fit in behind her to spoon. He put one arm over her stomach and one under her head so she would be lying on his shoulder. Sunshine snuggled her back into his chest and tried not to overthink everything that was happening and just go with it. Drake surrounding her body with his felt right. His thigh in between hers, his warmth seeping into her muscles to relax her.

"What movie did you pick out?" Sunshine asked.

"*Gladiator*—thought you might like to watch that since it's one of our favorites," Drake answered.

She breathed out a sigh of relief. "Thank goodness, I was sure you'd try to torture me with *The Notebook,* or one of the chick flicks Emerson insisted I needed in my collection."

"I would never do such a thing. I would only torture you in the bedroom." Drake tried to look innocent, which was hard to do when you looked like a fallen angel turned cowboy. Sunshine tried to keep her train of thought, and not jump his bones.

"Yeah you would, for spite." Sunshine turned back towards the TV. "Now hush."

As the end credits rolled, Sunshine dragged herself and Drake off the couch so they could finish cleaning up before he had to go home. Both of them had to get up early in the morning for work. Sunshine put everything in the dishwasher as Drake brought everything in from the dining room. She wasn't about to let him load it; it wouldn't be in order.

"Hey, baby, why don't you shake that ass for me while you're bent over?" Drake teased.

"Why are you such a pervert?"

Drake stared her down and she felt a tingle rush through her at his look. "Quit fussin'. You know you want every dirty thing I'm imagining doing to you with you bent over that way." Drake stalked over to her and pulled her head up so he could look her in the eye. He covered her hand with his and put it on his dick. She felt how much he was enjoying his thoughts. "I'm gonna give you a little bit longer, Sunshine, and hell that could mean a few hours as horny as I am, but before too much longer, I am going to be inside you."

Sunshine felt her panties explode. They disintegrated between her legs. Traitorous vagina. Hellfire. How was she supposed to anticipate that he had a dirty mouth and that it would be her damn turn-on? There was a part of her that screamed she shouldn't enjoy him talking to her like that, but her vagina told that part to shut the hell up. She didn't know he could have her wet and ready with a few words. She didn't even know he could talk that way. Drake had been hiding a lot of things from her, it seemed. She had never ever been talked to in that manner.

Sunshine ran her hand down the length of Drake over his pants and felt him get even bigger. Oh, she wanted that. "Drake, I think it is time for you to go home. We have some things we need to think about." Sunshine looked up at him and damn if that perfect face didn't make her want to say, *the hell with it, take me now*. She was fighting this thing between them for as long as she could.

Drake let her go and shook his head. "I've done made up my mind. The only thing I'm going to be thinkin' about tonight is you while I jack off like some damn teenager."

Sunshine was tempted to offer to help him out with that real quick, but fortunately she kept herself from blurting that. "You may not have anything to think on, but I still do. I don't want this blowin' up in my face."

143

"Honey, I won't blow up in your face unless you want me to." Drake had a shit-eating grin on his face.

Sunshine went slack-jawed before she could muster up enough breath to yell at him. "Drake, go get in the damn truck."

"Yes, ma'am." Drake turned towards the door and started walking out. "And just so you know, I will be the one barking out orders in the bedroom, but I may let you take the reins every once in a while."

She let out a small moan when he was out of sight. *Damn you, vagina, stop responding.*

# CHAPTER 14

## Battle Lines

The ride between them was silent besides the background noise of the radio. It wasn't long before they pulled into his parents' drive. She drove him up to the barn where he resided.

"You coming up?" He shot her a grin.

She shook her head at him. "Hell no."

"Come on up, I promise I won't behave."

"If I came up, you would be talkin' me out of my panties and these panties need to stay on their owner."

"Good, glad you are giving my dirty mouth some credit, but your panties can stay on. I can work around them." Her face was highlighted by the interior truck light, and he watched as a blush crept up her cheeks.

Sunshine peered over her steering wheel at his bull in the catch lot beside the barn, not looking him in the eye. "Still haven't forgiven you for stealin' him. Don't think I've forgotten that."

"Come over and see him sometime this week when it's pretty out." He'd let her change the conversation for a minute.

"Sounds good. I'll see you later."

Drake leaned over the seat to give Sunshine a goodbye kiss. He slipped his hand in the back of her hair, and angled her head up to him to move his lips to her ear. "You won't be worried about that bull after I get done making you forget." He slid out of the truck. "Night. I'll see you later." Best to leave her as heated and horny as he was. She gave him a nod when he got out of the truck. The knowledge that he could kiss her silent was a heady one.

Drake walked into his living quarters to find his brother lying on his couch. Brice turned his head towards him. "So, what's going on between you and Sunshine? And don't give me any bullshit."

Drake stared his brother down. Sometimes he wanted to beat the shit out of Brice, and this was one of those moments. "That isn't any of your damn business."

"I believe it is my business. Her family is our family. If you are thinking about sticking your dick in her only to have some fun, you need to reconsider. Sunshine isn't the type of woman for that. She's too good for that kind of treatment."

"I don't plan on only sticking my dick in her, you asshole. I don't know what I want or what I am planning on, but I sure the hell ain't going to treat her the way you would a wham bam thank you ma'am. I'm glad you are back home from school, but you need to stay out of my business. We don't have ovaries and I am done talking about this." Drake moved over to the fridge to get himself a beer as Brice settled back down on his couch and pulled a blanket over himself.

"You staying here again tonight?" Drake asked as he headed towards his bedroom.

"Yeah. I don't want to go in and wake Mom and Dad up. Night, D."

"Night, B." Drake shut the door to his bedroom and walked into the master bathroom to go through his usual routine before bed. Brice being there ruined his plans for self-gratification. His brother couldn't keep living with him. He needed to get his own place.

He'd meant it when he told Brice that Sunshine wasn't any other woman. Drake couldn't get her out of his head. He sure the heck hoped she was thinking about him. Every time he touched her or kissed her, all he wanted was more. He didn't quite know how to handle that. Sunshine was a beautiful, talented, and exciting woman. The only problem was that she came with a pasture full of cow patties, the biggest being their families. He had a lot going on at the stockyard right now, and with Duck and Cover.

Drake figured he should call and talk to Sunshine about what he was thinking. If she was that concerned about them starting something, then he needed to make sure they were on the same page. Pushing her sexually wasn't something he was going to do if she was that conflicted. He picked up his cell phone and dialed her.

"Joe's Meat House. You can beat our meat, but you can't beat our prices." Her voice came through the phone.

"You are nuts, you know that? I thought I would call you before you had the chance to overthink all night and wake me up at the butt crack of dawn to talk."

"Well, I'm still up. What is on your mind?"

"Sunshine, when the inevitable happens and we have sex, what do you expect from me? Are you expecting happily ever after and all that bullshit? Or dates, or what?" Drake scowled at his phone, out of his damn element waiting on her reply. He was certain he was screwing things up, but hell, he didn't know what else to do. He could be who he was, and that was it. He didn't hear her voice for a few minutes, but her breathing assured him she hadn't hung up on him yet.

"I don't know, Drake. I don't think we have to plan it out step by step, but if we do end up sleepin' together, I want it to be exclusive at the least. I don't want you sleepin' with other women. I would hope you would respect me that much."

Drake breathed a sigh of relief. "I wouldn't screw around behind your back. It would be exclusive till one of us wanted to end it." He felt his stomach drop at the mention of things ending, but they were adults talking about an adult relationship. Sunshine wouldn't be like Raegan and go crazy when things ended between them.

"About the date stuff...I don't know. Are we going to let the parents know? Is this goin' to be a public thing or a behind closed doors thing? Can we still talk to other people and date them, but not sleep with them?" she asked.

Drake felt his fist clench. "It's probably best to keep this from our parents and everyone else to start. If we don't, we are gonna have the entire county pestering the hell out of us. I think we should keep it behind closed doors for as long as we can. If we want to go out together here and there, we can go out to one of the other counties. When we decide to end this, there needs to be no hurt feelings between our families. As for dating and talking to other people, no. Unless you meet someone you think there's a chance with, then you can let me know and we'll break things off." The hell if he wouldn't make Sunshine change her mind if she thought she wanted someone else in her bed besides him. Drake had the urge to go punch Brice in the face to get his man card back. He sounded ridiculous talking about this shit. He was glad Sunshine had girlfriends. He hated talking about this type of stuff. He would have rather sent up smoke signals to her house.

"Alright, sounds impossible to keep everyone in the dark if we are at each other's places more than usual, but that'd be best. This stays between us—well, besides Willow and Belle. As for the dating aspect, neither of us should close ourselves off to other people since this will be goin' nowhere. I'm not lookin' to settle down anytime soon any more than you are, Drake. There are still a lot of experiences I want before I decide to take a walk down commitment road. There is somethin' I am workin' on, and I want to do it on my own."

"Same here. We can keep this fun and commitment-free, and end things all civil like whenever the other desires to. What are you working on anyway? You haven't talked to me about it."

"You're right and I'm not gonna talk to you about it, or anyone else." Sunshine left him no room for pestering.

"Okay, I'm going to the gym first thing in the morning. I need to get some sleep in. Night."

"The hell with the gym. Night, Drake."

Drake hung up the phone hoping there would be some sort of relief after making sure she didn't have any expectations that he didn't want her to have. She didn't seem shocked or worried about his want for lack of commitment. He didn't know if he liked what that said about her opinion of him.

His alarm clock slammed him awake. Damn Monday

mornings. He grabbed his gym bag off the floor and headed down the stairs. Footsteps behind him alerted him to Brice's presence.

"You comin' with?" he asked Brice over his shoulder. He stopped by the catch lot for a quick look over his bull. He seemed to be no worse for the wear with the transition.

Drake hurried to the truck to get out of the misty rain. His brother was lying back in the seat with his ball cap over his face. Brice wasn't a morning person like he was.

"Why the hell do we have to get up at the ass crack of dawn to go punish ourselves? Why not sleep another hour and a half and go tonight?" Brice mumbled to Drake.

"We have jobs, and today, and most days, we work long hours. I didn't ask you to tag along, or make you get up. Don't bitch." His brother could be a real titty baby. He had some concerns about where Brice was coming in on the business side. Brice had studied hard, but real-world application of business practices and a textbook knowledge were two different matters. Maybe that internship Brice did smoothed out some of the kinks.

His Dad would keep a close eye on Brice for a while to make sure he did what he was supposed to do. Drake wouldn't have to worry about him as long as his Dad was around to keep him in check. He didn't need babysitting his brother at work to be added to his workload.

Drake swiped his card at the gym and let Brice in to sign the guest list.

"You gonna join and start workin' out with me and Bishop? We work out three days a week, if we can make it."

"Yeah, if I don't, I'll be looking like a string bean. Can't seem to keep any damn weight on, or muscle mass."

Drake listened to his brother complain about his lanky build. If he wasn't careful, he would have the opposite problem and put on too much weight. He didn't know how often he would keep up his early mornings if he started working Sunshine over at night. One thing was for sure—he'd be getting his cardio in. He threw his bag down near the wall. Bishop had beat them there and was running on one of the treadmills. Drake and Brice joined him for a quick fifteen-minute warm-up.

"How many miles have you done?" Drake asked Bishop as he stacked weights on the leg press.

"Two. I haven't been here long. There was a lady that left after I got on the treadmill. I'd met her before. I think she's one of y'all's friends. Belle?"

"Oh yeah. How many miles had she done? A hundred?" Drake chuckled. Belle was one hell of a runner.

"She said she was doing ten today, but that her normal was twenty or more. The hell with that. I'd rather go without sex for a week than run that far once." Bishop shook his head.

"You didn't hit on her, did you?" Brice asked Bishop.

"Hell no, she wouldn't give me the time of day if I did. I suppose we aren't each other's type. I prefer my women with more curves. She's not the type I fancy." Bishop grunted as he shoved the leg press up.

"Belle is hot. I don't know what you're lookin' at," Brice said. Drake watched their exchange with little interest. He had his own lady problems to deal with.

"Yeah, she is. I didn't say she wasn't. Are you wantin' me to hit on her?" Bishop asked as he stood up.

"Hell no. I was I just making the statement that she's hot."

Drake went next, and then took twenty pounds off before his brother sat down. He didn't want him straining his knees.

Brice gave Drake a stubborn look. "I saw you take those plates off."

"You haven't been working out on a regular basis. No sense in getting hurt right when you start your job with us." He motioned for Brice to get started.

"Any thoughts on what we spoke about previously?" Bishop asked as he watched his brother's form.

"Yeah. I've got some ideas and figures runnin' through my head." Drake cut his eyes to Brice. His brother didn't seem to be listening, and had his earbuds in.

"Got to come clean with you, even though the artificial insemination is the best choice in my opinion, that was suggested for selfish reasons. I'm looking at opening a lab up here within a year. It'd help if I already had a large client lined up, especially one who had business ties with more potential clients," Bishop said.

"No worries. You wouldn't screw me over in business. I'll be expecting a discounted rate." Drake reached out and shook Bishop's hand. He wasn't upset about Bishop hiding his main plan from him, because if he did screw Drake over, he'd be quick to ruin any plans of a future business for him here. Bishop's family had reach in Mississippi and Tennessee, not so much in Alabama.

"Of course. Slip the word around to those you think would have interest," Bishop said.

"Will do."

"You gonna talk to Brice about what you have planned for

the future of the stockyard?"

"Not until I see how he does with what we have going on now."

"He is smarter than you or your Dad give him credit for. He isn't the same hell-raiser that went off to Miss. State."

Drake grunted a yeah towards Bishop while he unloaded the rest of the plates off the leg press. His brother took his earbuds out and serenaded him and Bishop with the song coming over the speakers in the empty gym. He wanted to stab his eardrums when Brice hit a particular high note in "Girls Like You" by Adam Levine.

"Brice, no wonder you can't keep a woman. Your singing is shit," Drake kidded his brother as he heaved the weight up off his shoulders and back onto the squat rack.

"I could keep one around if I wanted to, and if I recall, didn't a certain redhead go psycho the other night because of you?"

"Yeah, but I didn't want to keep that one around for damn sure."

"What about Sunshine? You gonna keep her around?"

Drake stopped what he was doing to face his brother. Bishop made a quick step towards them.

"Brice, we had this conversation last night, and I don't think anything has changed since I went to sleep. Keep your mouth shut about me and Sunshine. She and I prefer to keep our private life private. I'd hate to have to remind you who's the bigger and older brother, but I'm not above kicking your ass when it comes to her." He watched as Brice's ensuing grin went to his eyes. Fuck, he stepped right into that one.

"You're messing around with Sunshine?" Bishop asked him. Drake could read the shock across his face. He turned towards his snitch of a brother.

Drake headed to the showers, not in the least inclined to hear Bishop or Brice rag on him. "Not yet, Bishop, but that's my mission."

# CHAPTER 15

## Dirt Roads

Sunshine met Bishop in the next county over at Casa in Muscle Shoals, because let's be honest, who doesn't love Spanish-inspired food? She got there before him and got them a booth tucked in the back corner of the nonsmoking section.

She had met Bishop Matthew Hamilton III through Brice when he was off at college. She'd come down to hang out with Brice but ended up hanging out with Bishop that night instead. Brice had been passed out on the couch. Bishop was sharp as a tack and made her laugh when he drew dicks all over Brice's face in permanent marker. Brice woke up pissed, but he deserved it for passing out drunk before she could get there.

She knew Bishop well, but when it came to business, if she wasn't the person for the contract, she wouldn't get it. Playing favorites isn't how the Hamiltons got to where they were. They only dealt with the best, and she wanted to be the best, without having anything handed to her.

Sunshine smiled when she saw Bishop walk through the door. She seemed to be surrounded by handsome men these days. Bishop was around six foot one and solid. He looked as if he would be more at home on the football field as opposed to the

155

back of a horse, or behind a desk. He had a sly smile that hinted that he may be up to something. His hair was cut short to his scalp and his brown eyes hinted he that knew something you didn't. He gave off the distinct badass vibe that made women want to try and tame him. She had recognized his appeal years ago when she first met him, but he was out of her depth when it came to sex. Brice had told her that Bishop was kinky, and at the time, she didn't have a drop of experience under her belt to even ask what he was into.

Sunshine got up from their booth to hug him. He pulled her off her feet and squeezed her tight and sat her back down as if he may have broken her. Sunshine settled back in her seat and smiled over at him as he sat. "Hey, handsome. You greet all your business clients that way? If you do, sign me up for a meeting twice a week."

"If they are as sexy as you, I do. I'd be an idiot not to." Bishop winked at her. Sunshine couldn't help but blush a little at the compliment. Bishop did that to a woman. He was a flirt. He would flirt with any female, no age limit. He was a horndog.

"If you didn't say that to every woman you meet, I might be flattered, but seein' as you do, I am not." Sunshine winked back at him.

"Damn it, better luck next time. What are you getting to eat?" Bishop asked. Neither bothered to pick up a menu. When Bishop was in town, he and Brice made it to Casa at least once during his visit. Meanwhile, Sunshine was there once a week.

"Fajitas. My usual. I ordered a cheese dip, and you a sweet tea." Sunshine motioned to the glasses on the table.

"Did I mention that I want you to marry me? Because I do,"

Bishop declared before taking a big drink of sweet tea.

Sunshine rolled her eyes. "You have on occasion, but I've yet to see a ring on my finger or any trace of you being faithful. Gonna have to say that I am turning you down."

Bishop shook his head at her and grinned. "You want to talk business now or after we eat?"

"I prefer now, get it out of the way." She waved the waiter down and ordered.

"Okay, I went over to Moonshine farm today. The stock is looking healthy, and I've looked over the statistics of the herd and their output over the last three years. Same as I told you before, the quantity is what is lacking." Sunshine's heart dropped as Bishop continued. "That hasn't knocked you out of being bought by Mr. Alexander, but I want to forewarn you that the other player has bigger numbers and also some great quality. I'm trying to work out something and find another buyer in the state that wants to buy another young registered herd, but it isn't something I can promise."

"I understand. I will have the numbers within two to three years. I have been concerned with building quality at the beginnin' versus quantity. I want the herd's statistics to speak for themselves. I appreciate the confidence and you tryin' to get a broker to take a chance on me. Who is the other person vying for the contract?" Sunshine asked with a sinking feeling in her stomach. She knew it was a long shot that he would spill the beans, and then Bishop confirmed it.

"You know I ain't going to tell you that, no matter how pretty you are." Bishop grinned. The laugh lines around his eyes crinkled and softened his words to her somewhat.

"Can't blame a girl for tryin'." Their food arrived and she dug in. Sucked balls to hear she was a long shot after an already rough morning of losing a heifer and bull calf during birth—a bull calf that happened to have been meant for the Moonshine herd. She needed this sale. She needed to get out from under that loan.

Sunshine swallowed down a large bite of fajita before askin', "What's happenin' on the lady front?"

Bishop shrugged his broad shoulders. "Nothing of any interest. I've been keeping more to myself, trying to reform. The female population is upset, and close to rioting, but I am managing." Bishop gave her a smile.

"You are full of shit, Bishop Matthew Hamilton. You've not been in town this time but a week, and I guarantee that you've got your eye on someone to get in your bed."

Bishop shook his head at her. "I swear, I am reforming as we speak. My wonder down yonder is staying in my pants."

She laughed. "Um, we will see how long this reform lasts."

She made idle chitchat and caught up on him the rest of the meal, no more business talk or talk of his sex life. The both of them had to keep the business and personal separate to maintain their friendship. She couldn't let emotions get involved, and both parties had to be committed to that goal for their friendship to stay solid.

She gave him a tight hug as she left. On her way back to the Moonshine herd, she called Belle and Willow and asked them to ride around with her later. Thank goodness they agreed. She had a lot of crap she needed to talk to them about. It had been a pretty hard day on the farm even before that lunch meeting with Bishop, not that she would talk to them about that, but then she also hadn't heard from Drake. Not that she minded, not at all, but she figured she wouldn't sit at the house thinking about it. She would be damned if she would be the type of woman who sat around waiting and moping over a man.

She did a quick but thorough inspection of the cattle and headed to pick up Belle and Willow. She pulled up in front of Willow's alluring home. A two-story Victorian with a wraparound porch, jasmine climbing up some of the poles, and flower beds overflowing with different types. Not that Willow did any of her own landscaping. Hell no, she hired that out. Sunshine saw that Belle's car was there. She honked the horn.

"Hey, hobags. How are they hangin'?" Sunshine asked as they climbed into the front seat.

Willow grabbed hers and seemed to try and weigh them.

"They aren't hanging. They're still perky. Thanks for inquiring."

"I second that," Belle said as she snapped her seat belt.

"Smartasses. No plastic surgery necessary this year. Good to know. Now, how were your days?"

Belle whipped her head around towards her so fast that her honey-blond hair covered her face. "I will tell you how my day was. It was shit. Shit on a stick. It was the equivalent of going to the ice cream truck and thinking, 'Hey, I am going to get an ice cream,' but no they are out of ice cream and instead you get shit on a stick because there is no damn ice cream."

"Okay, amazing metaphor, but what exactly does it represent?" Sunshine pulled to a stop at the four-way in town.

"I am concerned about the shit on a stick. I mean why shit

on a stick? Why not shit on a cone, or a plate? It seems it would be difficult to put shit on a stick, unless you have taken a lot of iron maybe?" Willow asked with a straight face.

Belle scowled at Willow. "That is all you have to say about my metaphor? You are concerned about how the shit got on the stick? I should punch you in your cooter. Brice Beauregard Caldwell is my problem. The man won't leave me alone. Everywhere I turn, there he is. I went to the Swine and Dine today for a quick lunch and bam, there he is. Brice, for some reason, thinks I have a problem with him, and whatever imaginary problem there is between us, he needs to fix it."

Sunshine looked over at Willow and gave her a *what the hell* look as Belle continued. She hadn't heard Belle get testy, or even express the least bit of emotion about a guy since the last douchebag she dumped.

"How does this translate to your day being shit on a stick?" Willow asked.

"I wanted the last piece of chocolate pie. I had been eyeing it all lunch long. I wanted it worse than a dog in heat wants to hump. I wanted the damn pie!" Belle gestured wildly with her hands as she spoke, a sure sign of distress from Sunshine's more reserved friend. "I was at the cash register and Brice walked in the door and ambled up to the counter beside me. I was fixing to ask for my pie to be delivered, but before I could get the waitress's attention the bastard stole the pie. He leaned over the counter and gave a *come do me now* smile to the waitress and asked her to please get the last piece of pie for him to go. He made ordering a piece of pie from her sound sexual. I thought she was going to lie on the counter and say, *here you can have a piece of my pie*, or he was going to tell her she could have a piece of his pie, or maybe they could rub their pieces of pie together and make babies!"

Sunshine looked over at her, confused. "Is this about the real pie, or the fact that you thought Brice was going to get sexy pie from the waitress?"

Belle huffed. "It's about the pie. I mean there wasn't a problem between us, but now there is. I wanted that specific piece of pie."

Sunshine couldn't help but think Belle was talking about getting a "piece of pie" from Brice herself, and not the edible kind.

"Okay, are you over your craving for this certain 'pie'?" Willow made air quotes around the word *pie*. "Or are you thinking about getting you a slice of this 'pie' at a later date?"

Belle gave Willow a hard look. "I think I need to get over my craving for this particular pie. I mean I could get diabetes and die from too much pie. Or I could get attached to said pie and crave it for the rest of my life and then the pie factory will be shut down."

Sunshine gazed over at her. "Don't question it or doubt yourself. If you want pie, get some pie. If the pie factory does get shut down, there is another bigger and better pie out there waiting to take the other pie's place."

"Yeah, but when it turns out to be your favorite pie all other pies are just replacement pies." Belle put her hands over her face.

Sunshine waited a while before she spoke again. "Well, penises and their owners are confusin'." Willow and Belle both turned and nodded their heads at her in agreement.

"Whose penis, or owner of said penis, did something to you?" Belle asked.

"Drake is the owner of said penis. He and his damn penis have confused me. I do believe we have agreed for us to be exclusive in our 'pie making.' We aren't telling anyone though." Sunshine looked over to judge their reactions.

Belle nodded and motioned for her to continue. Willow sat in the middle of the truck and appeared to be thinking deeply this whole *pie* conundrum.

"But my vagina wants to meet his penis and for them be on a first-name basis, but I think I'm getting in over my head here. I want a piece of his pie, well his whole pie, but I feel like I'm being a ho." Sunshine huffed as she drove towards the edge of the county and the less-traveled backroads. "Any thoughts, opinions, or judgments from the choir?"

"Do it, because if you don't, you are going to regret it and always wonder *what if*. You are not an ask permission type, Sunshine. You are an ask for forgiveness person. There are never any guarantees about any relationship, but I do believe if Drake said he was going to be exclusive, he will be, and that he will also be fantastic in bed," Belle advised.

"I think you might need to think about what you said there and maybe take your own advice," Sunshine said with as much kindness as she could. She didn't want Belle to think she was trying to be a bitch, but she needed to take a chance on Brice.

Willow nodded in agreement. "You both need to get all the pie you can. Pretend it's a buy one, get one hundred free sale. Then tell me all about the different types of pie you have."

Sunshine laughed. "All those in favor of Sunshine's vagina and Drake's penis bein' introduced and getting a piece of pie, raise your hands." Sunshine looked over at them, smiling. It was unanimous. She did believe she'd decided to start a sexual relationship with Drake. Not that she would, or wouldn't, have made her decision based solely on what they said, but she would have taken their opinions under advisement.

"Now, all those in favor of Brice and Belle getting a piece of pie, raise your hands." Sunshine and Willow both raised their hands while Belle glared at them. Sunshine's smile fell. Well, shit. "Guys, I am not real experienced at makin' pie. As a matter of fact, I have had very few pie makin' classes. Those experiences in pie makin' were, to say the least, disappointin'."

Willow chimed in. "Yeah, I remember you telling us about quickie McGee and lackluster Luke. Sad, and I'm sorry your pie-making encounters have been less than, well, less than, but you have nothing to worry about. You'll be naked and that's all it'll take for him to get happy. He won't even notice if you aren't all that experienced at making pie. You will be learning each other's wants and bodies. There are going to be embarrassing and weird moments in any pie-making experience. That's all part of getting intimate with someone else."

"I know I don't tell you this enough, but y'all are brilliant and I love you." Sunshine smiled at them. They were the best two friends she could have. They pulled back into Willow's since they all had to work the next day.

Belle hopped out first. "You have all the pie you want, Sunshine. I'll live vicariously through you."

Sunshine yelled back at her. "Why don't you go get your own pie?" Belle flipped Sunshine off behind her back and kept walking.

Willow jumped out next. "You tame that penis, Sunshine.

You tie that thing down, and make it commit to your vagina and your vagina only!" Willow yelled as she drove away from her house. She hoped there were no people nearby to hear Willow's brand of encouragement.

Sunshine felt better after an evening hanging out with the girls. She did want pie after that talk, and not the sexual kind, but the real thing. Some pecan pie with ice cream and caramel on top sounded amazing. She could, however, also eat that real pie off Drake's body and have the best of both worlds. She drove around for a bit longer, takin' the long way home. She decided to stop in at The Cardinal and get her an apple pie with ice cream and caramel on top. Might as well eat something to sate that sweet tooth of hers.

Sunshine glanced over at the clock on her dash as she pulled in the driveway. Ten o'clock. She needed to be in bed within the next hour if she was going to be able to function tomorrow. Her truck lights fell on her front door, and she knew she wouldn't be going to bed any time soon.

# CHAPTER 16

## Sneaky Varmint

Drake opened up John Wayne when he saw her truck lights in the drive. He stood there, waiting on her. His day had been a good one, and her smile made it great.

"Hey, cowboy," Sunshine said as she walked past him through the door, pausing to take her boots off.

"Hey, cowgirl." Drake reached out and pulled her to him. "Where've you been?"

"Would you believe me if I told you Belle, Willow, and I drove to Tunica, went to a strip club, and won five thousand dollars?" Sunshine grinned.

"Hell no."

"I stopped by and got Belle and Willow. We rode around a bit, talkin' about pie, shit on a stick, and our boobs." She gave him a sly grin. He assumed there was something he was missing there.

"None of that makes a lick of sense to me, but the boob talk I can weigh in on." Drake leaned down to kiss her. He parted her lips with his tongue, and she took what he offered her. He swallowed her moan as his hands grabbed her butt and pulled it close. When her own hands started creeping up his shirt, he pulled back before he lost his sanity and reasoning skills.

She walked away from him into the kitchen. "What'd you do this afternoon?"

"Worked. I didn't get off till late. Ran by and ate some supper at Mom and Dad's. Decided I'd come here after I had my shower." He left out the part about running to check on Duck and Cover. He wanted to keep that to himself for a while longer. At least till he found out if his herd got bought out.

"You want a beer?"

"Nah, I'm good. Brice and I had one together before I left."

"Brice knows you're over here?" She raised her eyebrows. "The little shit may tell on us to get back for all we've pulled on him over the years."

"He's been stayin' at my apartment nonstop, so yeah, he figured it out."

"Um, you trust him?"

"He won't say anything to our parents. He's done a lot of growing up in the past year, I think." He gave her a shrug. Wasn't much he could do about it now. He didn't want to tell her that Brice had told Bishop. She'd get pissed at Brice, and then he'd have to listen to her call and yell at him for a good twenty minutes.

"How was it working with Brice today? He drive you insane?"

"Not bad, better than I expected. His work ethic as a teenager and the work ethic he showed us today are polar opposites."

"Really? He didn't goof off all day?"

"No. He showed up on time, but he did ride with me. He put in a hard day's work in his office, and I had nothing to do with that. He figured out a way that we could save a thousand dollars in overhead every two weeks. Shocked the hell out of me and Dad. All in all, I think it is going to be good to have his energetic perspective in the business matters. He has a better personality to deal with people than I do at times."

"What'd your Dad say?"

"He told Brice that finding that cut in our overhead was a start on paying him back for his education." Drake had laughed when his Dad said it, but his brother didn't say a word. He'd walked out, their Dad following. He had looked over the rest of the paperwork Brice had done, and he'd been more than impressed. His brother had streamlined the accounting sheets. He had a feeling Brice's expensive degree and internship were gonna pay off for all of them.

He'd done an effective job of making Drake feel like a dumb ass, but Drake's job wasn't finances. Drake's job was to keep the big buyers and sellers happy, and keep up with all their personal cattle. His Dad's job was to oversee things, but in reality, he sat back and stepped in when he thought Drake might need help. Today had given him hope that he would continue to have time for Duck and Cover.

"That was a harsh thing for your Dad to say." Sunshine frowned. She'd be calling Brice later and checking up on him if Drake had to bet.

"He can be a hard man, but he's a good businessman. If Brice or I needed to go, he'd fire us in a heartbeat." He understood his father, and he loved the man. Ben had raised him and Brice to have strong work ethics, and values. His Dad wouldn't put up with anything less than their best when it came to his business.

"By the way, how did you get in my house?" Sunshine went to the front door and locked it. She put her hands up before he could get offended. "Not that I mind, but I need to know if I left the door unlocked."

Drake sat down at the bar and held Sunshine's spare key up for her to see. "I know where you keep the spare. I let myself in."

"Did you park your truck behind the barn?"

"I didn't drive. I rode Chief over tonight. Thought it might keep our parents from knowing I was gone, or where I was at."

"Good plan. Sure didn't expect for some sexy man to break into my house tonight, but I'll take the surprise since it's you." Sunshine winked at him. She had some of the most beautiful hair he had ever seen on a woman. Not that he took the time to notice a woman's hair much. Sunshine's hair made him think about how it would feel when she dragged it down his body heading towards, what he assumed would be, the best blow job he had ever had.

"Why don't you go ahead and have your bath." Drake got up and walked over to where she was standing, leaned up against the bar, his need to touch her disconcerting to him as he rubbed her shoulders and she leaned into his touch. "Throw your dirty clothes down and I'll throw them in the washer. Then we can lie in bed and watch a movie." Drake laid a kiss on her cheek. He needed to get her upstairs and out of arm's reach for a bit.

Sunshine turned towards him and gave him a skeptical look. "You are going to put a load of laundry in, and then lie in bed with me to watch TV?"

Drake tried to look wounded, but by the chuckle she let out, he failed. "Hey, I wash my own clothes. And yes, to watch TV. Maybe also feel you up a bit, if you'll let me." Drake raised his eyebrows at her, making a quick grab at her boobs. She deflected his advances with a karate chop. Damn her reflexes.

"That last sentence is a tad more truthful, but keep your penis to yourself for the time bein', understand? I'm goin' on up. Don't be tryin' to sneak a peek at me in the shower, you perv."

Drake was tempted to follow her up and take what he wanted. It wouldn't take much and she would be ready for him, but tonight wasn't the night for that. How he could think now wasn't the time for sex, hell he didn't know, but it didn't seem right. He picked her clothes up off the floor where she had thrown them over the railing and walked to the laundry room. He sorted through some of her dirty clothes and threw a load in the washer. He figured he'd get her clean ones out of the dryer while he was at it. He was a freaking domestic son of a bitch when he needed to be.

His phone buzzed at him—it was a text from Brice. He'd been right. Sunshine had already checked up on his brother. He was bitching at Drake for telling Sunshine what their Dad had said. Drake flipped him off with an emoji and silenced his phone.

Drake headed up the stairs and hoped Sunshine would have enough sense to close the door so he wouldn't be tempted more than he already was to barge in. Disappointment still hit his stomach when he found the bathroom door closed. He made his way to the bed and laid the laundry out on it. He noticed a sexy piece of underwear in the pile and pulled it out—a bright red thong with see-through lace in the front. He got hard just holding her damn panties. If he saw her in them, he would cum in his pants.

A small creak filled the air and Sunshine walked out of the bathroom wearing a Christmas pajama set. The tank top said naughty list, which happened to be the exact list he needed her to be on. He was still holding her revealing pair of panties. His muscles tensed and his eyes were directed at her boobs as they bounced with her steps. He struggled not to go after her. She was a smoke show.

"Drake, look me in the eye." He reined himself in to follow her direction, and found enough control not to go caveman on her and bang her up against the wall. It was a close call.

"Sunshine, I want you to wear these panties for me one day. I plan on taking them off with my teeth." Drake put her panties down and walked over to her. He could see that she wanted him. Her nipples were hard against her tank top and her eyes were glazed over and heavy lidded. He pulled her up close and kissed the top of her head.

"But I know, not tonight. What do you want to watch before bed?" Drake asked as he moved the clothes off the bed and put them in stacks on top of Sunshine's dresser. She could put them up herself later. If he found any more revealing panties, he would be getting her to put on a fashion show. A dirty, lewd, erotic fashion show. He added that to his fantasy list starring Sunshine.

While Sunshine got situated for bed, he pulled his shirt and ankle socks off and crawled in beside her. He held his arm out and she curled up under his arm and snuggled into his chest.

"How 'bout we watch whatever you want to? I'll never be able to stay awake long enough to watch one of my shows." She handed him the remote and laid her hand across his stomach. He decided on Sports Center. He hadn't had time to watch it over the last few days and needed to catch up. It was in her favorites list. She watched Sports Center with him and Brice often so she wouldn't mind his choice. Sunshine started to trace his abs with her fingers. He tensed as she touched a ticklish spot here and there. She was driving him mad. Did she not know he was hanging on to his self-restraint by a thread?

"Sunshine, stop."

He figured to the reason for his request was evident since she had nothing to say in response. Instead she dropped her hand, arm across his stomach, and threw her leg over his. He could do this. He could cuddle with her and not hump her. Damn it.

"How was your day?" he asked during a commercial break. Drake rubbed a hand up and down her back as he waited for her to answer, trying to torture her as much as she did him.

"It was a rough one. Lost a calf and a heifer today. I had to get the pullers out and neither of them lived. It comes with the territory, but still doesn't make it any better when it happens."

"Oh shit, that makes the day go to hell in a hurry."

"That isn't all. Then I had a blow out on the tractor while I was movin' some hay. Sugar Baby decided she was pissed and broke a board in her stall. I got to hang out with Belle and Willow and that helped relieve some of my stress. Then this guy showed up to my house and kissed me senseless. That made it some better." Sunshine gave him a soft smile. Her laundry list of a day ended with a yawn.

Drake stopped rubbing her back and hugged her. "You could have called and told me about it. I probably wouldn't have been able to get away to help you right then, but you never know. I could have at least listened to you gripe about it."

Sunshine shook her head. "Nah, I had it handled. No sense in whinin' about it, let alone botherin' you with it. You've got your own craziness to deal with at work. I called Dad and he came and helped with the flat tire. Hated to bother him, but I didn't have the strength to get the tire changed."

"You've called me to bitch about stuff during the week for years. Last week you called to yell because you thought I had been coming over and feeding your horses more than usual causing their shitting to increase and only I would think to do something that diabolical to irritate you." His laughter had her head bouncing up and down on his chest. She gave him more credit than he was due for scheming against her.

"When you say it out loud, I sound ridiculous. I have good reason to suspect you when it comes to any type of circumstance that is a pain in my ass. You have been behind a good many of them. Case in point: buyin' that bull." Sunshine pinched his nipple when he kept laughing and he jumped.

"Watch it, or I won't keep my hands to myself anymore." Drake made a motion to pinch her nipple and she batted his hand down before he could touch her.

"Whore. I will damage you if you give me a titty twister," Sunshine threatened him. She leaned her head back so he could see her smiling at him. He gave her a quick kiss, before she yawned and snuggled back up to his side.

"What do you plan on doin' with the bull anyway? Store his semen and sale it?" Sunshine asked him. Thank goodness she gave him an easy out. She must have been puttin' some more thought into his purchase. That wasn't something he needed her to do.

"Umh, now that is a good idea. We might need to hire you on to help Brice." He didn't confirm or deny what she thought.

He wouldn't outright lie to her about it. "Let's go to sleep. Work is waiting on us in the morning."

He turned off the TV and slid down further in the bed, repositioning himself and Sunshine on their sides where they'd be more comfortable. He splayed his hand across her belly and pulled her close. It was torture with her ass right against his dick, but it felt good to be lying there with her.

"Night," Sunshine mumbled, almost asleep.

Drake leaned over and kissed her cheek. "Night."

He was anxious to get his sleep in and wake up to her. He had agreed to keep his hands to himself that night, but she hadn't said anything about tomorrow.

# CHAPTER 17

## Mornin'

Sunshine woke to a hand between her legs, doing wicked things. She moaned and arched into Drake, searching for more pressure and friction. She was ashamed to say she whimpered when he pulled his hand away. Well, she believed she did. It could have been her vagina that was staging a mutiny and decided to speak up.

"Not yet," Drake growled. He flipped her over onto her back and got on his knees between her legs. "I want to see your face."

Sunshine about screamed out in happiness over that statement. Damn, Drake looked good in the morning. Eyes blazing, his face was scruffy and his hair was all over his head. Sunshine couldn't even think of a response. She swallowed her tongue when Drake jerked her shorts down and spread her legs before she could think to shut them tight.

"I've been thinking about what you were going to taste like, look like, and sound like for days. I plan on finding out right now." Drake put his face level with her most intimate parts and put his shoulders between her legs to keep her from closing them.

"What are you doing?" Sunshine asked, hoping he was going to do what she thought he was. She had never had that done before. The two guys she'd been with had both said that wasn't their thing. Thank goodness she had the good sense to shave last night. You know, just in case.

Drake didn't say a word in response. Sunshine about came with the first swipe of his tongue. She knew she sounded like a porn star moaning but she didn't care. There were no words for what he was doing to her. She could feel the tingle and tightening at the base of her spine moving towards what she knew was going to be an amazing orgasm. She ran her fingers through his hair and held on. She could feel him grin against her when he did something she particularly liked and she started to try and climb up the bed, away from him. She figured she was going to pass out from the pleasure. She didn't though. She exploded, and felt as if she was torn in two. Her back bowed so hard she thought she may break.

Sunshine thought she was going to cry when Drake's continued his onslaught. When the fireworks within went off inside her again she hadn't know she could have orgasms back-to-back. Sunshine opened her eyes after a few minutes to see Drake grinning at her. She suddenly felt embarrassed, which was not her usual MO. This was Drake, the guy she took baths with when she was little. Hell, he knew her as well as anyone and now he knew her better than anyone. *This* was intimacy.

"Damn if you don't taste good."

Sunshine felt herself blush at his words but remained silent.

"Come on, baby, talk to me." Drake laid a kiss against her pelvis.

"Whoa, and could you not lie there and look at her like that? It's embarrassin'," Sunshine said, not meeting his eyes as she continued blushing, trying to get him to move from between her legs.

Drake moved over to her side and pulled Sunshine up against him. "There is nothing to be shy about. If I want to stare at you, lick you, kiss you, and give you multiple orgasms, you lie back and enjoy it."

Sunshine shrugged, keeping her face buried in his chest. "I've never had that done before and it was a lot more intimate than I'd imagined."

Drake furrowed his eyebrows and frowned. "I don't know why no man has ever done that for you, but I can tell you that I loved it as much as you seemed to."

She felt her cheeks become more heated. She had never heard him talk in that manner, the past few days aside, and it was a new part of him she was trying to adjust to.

"Baby, you're gonna have to get used to the way I talk when it comes to sex. I'm gonna say dirty things to you, and you're gonna enjoy it. Don't even try to deny it. I can tell by the way you react. Everyone has their own kinks and we will find out yours together, one of which appears to be my dirty mouth."

Sunshine squinted up at him. "You are weird. This is weird. I've stepped into an alternate universe."

Drake laughed and pulled her closer. "I agree that things have been unexpected."

Sunshine could feel him hard against her stomach. She stammered. "Drake, do you, uh, um, want me to maybe help you out with that?" She then got pissed at herself. Where the hell was her forwardness, her lady balls?

"No, baby, the first time I'm with you, I want to be inside you, not your mouth. Even though it is a very beautiful mouth and I plan on doing that too." Drake's alarm went off. Sunshine leaned up as he kissed the little squinty lines between her eyebrows, then lowered his mouth to kiss her lips.

Sunshine's alarm started going off next and she rolled away from him and turned it off. Damn man was too sexy for words. She was out of her league with the sexual stuff, but it looked as though she was gonna get introduced to the finer points with Drake doing the teaching.

"I'm gonna go grab a shower," Drake told her as he got out of bed and headed to the bathroom. "Don't come in because I think I may also have to take a shit." He turned around and winked at her.

"And there's the Drake I know well. I was wonderin' when he was going to come back. And to think I let you kiss me with that mouth." Sunshine laughed and pulled the pillow over her head.

"You love my dirty mouth. Don't pretend you don't," Drake said as he shut the bathroom door.

Sunshine mumbled into her pillow, "Damn right I do."

"I heard that," Drake called out from behind the door.

Sunshine smiled and snuggled back into the bed and blankets for a few more minutes of rest. She was enjoying their time together. She always had, but now this new, whatever it was, was more enjoyable and exciting. The things he could do with his mouth and fingers… Dear heavens above, she would never be able to look at him the same, no matter when they ended things. Their family dinners were gonna be a new experience because she was gonna look at that mouth and know the wicked magic he could work. She rolled over when she heard him come out of the bathroom.

"What is on your to-do list today? Besides give Sunshine an

orgasm. You can go ahead and mark that off." She had found her sass.

"Damn, I am already ahead of the game today. All other accomplishments will be dim next to that one, but I have some paperwork. Need to work a few calves out of the herd to put in with the other heifers. Plan on working the new horse I bought a couple weeks ago with the cattle today to see what he's got. I thought you might want to come look at the new bull or even help me, maybe?"

Sunshine finished putting her hair up and put some toothpaste on her toothbrush. She noticed her toothbrush was wet again, but she didn't say anything. He would surely have something dirty to remark in return. She turned towards Drake and leaned against the granite bathroom counter top. He looked damn sexy leaned against the doorframe with his sexed up hair, and smuggling a weapon of _ass_ destruction in his pants. She tried not to snort at her joke as she spoke, "I've got a few things as usual to do around here, but I may be able to break away sometime this afternoon. Text me and let me know when and I'll see where I am in my workload." Sunshine turned, dragging her eyes off of Drake's man parts, and started brushing her teeth. He walked up behind her and pulled her against him.

"I saw what you were looking at, and I will tell you what was running through my mind." Drake dragged his hands up Sunshine's sides, bringing her top with them. He stopped right before he uncovered her breasts. He bent and kissed down her neck, back up to her ear where he whispered, "I was thinking about jerking those hot shorts down, bending you over that counter, and taking you from behind while we both watched." He bit down on her ear and goosebumps broke out down her arms.

Her shorts were soaked. The images going through her mind from his words were almost enough to make her disintegrate. Damn man was a danger to her. Her vagina wanted to cheer. She muffled it in case he had vajayjay ESP.

He walked away from her, and she listened as he pulled his clothes on in the bedroom.

"Well, this has been an interestin' mornin'." She walked over to the doorway and shut and locked it before jumping in and taking a quick shower, being careful not to get her hair wet. She wrapped her towel around her before walking out of the bathroom to her work clothes dresser. Drake was sitting on the bed watching her. Sunshine figured payback was necessary.

She dropped her towel and slipped on her work clothes while Drake watched. She'd heard a strangled noise from behind her when she bent over to pull on her panties. She turned towards him and could see the fire in his eyes. "I thought I would give you somethin' to think about today." She smirked at him. "Now, you still have to get Chief and ride home. I suggest you get going and get your day started." She walked over and slid between his legs to give him a kiss. "Have a good day, sugar."

Drake tugged her closer and deepened their kiss. His phone alarm went off again and he pulled away from her. "Yeah, I gotta go. I will talk to you later." He got up and hugged her one last time before heading for the door. "Have a good day, cowgirl."

Sunshine watched him walk out of the bedroom and gave herself a mental slap to make sure she hadn't hallucinated this entire scenario before she called out to him, "Bye, cowboy." She had to get her head out of her ass and get her day started.

She was sitting at her desk in the house, looking over feed prices, beef prices, and figuring how she could grow her stock, but still keep the quality, when her phone rang at about five o'clock that afternoon. "Charlie's Whorehouse, we got the ho if you got the dough," Sunshine answered with a smile in her voice.

Drake laughed. "Yes, I request Mistress Bitchin' Becky and her sexpertise."

Sunshine pretended to think a minute. "Um, let me check her schedule, but I don't think she is free till hell freezes over."

Sunshine couldn't see Drake, but she was certain he was shaking his head at her.

"You gonna come over here and help me with these cows? Or am I going to have to find Becky?"

"I will be there with bells on, but you have to grill me a steak tonight for my free labor," Sunshine bargained. She closed out some documents on her computer and straightened her desk.

"Done, and I'll throw in a baked potato. You're welcome."

"Okay, sounds like a deal. Give me about twenty minutes. I gotta get Deacon saddled and I will be over there in a jiff. Bye." Sunshine didn't wait for his response. She hung up as she got up from her desk and headed out to the barn, making sure not to forget to lock her house this time. Not that anyone had any problems with stealing, but it made her feel better since she lived alone.

Deacon pranced around in the corral, showing off. Bo was his audience, but that was all Deacon needed. That horse was a ham for attention, but he was a wonderful horse. They say you get one great horse in your lifetime. She had to disagree, so far she had two, but Deacon did outshine Sugar Baby. He was her go-to horse for any and everything, especially for working cows. Sugar Baby was great at working cows too, but she didn't have the size and stamina that Deacon did.

Plus, Deacon was beautiful. She clucked at him and he came over to the fence for her to love on him a minute. She opened the gate and let him follow her without worrying to hook a lead rope to him. He was her baby and he followed her wherever she went.

Sunshine walked into the barn and pulled out her saddle and Deacon stood still while she climbed up on a step stool to get it situated. He was a tall horse for her. He stood sixteen hands high, and a stool was necessary for her to get the saddle and bridle on him perfectly. She would have him cinched in and strapped up in no time. She jumped up on his back and they headed down the driveway at a trot. Deacon and Sugar Baby got shoed two weeks ago, so she wasn't worried about his feet any on the gravel drive and road. It was an uneventful ride over to the Caldwells' farm, only taking about fifteen minutes or so, not long enough to dampen her, or Deacon's, excitement for working cows.

# CHAPTER 18

## Shake a Stick At

Hooves in the barn alerted Drake to Sunshine's presence. As she rode through the hallway of the barn, she looked regal as if she ruled the South from the back of her horse. He didn't think she could be any more beautiful than she was in that moment. She didn't have on anything special in particular, just her regular T-shirt and pants, but there was something in her smile. The way she looked relaxed on Deacon's back made him happy.

Sunshine slid down and walked up to where he was brushing out his new horse. The horse was built the way it should be—thick, muscled, and proportional. She wasn't as tall as Chief—she was more compact—but she was still a big horse. He and Sunshine both had a thing for Carmella-colored horses, and this one was a beauty with good breeding. Which was why he wanted her in the first place. Axel wasn't nothing to shake a stick at, he was sure of that.

He figured he'd keep her for a bit. Bishop had shown some interest in her and had mentioned wanting to buy her if he thought she had enough stamina.

"What's her name? You gonna call her by what's on her papers or by somethin' different?"

Drake finished saddling her up before he answered. "I'm going to call her Axel, but her name on the papers is Axel Weld Bender. Now, enough about the horse. Come here and give me a kiss." Sunshine walked into his arms and leaned up and bit him on the lip. Drake jerked back from her reach. That hurt.

"What the hell was that for?" Damn woman was crazy.

"Don't forget you stole my bull. I saw him out there in the catch lot. Don't think I've forgotten that, you ass." She gave him a glare.

"That didn't mean you had to bite me."

"He's freaking gorgeous, and he should have been mine."

"Alright, let's get to work. Maybe your freaking mood will cheer up a little by the time we are done instead of being a pain in my ass."

He got on Axel and rode out of the barn without a glance back. She could take the hint and follow if she wanted to help. After that bite on the lip, she could leave if she wanted to. He could deal with her mood swings, but when she did shit like that it fired him up.

Drake went to the pasture west of the house where they kept the heifers. He motioned for Sunshine to hold Deacon back for a bit so he could see how Axel worked the cows. Axel moved in and out of the cattle with ease and precision. She did better than he thought she would with his big ass being on her. He signaled to Sunshine for her and Deacon to get to work.

Drake looked on as a heifer made a quick move and broke away from the herd, and Sunshine let Deacon have his head. He'd been wrong when he thought she couldn't get more beautiful. She rode with ease as Deacon cut the heifer back in.

When her attention was else where he looked his fill. Her hair was up and off her neck. She had her bandana around her forehead, and sunglasses on. Her eyes were expressive, telling him what she was feeling instead of what she hid with her words. He didn't care for when she wore her sunglasses. He couldn't anticipate her actions as well. If she hadn't had them on earlier, he might have avoided being bit.

She sat the back of a horse as if she was born there, could talk cattle with the best of 'em, had a woman's body, curves everywhere they were supposed to be, a good Southern Lady, and his parents loved her. She would be his perfect match if she weren't his longtime friend. She had too much shit on him to be stupid enough to fall for him. He couldn't go longer than ten minutes without aggravating her.

Sunshine was rough and tough on the outside, but on the inside, she was the same as peanut butter, sweet and gooey. No one saw that part much. He figured she was too busy showing everyone what a badass she was. When Sunshine was made, the mold was broken. That cowgirl was as strong-willed as any cowboy, and sassy as the day was long.

Yep, he was fine, everything was fine. His anger at her passed with a quick kick out the door from lust. He wasn't getting as hard as a rock watching her work, nope. He needed a kiss from her.

Part of him wanted to carry her over to Duck and Cover and see what she thought about his herd and the possibility of them adding a registered sale night at the stockyard. Her opinion would matter about his cows. She had placed in FFA competitions multiple times at their conventions in cattle judging. But the idea of doing that didn't sit quite well with him just yet, he held himself from mentioning it.

He and Sunshine got the cattle moved over and were headed back towards the barn. They had over six hundred acres, with around three hundred head of cattle in this one spot, and that wasn't counting the other properties and cattle. It was constant upkeep and work, but he and his Daddy enjoyed it as much as Sunshine and her Daddy did. She rode up beside him and motioned for him to stop.

"Give me a kiss."

"You think I should give you a kiss after you bit the hell out of me earlier?"

"No, but I want one. Just don't bite me back, please?"

Drake watched Sunshine try to fake being contrite. It was humorous. Not that Sunshine wasn't a good person, or likable, or even sweet sometimes, it was that she tended towards rough edged and blunt.

He leaned over and gave her a quick kiss, then pulled back.

"We shouldn't do this, but I'll race you back to the barn. Let's see what Axel has got under her hood."

He clucked Axel up to a run and Sunshine and Deacon were on their heels, Axel's short, quick strides eating up the distance. Loud, thundering hooves beating against the ground, bellowing breaths, and laughter rang in his ears as Sunshine and Deacon streaked by him. Damn it, his weight had held Axel back. If he'd been on Chief, he would have beat her. First, she'd beat him on Bodacious, and now in a horse race. His pride was taking a hurting. The taste of defeat went down smoother, being that it was Sunshine that served it up.

Sunshine raced through the opening of the gate and slowed

down to a walk as she sailed into the barn. Drake jumped off of Axel and pulled Sunshine down from Deacon, pushing her up against the stall door before either of them could think twice about what he was doing.

Drake leaned down and slipped his tongue into her mouth, tasting that sweet honey that was waiting for him. Seeing her riding Deacon as if she were the happiest woman on the face of this planet had him needing to taste her excitement. They both had the same love for riding.

She melted into his kiss and he enjoyed the dance of their tongues. The subtle give and take. The increase in tension and sexual longing. The rhythmic foreplay that mimicked what was to come. It was all a buildup, and the release was gonna be damn good for the both of them.

He slipped his hand up her shirt and ran his hand over her breasts. She arched into his touch and gave a soft moan when he rolled a nipple between his fingers.

She leaned away from him, easing out of the kiss, and moved his hands away.

"Honey, we are in the barn and anyone could walk in. Let me on up to the loft and get those steaks out and ready to grill."

"Mom and Dad are gone with your parents to eat." He tried pulling her back to him, but she sidestepped his grasp.

"Yes, but Brice isn't, and you said he's been over here every night since he's been home."

He gave her a nod. She went to put the brush back up and turned towards the stairs to the living quarters, heading on up and leaving him with his thoughts as he finished putting Axel up. Damn Brice was cockblocking him and he wasn't even there to know he was doing it.

"I still want that bull," Sunshine hollered at him from the top of the stairs.

"Not happening." She was persistent, he'd give her that, but she wasn't getting his bull.

He heard the echo of footsteps a few short minutes later and turned to see his brother. Shit, how was she always right? "What's up, B?"

"Nothing. Came out here to see what you and Sunshine had planned."

"I had plans that involved Sunshine's body, but since your ugly mug showed up, that's changed. You want a steak?" Drake didn't want him intruding on his time with Sunshine, but he wasn't gonna leave his brother out.

"Hell yeah, sounds good." He wasn't surprised by Brice's answer. He may be the skinnier brother, but he could put the food away.

"Come on, let's get the grill ready. Sunshine is upstairs getting everything ready to bring down."

He and Brice walked to the outdoor kitchen his parents had built by the pool. She found them with their feet propped up on a cooler near the grill.

"I see you gentlemen are working hard, cooking my supper." Sunshine walked up behind Drake and laid a hand on his shoulder. She handed him and Brice a beer. Drake got up and pulled up a chair for her beside his.

"Figured we've earned the luxury of putting our feet up today." He checked the temperature of the grill and threw the steaks on. He listened as Brice and Sunshine bickered back and forth, hearing a bit that caught his attention.

"I had come down to see you. It just so happened I was also talkin' to him at the time, but I was there to see you," Sunshine was telling Brice.

"Bullshit, as soon as you got down there, hugged me, and exchanged hellos, you were out the door with Chase." Brice called her on her lie.

Sunshine huffed. "Fine, you're right, being youthful and full of lust, I was more than eager to meet up with Chase. Alas, he was the leader of the douche brigade. Remember that date didn't last long, and I was back at your apartment and spent the rest of the weekend with you. I even made you breakfast and everything. What's a little shacking up between friends?"

Brice smiled over at Sunshine. "You did spoil me whenever you came down." He leaned over from his chair and kissed Sunshine on the cheek. "Love you, Sun."

Drake was blown away by the smile she sent Brice. "I love you too, B. Wouldn't know what to do without you." He wanted to punch his brother for daring to kiss Sunshine, even if it was on the cheek. Sunshine had always been Brice's honorary big sister, and she took the role seriously.

Drake spoke up. "I didn't know you went to visit Brice often."

Sunshine gave Drake a *duh you're a dumb ass* look. "Of course I went and visited him at school. You knew that. Belle even went down with me once to see why I'd been goin' off so often. Why wouldn't I?"

"You didn't come over to my apartment and visit me much."

"We saw one another enough on campus. Besides, you don't know everything about me." She gave him a wink. "We were both out doing our own things. You've got some skeletons in your closet, same as me."

Brice gaped over at Sunshine. "What are you talking about Belle coming down to visit when I was in college? I don't remember that."

She looked at Drake, then back at Brice liked he'd lost his mind. "Uh yeah, she did. It was your junior year. We came down to visit and were going to stay at your place that night, but you got plastered, then Belle came down with something and we left. It wasn't an eventful weekend."

Drake watched as Brice got up from the table, leaving his steak half eaten. "Seems as if little brother has some explaining to do."

Brice nodded at them. "Yeah, I do, but not to y'all. Love y'all. Bye."

"Love you, B," he and Sunshine both answered.

"That was strange. How could you not remember someone coming to your house?"

Drake laughed at that. "I had a few blackout drunk nights before I grew up."

"Yes, I know. I've had the unfortunate pleasure of being there for some of them."

"Hey, I wasn't that bad." Drake pulled Sunshine into his lap. Thank goodness Brice was gone. He was ready to have his hands on her.

"Not that bad? I've held you up while you peed. I held your hair back that time you grew it out while you puked. I've also kept you from going home with twos that you thought were tens at the time."

Drake smirked. "Okay, maybe it has been that bad from time

to time." He leaned in and kissed her. That shut her up. He wanted his lips on her more than he wanted to argue.

Sunshine pulled back from his kiss. "I've got to go home, think about this some more, overanalyze it, sleep on it, and then think some more." She grinned at him.

"I can sneak over there later and sleep with you again." He wiggled his eyebrows at her. "I will give you a happy wake up." He grazed his hands over the seam in her pants and watched her squirm, her face turning red.

"Yes, you could. You have more than proven that point, but I think you better not. By the way, I'll be bringin' some cattle by the sale barn tomorrow. You want me to bring us some lunch when I do?"

Drake smiled at that. "If I can eat dessert off you." She would be a welcome respite in the middle of his workday.

"You perv, wanting in my pants every chance you get these days, I tell you." Sunshine laughed, but he could see the twinkle of mischief in her eyes. Damn if he didn't want to explore her some more.

"You want me in your pants," Drake said, grabbing her butt and squeezing.

"That is true." Sunshine jumped up and headed to the door before he had the chance to talk her into staying. She was too smart for his own good.

# CHAPTER 19

## Small Town

Sunshine and her Daddy had gotten the cattle loaded early that morning. She needed to stop at a couple of places before heading over to the see Drake at the stockyard.

Her first stop was at Winston and Sons lumber yard. She threw her hand up at a passing car as she went into the business office to order a shipment of new fence posts. When she opened the door and glanced behind the desk, she was surprised to see the eldest son, Reece, sitting there looking pissed off and gorgeous. He had been a couple of years ahead of her in school, but that hadn't stopped them from being friends. That man was six foot two of delicious with golden hair that made women cry with envy. He had it pulled back in a ponytail today. Dark blue eyes surrounded by thick lashes that stared a hole through your soul, and full lips that made you want to kiss them to make them stop frowning.

If it weren't for Drake, she would have to think about making a pass at Reece. Hell, she was going to flirt with him anyway. This was the first time he had been back in town in months. She heard he'd been off doing God knows what God knows where. That was folks talking out of their asses because they were jealous they didn't have the courage to get out and see the world.

Sunshine moseyed over to the desk and propped her elbows on the counter, grinning at him. "Hey, handsome, you come here often?"

Reece grinned back at her, walking around the counter to give her a hug. "I would if I knew I was goin' to have beautiful women such as yourself walkin' in here."

Sunshine hugged him then pulled back to look up at him. He looked weary around the eyes, but he was still a hottie. "Flirt. I know you say that to every woman that walks in here. I have missed seeing that pretty face you have around. You back in town for a while?"

Sunshine noticed his face fell a little at her question.

"Forget I asked, anyway." Sunshine moved back over to the desk and reached over the counter to get the order form.

"Since you *are* back in town for the moment, why don't we get together and hang out some? Everyone would enjoy seeing you."

Reece walked back behind the counter and sat back down on his stool. "Yeah, I need to. I got back in town last night, and I had planned on letting you know today. Before you decide to crawl up my butt. What's it been, about six months since I last sat down and had a beer with all of your crazy asses?"

Sunshine wrote down her order and handed it to him. "That it has, darlin', that it has. And by the way, my number hasn't changed. Since I haven't heard from you since you last left, I figured maybe you lost it." Sunshine raised a disapproving brow at him.

Reece had the good sense to look ashamed. "I had things I needed to sort out and I didn't want to talk to anyone."

Sunshine gazed at him. He appeared tired and weighed down. "Don't forget that we love you around here, and there is something to be said for friends that have been with you since childhood. We tend to be understanding. We also know all the dirt on you, so start talking to us or we are going to blackmail you." Sunshine walked behind the desk and gave him another hug because he looked as if he needed it. She didn't care to see her friends hurting. Reece patted her on the back and let her go. She gave him one last squeeze and leaned up and kissed him on the cheek when she heard the bell above the door ding. Sunshine turned to see her G-Momma walk through, well, more like *strut* through the door. Well, shit.

Ida Terry Gibson was a woman to be reckoned with. She was a man killer these days. She had racked up many a date since G-Daddy passed. Sunshine couldn't keep up anymore, but G-Momma would never marry them. The minute they started mentioning commitment G-Momma ran them off. Hell, Sunshine was at the point she didn't even try to remember their names.

G-Momma was standing there in her leather pants, leopard top, red high heels, and hair done up to Jesus, not looking a day over sixty. She was somewhere around seventy-something, but no one knew anymore. Anyone that had known her G-Momma's real age was either dead, maybe killed off by the mob connections G-Momma swore she had, or was senile. Sunshine loved her G-Momma to bits, but she wanted her married off even more so than her own Momma did. Her G-Momma looked as if she struck gold seeing Sunshine standing there with Reece. Lord have mercy on them all.

Sunshine walked over and kissed her G-Momma on the cheek. "Hey, G-Momma. I didn't see you at Sunday dinner. Where were you at?"

G-Momma fluffed her blond Texas beauty queen hair with her freshly manicured nails. "Now, baby girl, you know a lady shouldn't reveal all her secrets." G-Momma turned towards Reece and leaned over the counter with her V-neck top draping open to show off some impressive breasts for her age. "Hey, handsome, you come here often?"

Sunshine about shit a brick, and Reece busted out laughing. "I guess it is genetic."

G-Momma looked over her shoulder at Sunshine. "If she was hittin' on you then you are right. Us Gibson women have good taste, and I would bet my last dollar you would taste mighty good."

Reece turned red in the face as he motioned over to her. "Indeed. Sunshine used that same line on me not ten minutes ago. I guess she inherited her finer points from her grandmother."

G-Momma looked over at Sunshine and raised her arched brows over eyes that were identical to her Momma's.

"Seems you did get somethin' from me after all, sweetheart, besides my good looks. Those are what you should thank me for the most." G-Momma turned back towards Reece. "I need sixteen 4 x 4's delivered to the house this week, please."

Sunshine was surprised that was all G-Momma had to say, but it didn't take long, and she wasn't disappointed.

Before G-Momma reached the door, she turned back around and winked at Reece. "Oh, and Reece, when a man delivers me his hardwood I prefer that he does so shirtless. Maybe we can work out"—she paused, looked him up and down and smirked—"some type of payment?"

Sunshine sighed and put her head down. "Shit fire."

Reece grinned. "I will see what I can do, Mrs. Gibson."

Sunshine was shaking her head as G-Momma waltzed out the door. "That woman will outlive us all."

Reece smirked at her. "If I were an older man, I would take her up on that offer of 'payment,' and maybe even set myself up as her next husband."

Sunshine gagged. "You are a disgusting individual."

Reece laughed. "I can't help that your grandmother is a GILF, you know, a grandmother I'd like to—"

Sunshine was quick to interrupt him. "Don't you dare finish that damn saying, you nasty whore. Ugh, she is seventy-somethin' years old." Sunshine hurried towards the door, flipping the bird at Reece on the way out. "I also want your hardwood delivered shirtless, Reece," Sunshine hollered out before the door shut behind her. She turned to see him bent over laughing. Good. He needed some humor in his life.

Sunshine jumped in her truck and headed over to the new bookstore in the square called Pages. They served coffee and deli-style food along with new releases and used books. It was a nice new addition to the town. Sunshine, being an avid reader, was one of the shop's frequent patrons. She never ordered a book online anymore, preferring to support local businesses. The shop owner, Magnolia Emerson Caraway, who preferred Emerson or Em, and Sunshine had become friends over the last few months. They had bonded over their shared love of books and coffee.

"Damn men in this town have lost their minds," Sunshine mumbled under her breath as she walked through the old French doors at the front of the shop. She was met with the welcoming smell of coffee and books. There were a few wooden booths along the right wall and a good many sturdy chairs and tables. There was a C-shaped bar in the center of the store with old random stools underneath, ready to welcome the next coffee-lover or hungry patron. There was a glass case built to the left of the bar that housed delicious baked goods, which lured Sunshine in every time. The bookshelves and comfy chairs were to the back behind secret doors hidden in the wall behind the bar. It was by far the most amazing bookstore Sunshine had ever been in, and it was in her hometown, which made it the best.

Emerson was behind the counter, serving coffee and taking orders. She nodded to Sunshine and motioned for her to have a seat. Emerson was about an inch shorter than Sunshine and the opposite of her in terms of hair and eye color. Em had gray eyes versus Sunshine's hazel, and chocolate-colored hair versus Sunshine's blond. Em was the real-life version of a pinup girl. Her curves were bountiful and she was voluptuous. She assumed that Em appeared in most every man's fantasies in this town.

Emerson put a caramel latte in front of Sunshine and asked, "How's it going today, sis?"

"Good. How has business been?"

"Busier than a hooker's door knob on dollar night. What'cha want to eat?"

"I need two chicken salad croissant plates, and two strawberry pretzel salads to go."

"Two? Um, who's the other for?"

Sunshine took a sip of her latte and tried her best to school her features. "Drake. We have a lunch meeting today."

"Is that what the kids are calling it these days?"

"No, they are calling it pie." At Emerson's confused expression, Sunshine added, "I'll tell you about that later."

Emerson went and placed her order with the deli cook, then came back to chat while the one waitress that worked for her handled the other customers.

"What have you been out doing this morning?"

"Had to go by the Winston and Sons to order some post to be delivered. Ran into Reece, and G-Momma. Small towns and all that."

"What'd G-Momma have to say for herself today?"

"Oh, her and Reece were yanking my chain. Damn crazy people. Reece was talking about bangin' my G-Momma if he was older, and G-Momma propositioned him. No shame with either of them."

"Your grandmother is spunky for her age. I doubt any man would be able to tame her."

Sunshine smiled at that statement. "You are right. No man has ever tamed G-Momma. G-Daddy was always just along for the ride. Reece may be the man for the job. He is a fine piece of grade A prime ass. Not that I'm interested, he's a friend."

Reece was hot, but he didn't even get her lady boner up anymore. Seems one round with Drake's tongue and she was ruined. What the hell kinda devil penis magic was he gonna be able to work on her? They hadn't even had sex yet and she was hooked.

Emerson shook her head in agreement. "Reece is a fine piece of ass, he came in this morning but he seemed restless, and moody."

Sunshine grunted in agreement while she took another sip of her latte.

Emerson leaned down, her breasts propped on the counter as she continued. Sunshine couldn't help but look. They were nice boobs. "He wasn't overly friendly to anyone, but not rude. Kind of looks at you as if he knows everything about you. Couldn't help but notice the man. Quit looking at my boobs, you nincompoop." Sunshine laughed when her friend gave her a light pop on the head.

"That is an accurate assessment, both of me looking at the goods, and of Reece. He is friendly, but he needs to know you. He doesn't waste time on small talk. With those eyes of his, I wouldn't be surprised if he did know every secret about you that there was to know. Your boobs are perfect, by the way. I'm envious."

"You have a great rack. Now, I have to go pretend to be an adult and run my business. Maybe my next customers won't stare at my boobs the entire time they're looking at me."

Sunshine smiled, showing all her teeth, and shook her head. "I doubt that. The girls are out there loud and proud today." Emerson walked away to serve another customer, ignoring Sunshine's last statement.

Sunshine finished up her coffee and got her to-go order. "Bye, Emerson. I'll see you later. I'll need to come back and scout out the books. Leave a few off to the side if you see anything I may be interested in. If you have time." She gave a wistful look at the secret doors. She didn't have the leeway today. There was more to be done. She still had to stop by the feed mill before heading to the stockyard. She hoped Drake had time to eat her in the office. She shook her head at her train of thought. Damn it, meet with her and eat lunch in the office. Yeah, that was what she meant.

# CHAPTER 20

## Crazy Heifer

Drake's day had been chaotic. Everybody's cows had been bat-shit crazy. There had been problems getting the cattle separated and unloaded all damn day. They were about at maximum capacity. That was good for business, but they were going to have to set up extra holding pens. The sale was tomorrow night and there was still another day ahead of this. What wasn't good for business was when he wanted to snap at his employees and acted like a complete jerk because he hadn't gotten what he craved from Sunshine yet.

"Drake." He turned to see Brice heading for him.

"Yeah, what is it?"

"You want to go get some lunch?"

"No, thanks. I've got plans."

"Okay, checking before I head out." Brice gave him a wave.

Drake stayed on the catwalks, pacing to calm himself. His Dad had mentioned his bull purchase to him in passing today. That had put a damper on his mood first thing. He'd given him the same spiel he gave Sunshine. He was gonna flip him at the registered sale. His Dad gave him a knowing look and walked off. He was gonna have to come clean with him. No sense in continuing to keep it from him.

He'd need to get a solid business plan laid out on paper to show his Dad before he told him. Maybe with the right finical numbers he could get him to agree to at least try a registered sale night and convince him that using AFI on their non-registered cows would be beneficial long-term.

That was one more damn thing to add to his to-do list. Speaking of his damn to-do list, he saw a heifer jump a panel. "I be shit." Right here at damn lunchtime when they were shorter staffed. He ran downstairs and helped get it put back in the correct holding pen, but not before he was chased up and out of the small catch lot by the damn thing. He headed back upstairs, away from the crazy heifer, to walk along the catwalks. She'd scared the shit out of him when she turned on him that quick to take a run at him.

Sunshine pulled up to the stockyard and his employees helped her unload the cattle. He waited as she signed the ticket, and she checked to see if all of them were separated as they needed to be. She headed up the stairs towards where he'd been waiting to see her pull in.

"Head on over to my office," he yelled across the barn at her when she got close enough to hear. She nodded and carried their food with her.

Drake strode in the door ten minutes later, shut the door, and shoved Sunshine up against the wall. "Hey, baby, nice to see you, you look beautiful, thank you for the food, and that covers it." He put his lips over hers and she opened to him and their tongues began the foreplay he loved so much.

Sunshine jumped up and put her legs around his waist, and

Drake pushed them up against the wall again. He had a thing for having her up against something, and that seemed fine by her. He stayed in their embrace, kissing her hello all while trying to somewhat appease his horny self.

Drake pulled back and laid his head against hers. "You sure know how to make a man happy, Sunshine—you, food, and a smoking-hot make-out session. Uh, damn, woman. I could eat you up."

Sunshine laughed and patted his shoulders for him to let her down. "Hey, I do what I can. It is a good thing our food was cold anyway. Took you long enough to get up here. I got us both chicken salad croissants and strawberry pretzel salad for dessert."

"Sounds good. Emerson make it?"

"I don't know. She's hired a part-time cook for the deli for her busy days. Today was one of her busy days."

"Good. We need more small businesses opening in town."

"What has been goin' on that has you frowning?" she asked him.

"Crazy ass cows today. We had a damn heifer climb over a panel and chase me and three workers. She about got my big ass, I shit you not. It took forever to get her in the shoot. And then earlier, I had to run back home because I forgot my laptop. That made Dad happy with me. When I got out to my truck to rush home, Brice had put a damn rubber snake in there. I about had a heart attack at the age of twenty-eight."

Sunshine leaned over and gave him a quick kiss. "Suck it up, buttercup. Your day hasn't been that bad." His day had been that bad and then it got worse when Brice came through the door and sat down to make himself comfortable.

"B, what a surprise." Drake gave his brother a look.

"Hey, Brice," Sunshine said.

His brother walked over and gave her a hug before he pulled up a chair to his desk and joined them for lunch.

"What's new?" Brice asked, over a bite of what looked to be a half eaten slice of the Swine and Dine's famous chocolate pie.

"Reece is back in town. He called me and wants all of us to get together in a few weekends," Drake told them.

Brice nodded his head. "Sounds good to me, let me know when and where."

"I saw him this morning." Sunshine said.

"Where did you see him at?" he asked her.

"Winston and Sons. Had to put in an order for some fence posts."

"Did he say where he'd been, or what he's been doin'?" Brice asked.

"Nope. Said he'd needed some space. I told him we could respect that and he could talk to us about it when he was ready. Then G-Momma walked in, and of course it turned into a shit show." She gave them a rundown of how G-Momma had embarrassed her, and what Reece had said. Hell, G-Momma could embarrass anyone. That little old lady had a potty mouth on her. He was certain she had grabbed his ass on more than one occasion.

Brice horse-laughed. "You have got to be screwin' with me. Reece, that dirty old bastard."

"That is what I said. The worst is when she offered to work out 'payment' for the hardwood." Sunshine shook her head in disgust. "Of course, I also asked for my hardwood to be delivered shirtless, same as my G-Momma. I do hope Reece will not deny me that pleasure."

Drake laughed. "Your G-Momma is a woman to be reckoned with, as is her granddaughter." He and Sunshine bumped fists in agreement.

"You're damn straight. I want to live my life to the fullest same as her, though maybe not with so many boyfriends."

"How about any boyfriends, or husbands, Sunshine? You got that big house and all now. You not looking to add a husband anytime soon?" Brice asked. Drake turned to give her his full attention. This wasn't stuff they took time to discuss.

"No, I'm happy with it being only me. Maybe in a few years. I'm interested in doing what I want to do, when I want to do it, and who I want to do it with. I don't believe I will trade in my freedom for picking anyone's underwear off the floor anytime soon."

"What about you, Brice? You interested in settling down? You know, this being between us." Sunshine rolled her eyes at Brice.

"As a matter of fact, I wouldn't be opposed to it if I found the right woman."

Sunshine's face showed the shock he was feeling. "Are you shitting me right now?"

Brice shook his head that he was not.

Drake chimed in. "Little brother, you have surprised me. I figured you would be at least forty when you settled down given how much tail you chased at Mississippi State." And Drake figured he himself would be to.

"When are you thinking about settling down, Drake?" Brice asked.

Drake cut his eyes at his brother. He could be a complete asshole. "I don't know. No time soon, but if the right woman came up and slapped me in the face, I guess I would consider it. I enjoy my life as it is. Mom and Dad's relationship has been a good example, but they are the exception, not the rule. How about let's change the topic?" Damn this touchy-feely conversation to hell.

"Okay, back to Reece. Let him know that in a few weeks, we will all get together. I'll let everyone on my end know about it," Sunshine said.

"Brice, it's time for you to leave, and quit playing chaperone."

"Thanks, I can tell when I'm not wanted." Brice gave him a sneaky grin and gave Sunshine a hug before walking out.

"That was mean, but he has been around an awful lot when I am." Sunshine smiled. "I think it's sweet."

"It isn't sweet. It's him being an irritating little brother."

She scraped the bottom of the bowl on her strawberry pretzel salad. He would offer his, but, no. No, he wouldn't offer his. Emerson made a damn good dessert, and Sunshine wasn't about to get his. If she wanted more, she could stop on the way out and get another serving of it.

"What are you doing tonight?" Drake asked as she was swallowing her last bite.

"Nothing but my usual. I have to finish up paperwork, clean out the barn, saddle Deacon to ride for a bit, and then cook and eat some supper." Sunshine cleaned up their trash while he looked at some paperwork on his desk.

"What are you gonna do?" she asked him.

Drake stopped what he was doing to look her in the eyes. "I am going to be doing you. After you get done working, skip on the horse ride tonight. I don't want you wondering if it was the horse ride or me that made your thighs ache tomorrow. Don't cook anything either. I would rather have your cooking, but I will pick us up something on my way over, so you can relax before I get there. Oh, and no touching yourself or trying to ease the ache before I get the chance to." Drake smirked and leaned back in his chair.

Her mouth dropped open in shock, and he could see her thighs rubbing together at his words. "Sunshine, close your mouth before I decide to fill it with something, and then finish eating my dessert right off you. I don't think you want this lunch to end with us rounding third and heading home to the sound of cows and the smell of shit in the air. Now get your fine ass out of here before I change my mind."

"You are confident that you are gonna get what you want tonight, but don't forget I have a say in this." She stood up and walked straight out the door towards the exit but not before he had the last word.

"You do, but you've already made up your mind." He knew he was right, and she knew it too.

He got up from his desk and locked his office door before calling Bishop. He didn't want Brice or his father barging in mid-conversation about his personal business. It had been hell trying to keep the main man of cattle in the county out of his side dealings, and doubly so since that man was his father. He leaned back in his chair, listening to the ringing of his phone.

When Sunshine had been up in the office earlier, Drake had been making sure her cattle were logged correctly, and was looking them over in general in case he saw something he wanted to buy. Her and her Daddy's cattle were looking good. If they started up a breeding program, they'd give Drake a run for his money.

Frustration seemed to seep through his tone when Bishop answered on the fifth ring. "Hey, man, we need to talk."

"Okay, what's up?"

"I think I know who owns the other herd that Mr. Alexander is interested in."

"Did the person tell you, or are you making assumptions, hoping I will tell you who it is?"

"At this point, I'm making assumptions, but just in case I'm right, neither of us wants to talk about it with you, or each other. We are all going to keep it business. No mention of it to one another."

"Sounds good to me and makes my life easier. So, we never had this conversation?"

"What conversation?"

"Let's meet up soon at the gym for a workout."

"Sure, I'll talk to you later tonight, man. I'm fixing to head into a meeting."

Drake exhaled slowly as he hit end. He didn't know for sure if Sunshine was the other person in line for the contract, but he had a gut feeling she was. He was going to try and keep their professional and personal life as separate as possible. She had mentioned in passing having something in the works, but wouldn't give him any details. She had also been pissed he got that bull.

Drake rubbed at his chest, but the heavy feeling wouldn't lift. He stood up and closed the door behind him on his work and what he hoped wasn't knowledge that would later cripple him. He decided his workday would end early after his last pass through checking over everything. Most everyone was done dropping off their cattle by this time of day.

Drake thought Sunshine had looked damn good with her hat pulled low on her head, her long blond hair hanging out the back, tight jeans that were tucked in her work boots, and a light blue tight T-shirt. He had been hungry for food, but when he laid eyes on her, all he'd wanted was Sunshine. He watched her walk away, but only because he was certain that in few hours, he was going to have his hands on her again. Sunshine was going to be his by the end of the night. That was one thing he was damn sure of.

# CHAPTER 21

## Afternoon Delight

Sunshine finished up her workday in a rush. She would have enjoyed some of it and taken her time under normal circumstances, but today, she wanted to get it done. She was a woman and she had to get prepared. There was lady-scaping to do, legs to shave, hairs to pluck, things to buff, toes to paint, hair to fix, things to wash extra thoroughly, and clothes to decide on. She hurried into the house to start the beautification process.

Sunshine reached her bathroom and threw her phone in the dock to start some music, began running her bath, and stripped down. She jumped in and started the jets along with some bubble bath. Sunshine relaxed against the back of the tub for a minute before she started going through the same extensive shaving and cleaning processes that she went through before going to the GYN. Most women have those extra steps they go through before they go to the vajayjay doctor, and they are usually the same steps as when you might have a sexual encounter. It involves a sharp instrument and your lady bits and hoping and praying you don't remotely nick, or worse, slice anything, because if you do, it feels as if you are pissing fires of damnation out of your twat. Once you shave your lady bits there was nothing standing between you and ho-ish behavior.

Sunshine got everything cleaned and shaved. Then she lathered her hair up to sit back and enjoy her bath for a while longer and think. She hoped she didn't do or say anything stupid tonight. Imagined if she farted during sex. Maybe she needed to take a Gas-Ex just in case. You couldn't be too careful. She was pretty certain flatulence would be a mood killer. Her mind was coming up with ridiculous topics, trying to skirt away from what was going to happen, which seemed as good a preservation technique as any.

Sunshine rinsed out her hair, turned the jets off, and started to let the water out. She waited till there was barely any water left before dragging herself up out of the tub to reach for her towel. She turned towards the doorway while she was trying to finish drying off and screamed until she realized who it was and she got pissed. "What the hell, Drake? Let yourself in, no need in staying downstairs, come on up, and watch me bathe. I'm going to hide that damn spare key better."

"I've enjoyed the show. It didn't seem the appropriate time for me to start behavin' like a gentleman and make my presence known," Drake said as his eyes traveled her body.

Sunshine wrapped her towel around her. Not sure why since he had already seen everything she had. It was the only thing she could think of to do with her hands—that or rip his clothes off and push him to the floor to hump him. There was tension coiled tight in Sunshine's belly, and nervousness. She wanted him badly, enough that she wasn't thinking about the things that could go wrong, but everything that was going to feel right.

Sunshine walked out of the bathroom and stood in the

middle of the room and stared at him without making a move. She didn't know how to approach him. This was new territory for her and she was more reserved than she would be under normal circumstances. She needed her take-charge side. She was sure that side would come back as soon as she was comfortable with him.

"Sunshine, come here." Drake held out his hands to her.

She walked to Drake and took his hands. They were rough and calloused from work. His fingers were long and thick. He could palm a basketball with ease.

He pulled her in close and hugged her for a moment. "You nervous?" Drake asked her.

Sunshine pulled away from him and sat down on the bed, looking at him. "I have to say I am. Mostly that I am going to do something embarrassing and you are never going to let me live it down."

Drake laughed and grinned at her, his eyes heavy. "You're crazy, baby. Everything is going to be great between us. We will do what comes natural between us. There is enough sexual tension that the sex can't be anything less than amazing."

"Okay, but what if I fart or something? Quit laughing at me, you ass." Sunshine couldn't get the smile out of her voice.

Drake tried to stifle his laughter. "Baby, I don't think even a fart could kill the hard-on I have after seeing you naked. If you do happen to fart during sex, I promise to try my hardest not to laugh."

"You are a liar, but I appreciate your trying." Sunshine rolled her eyes. She watched as Drake's long, muscular legs brought him closer to her. The laughter was still there, but she could feel the tension coming off his body.

He stopped right in front of her. "Sun, if you aren't ready, that's okay. I can be a patient man."

Sunshine felt her shake her head. "No, I'm ready. I believe I've wanted you for years and never realized it. I've waited long enough." Sunshine stood up and dropped her towel. She let Drake look his fill.

She didn't mean for this evening to go this way. She had wanted this on her terms with her war paint on and a man-killer outfit, but this was how she was getting him. She felt bare of anything that could help her build her defenses.

Sunshine watched as Drake reached out his hands and ran them down her arms, bringing her closer to him. Sunshine could feel the knot building in her stomach. She reached between them and pulled his shirt up to his chest, motioning for him to take it the rest of the way off. She took her time running her hands down his stomach and over his pecs while he threw his shirt to the floor. Sunshine boosted herself up on her tiptoes and laid kisses to his neck and down his chest, then back to the other side of his neck. She felt his stomach clench when she ran her hands along the waistband of his jeans. She unsnapped the button and pulled at the zipper. She looked up to see Drake clenching his jaw. He was the finest man she had ever laid eyes on. His six-pack and that V-shaped muscle had her aching to lick all the way down to happiness. He had a small happy trail leading to what she knew was going to be an exceptionally large lollypop. She imagined herself skipping down a trail to candy land and almost snorted.

Drake stepped out of her reach. "Get on the bed. This first time is going to be all about you. You can explore later if you want."

Sunshine nodded her head, climbed up on the bed, and leaned back on the pillows to watch Drake undress. He pulled his pants off. He must have already taken off his boots and socks downstairs, and he was left standing in a pair of black Calvin Klein underwear that left little to the imagination. Damn, he was fine. She wanted to yell at him to hurry up, but she didn't. She wanted to savor the buildup.

Drake climbed onto the bed and rolled her over so they were facing each other. He ravaged her mouth with his tongue and she answered stroke for stroke.

Sunshine started arching against his leg, trying to get closer. She needed him to relieve the ache that was building there. She felt Drake shift beside her and he lifted her leg over his hip and stroked her with his fingers. Sunshine could feel how wet she was. She was willing. Drake slipped a finger inside her and she moaned and arched into him more. He pulled away from their kiss.

"Birth control?" Drake asked.

Sunshine took a second to focus. "Yeah, and clean. You?"

"Yes, I am." Drake slipped his underwear off with the hand that wasn't busy driving Sunshine mad. He pushed Sunshine onto her back and laid his lower body between her thighs. He looked down at her and smirked. Sunshine loved that look. He was more than she imagined.

She smiled and leaned up to kiss him. Drake broke away from their kiss, and moved down to her breasts. He pushed them up together and put his face between them. Sunshine heard a muffled, "I lub yur titties." Drake pulled his head up to smile at her. "Really, they are fantastic. You could smother me with them and I would die a happy man."

Sunshine laughed. "If you don't hurry up and get on with the show I may very well smother you."

Drake smiled and took a nipple in his mouth while he kept eye contact with Sunshine. Her laugh died in her throat. *Oh yes,* she thought while Drake licked and sucked at her nipples, switching sides to make sure both felt loved. He moved a hand between Sunshine's legs to work his skillful fingers. He moved his mouth back up to hers and then over to her ear. Sunshine about combusted when he nibbled and kissed her there. That was one of her spots, evidently. She was ready to ride his ass into the ground. She needed him now. Then she heard Drake say in a low voice, "We can wait. I'd be happy to wait for you to figure out what you want."

Sunshine about came off the bed. "Damn it, Drake. Now!"

Drake leaned back and bent Sunshine's knees up and spread them out for her. He came in between them, and made her move up a little more on the pillows, so she would have a better angle. Drake slid over her opening. He watched as she arched closer to him and closed her eyes. "Nope. Keep them open and watch."

Sunshine tried her best not to close her eyes as she watched him sink into her. He sat still, letting her adjust, but oh, that ache, that stretch. Damn that was the best thing in the world. That first push in was incredible. She didn't know how he fit in her, but he somehow made it work. She must have a magic vagina or something. It was one of them magician hats with a secret compartment. Sunshine couldn't help it, she giggled.

Drake looked at her with a raised brow. "May I ask what is

so funny during a moment such as this?"

Sunshine stopped laughing to answer when he pulled out and pushed back in with more force.

"Sunshine, eyes open and watching," Drake told her again.

She looked up at him with what she hoped wasn't a dopey expression, but right now she was so happy and content with him inside her. "I was thinking that my vagina must be magic and have a secret compartment, because I didn't think that much of you would fit."

Drake laughed and pulled back out of her again, and sunk back into her with ease.

"It's magic, alright." Then there was no more talking for a while. The only sounds to be heard were softs moans and the sounds of bodies in a rhythmic dance.

Sunshine watched as Drake quickened his pace and with each thrust, his pelvis was grinding against her, helping bring her closer to the edge with every stroke. Sunshine drove herself up against him matching his thrusts. She felt Drake lean his head down beside her ear. "You're mine. I want you every damn day, you understand?"

Sunshine managed to squeak out a "Yes." Goosebumps broke out down her body. Drake started driving into her harder and Sunshine felt the bed moving and the headboard slapping the wall. Sunshine couldn't hold back much longer.

"Drake, harder," she cried out. He gave her what she wanted and slammed into her over and over again. He slipped his hand down and pulled one leg up higher on his hips and slapped her ass. Sunshine could feel her orgasm barreling down on her. She looked up into Drake's eyes, and saw everything she had ever wanted, and damn if that wasn't terrifying.

Sunshine climbed towards the edge, felt herself clenching around him, and shattering. He was incredible. He drove deep into her one last time before letting himself go. When she gained coherent thought a few minutes later, it was, hell yeah, if that wasn't the best orgasm she had ever had.

Sunshine took the rag Drake retrieved for her and cleaned herself up. She threw it on the floor when she was done. It could wait. She rolled onto her side and snuggled up to Drake's stomach. She had no idea what to say or not say. That was the best sex she'd ever had. Hell, he may end up being the best she had till the end of time. She hoped her future husband would measure up.

Drake pulled Sunshine closer and kissed her shoulder. "That was the absolute best sex I've ever had, Sunshine, and you know I ain't only saying that." He had echoed her thoughts.

"Yeah, it was amazing." She grinned over her shoulder. "But I think I can do better."

## CHAPTER 22

Table for Two

He wanted to see Sunshine. It had been a couple of days since he last had. His work schedule and hers hadn't allowed for any late-night sneak-overs and she'd turned him down the previous night because she had some early-morning work planned. Meanwhile, he'd had to work the sale at the stockyard the night before that. At least he'd been able to hit the gym those few mornings with Bishop and Brice, and get in some much-needed time at Duck and Cover.

He looked around his apartment, and for once, Brice wasn't there. His parents had gone out of town for the night to a concert up in Nashville. Perfect night for Sunshine to stay at his place. He picked up his iPhone.

She answered on the second ring. "That was quick. Were you waiting on me to call?" He heard her huff at him and he laughed.

"No, I just got off the phone with Willow."

"Why don't you come over tonight, and bring a bag with something a little dressy in it?"

"Dressy?"

"Yeah, just in case."

"Um, okay. I'll see if I have anything dressy lying around."

"Mom and Dad are gone tonight. Brice is nowhere to be found. We can park your truck behind the barn," he told her.

"That sounds good. I'll be over in a little while. I've got a few things to wrap up here before I call it quits."

"Anything I need to come help with?" he asked.

"Naw, just some everyday stuff. I won't be too long."

"Okay. Be careful on your way over."

"Alright. Bye."

He heard knocking on his door about an hour later.

"What took so long? I thought I was gonna have to come get you and drag you here."

"Did you miss me that much? It's only been two days." Sunshine laughed as she gave him a hug and a peck on the lips. He watched as she threw her bag on the floor and lay down on his couch.

"I didn't miss you much. It's hard to miss a sassy-mouthed heifer like yourself." She laughed at him and shot him the bird.

"Oh yeah, I intend for you to do that later."

He went to his bedroom and made a quick call. Once he had a reservation time locked down, he changed his shirt and made a quick stop in front of the mirror to fix the curly black mop of hair on his head.

Drake leaned down over the couch and snagged a quick kiss from Sunshine. He watched as a grin spread across her face, highlighting her mischievous hazel eyes. "Come on, darlin', and get up. We are going out tonight. I made us a reservation." Drake pulled her up off the couch and twirled her around, dipping her back to snag another kiss. That one turned heated. He was going to have to reel himself in if he didn't get that perky ass of hers moving up and out of his sights. Not that he thought Sunshine would mind a good tussle in the sheets before they left, but he figured once they got started, they wouldn't stop for a while. Drake grinned at the wildcat in his arms. He loved her giggle as she grabbed his butt and squeezed.

"Your ass is amazing. Do you know how many women would kill for it? A helluva lot of them." Sunshine smiled at him and squeezed it again.

"Damn right. Women would kill to be in your shoes and gettin' to grab my ass." Sunshine smacked his chest. "You know what I mean, butthead."

She moved her hands from his ass to his chest and started running them down the front of his shirt towards his belt buckle. Drake watched as Sunshine's eyes got heavy. He pulled her tighter against him and stilled her hands from moving any farther south.

He leaned down and nipped at Sunshine's lip before moving his lips to her ear.

"We are going out to eat, but when we get back, I plan on banging you up against the door as soon as we get home." He licked the outer rim of her ear and felt her shudder. Drake pulled back and stepped away from her.

"How about we stay home and we can eat here?" Sunshine asked, walking back to him. When she ran her hands over the front of his blue jeans, he considered giving in. He was straining against his zipper as she stroked him through his pants. Drake clenched his jaw, gritting out his words. "I do plan on eating here tonight, but that is going to be my dessert and it is going to be off your body." Drake leaned back towards her to reach down and stroke her between her legs, feeling the heat through

221

her thin athletic shorts. He watched as Sunshine strained against his hand and tried moving closer to him. It was an effort to pull away. "Go get ready before I can't restrain myself and end up having you on the table."

"You aren't giving me any good reasons to go get ready. Only good ones to stay where I am." Sunshine eased her top up and over her head. Why, why had he decided he needed to take her out tonight, instead of staying in. Her boobs were perfect.

"Y'all are going to give me a heart attack. We never have a chance for a night out together with your owner. I'm standing my ground. Now, don't look at me like that. I know it, I want y'all to be in my mouth too, but I'm taking her out for some food. When we get back tonight, I will make it up to y'all." He was of course speaking to her titties. He gave Sunshine a grin when she rolled her eyes at him.

She glared as she pulled her shirt back over her head. "They don't want to listen to what you have to say right now."

"They love me, and we all know it. They told me just then, before you covered up those beautiful creations." Sunshine flipped her hair over her shoulder and went to his bedroom to get ready. He could do better than imagine what she looked like naked these days. What he was missing, standing out there with a door between them, ran through his mind.

"For turning me down, I may make you beg later tonight," she yelled to him.

"I'm going to the truck. Come on when you get done."

Drake questioned his sanity as he walked out to wait on Sunshine. If he stayed in the loft with her, he was going to barge in his bedroom and give her the satisfaction they both wanted. He sat there in his truck for about ten minutes when he saw Sunshine step out of the house in a long-sleeved dress and boots, her hair flowing around her shoulders. His heart did a quick uptick in speed and he tried to ignore the feeling in his chest at seeing her grin as she climbed into the truck. Why the hell he thought taking Sunshine out was more important than staying in with her was lost on him. Hell, he suspected she wasn't wearing any panties.

Drake made a quick drive over to the neighboring county to take her to Simp McGhee's in Decatur. They both loved the steak and shrimp there, and it was a private atmosphere. When he had made their reservation he had requested their most secluded seating. If anyone happened to see them, he had a story ready to tell. He would tell them a date had canceled on him, and since he had made the reservation, he asked Sunshine to go. No one would question that story twice.

"My favorite, thank you. Maybe you aren't such an asshole after all." Sunshine leaned over and gave Drake a quick kiss before stepping out of the truck. "This almost makes me forgive you for denying me earlier." She and Drake walked side by side across the street before entering the historic building. There was a light jazz band playing in the corner. The cherry-colored bar was populated with some businessmen who appeared to have had a few beers too many. The hostess seated them upstairs in the farthest corner away from the other diners.

He didn't bother to pick up a menu and neither did she. The waiter came over and took their drink orders. Drake went with a Summer Ale and she went with the house red. They both ordered the Dean's Delight, beef filet and shrimp over a Cajun

Alfredo sauce-drenched pasta. Delicious and filling. He hoped he would have the energy to rock Sunshine's world after the carb-coma-inducing meal.

Drake glanced over at Sunshine. She was looking at him with a grin, some of her hair had fallen across her face, giving her a more mischievous look. He wanted her, a lot more than he was ready to admit to himself.

"Why didn't your Mom and Dad go with my Mom and Dad to the concert?" he asked her. He shoved a delicious bite of steak in his mouth. My gosh that steak was like butter, melted in your mouth.

She gave him the one-minute finger. He'd caught her mid-chew. "This plate of food is the best damn thing in this county."

He gave an exaggerated cough. "Excluding present company."

She rolled her eyes at him. "To answer your earlier question, they did end up going last-minute."

"I thought Mac was too slammed at work to get away." His Dad had asked him and Brice if either of them had wanted to go when Mac and Sophia thought they couldn't. Neither he nor Brice had taken them up on their offer. Brice said he had somewhere to be, and Drake had planned on seeing Sunshine some way somehow tonight.

"Daddy was able to get a hold of one of his Foremen to delegate a couple of things to him. He called me, and I assured him I'd take care of all the cattle tomorrow."

"Yeah, Dad and Mom haven't had a night out in a while. It'll be good for them to get out. Dad's main hobbies are work, and Momma. He needs to get away. And lighten up."

"Has he been handing the reins over to you any at work?"

"Hell no. I do my job, but he won't let me have much input when it comes to big decisions." That chapped his ass too. He'd been working at the stock with his Dad since he was old enough to remember. He'd done about every job you could do there, but his Dad didn't seem to trust anyone but himself when it came to decisions concerning the stockyard's future.

Sunshine reached over and grabbed his hand. "I'm sorry. He has always been hard on you boys."

"What about your Dad? Are you gonna end up running Blackwell Construction?"

"Way on down the road. You know he's never once pushed me into his line of work, but he did want me to get my business degree. He's asked me on a couple of occasions to come to meetings, and he has a system setup with an advisor in line to help me run the business. When he's ready for me to learn more, he'll tell me."

She could be a bit self-centered. Her Momma and Daddy had coddled her. His parents had coddled her. She was the only child of Sophia and Mac, and Sophia was the only child of G-Momma and G-Daddy, God rest his soul. Needless to say, she hadn't had to work too hard at anything, but she was a hard worker despite all that. She hadn't taken advantage of the situation, but it appeared she had let her only child self-centeredness blind her to what her Dad may need or want of her.

"Sunshine, you may need to put in a little more effort than that before you start running your Dad's business."

"I'm aware of what it takes to run a business, Drake. I am more than capable. I run the cattle side of Dad's operation."

He dropped the touchy subject and made small talk about her day, their town, and the people they had in common. It was the best date—if you wanted to call it a date—he'd ever had. It hadn't been anything other than dinner, but the company had made the difference.

He pulled back into the driveway after a drowsy ride back. He was relaxed from the food and the drinks when Sunshine looked over at him and ruined his mood.

"I'm not wearing any panties under this dress." She smirked.

She was trying to destroy any sanity he had left. The she-devil made sure to lift her dress just a smidge while getting out of the truck. Enough to give him a little peep show of what he wanted. Hellfire.

Drake jumped out of the truck and kept himself in check long enough for Sunshine to walk past the tailgate. He swooped her up in his arms and carried her through the front door, kicking it shut behind him. Sunshine was clenching his neck and giving him a soft smile.

He pressed her up against the door and moved her to a more comfortable position. He slid his hand under her dress and didn't waste any time sinking two fingers deep into her heat. He could feel her contract around his fingers and heard a small thud from her head resting back against the door. She was soaking wet. Damn it, he needed her.

He heard her whimper when he pulled his fingers out. He let her slide down his body and pulled her into the kitchen. Grabbing the hem of her dress, he dragged it up her body. She helped him ease it over her head.

He jerked his shirt out of his pants and undid the buttons

before slipping it off. Pulling her naked body against him, he slid his denim clad leg between hers. The abrasive texture of his jeans was almost enough to make him cum in that moment. Sunshine squeaked a surprised "Oh" when he sat her up on the kitchen table and buried his face between her legs.

Drake could get drunk off hearing her moans. Sunshine tried to wiggle away from his mouth the closer she got to orgasm. He grinned against her as he continued to stroke her with his tongue. He felt her legs clench around his head and looked up to see her head fall back in ecstasy. That sight made him feel invincible. When he was certain he had wrung out every shockwave he picked her fluid body up off of the table and carried her to bed. He laid her down against the pillows and undressed the rest of the way.

Sunshine looked like the cat that stole the canary as she watched him walk towards the bed. The beautiful picture she presented made him want to beat his chest and tell the world she was his. That brought a sober thought to his mind. That she wasn't really his; this was only for the time being. He snapped out of that bitter thought.

At least, she was his for the moment.

# CHAPTER 23

## Worn Thin

Sunshine had rolled out of Drake's bed before his alarm woke him up. She had to get to Moonshine bright and early. She grunted as she pulled at the damnable thistle that had dared to rear its ugly head within her catch lot. Her thick work gloves protected her from the painful thorns, but she could feel anxiety creeping up into her chest, and she had to fight to keep it at bay. She was going to pin her frustration on this damn weed, and not the fact that she was anxious about selling Moonshine, keeping her parents outta her personal business, and what she feared was the beginning of the end of her and Drake. She had gotten what she wanted from him, and she assumed the same for him. For shit's sake she had to get it together.

Sunshine stood up and stretched her back out from bending over. There were too many things on her mind to focus on any one thing that needed to be done. She had a running list making the rounds within her head: spray the fence line, spot spray the pasture, put out salt, look at the spring feeding the pond, fill the feeders, check cows, heifers, and calves to the ledger. It had piled up on her and she needed to move the weight off and get back on track, but her mind seemed to want to dwell on Drake.

He was a damn dream in bed, and they were having a wonderful time, but she needed to focus on the important matter at hand—getting her herd sold. Her focus was wavering too much at the wrong time and she needed to be getting shit done. Sunshine got into motion, cranking up the four-wheeler with her spray tank in the barn. She'd pre-mixed the chemicals at home and had poured them into the tank. She spent the next few hours spraying the fence line, the thistles, and a few briars.

She pulled in behind the trailers and saw Atticus wave at her from his back porch. She pulled the four-wheeler to the side of the fence and shut it off.

"Yes, sir?" Sunshine asked him, wiping the sweat from her brow with the back of her hand and squinting at him due to the sun beaming at her from behind the trailer.

"You've been slackin'." He had a slight grin, erasing some of the scolding from his words.

"Yep, I have been. No excuses. I'm going to try and get over here more these next few weeks. Seems something else needs to be done every time I come."

Atticus gave her a slow nod and leaned up off the porch railing. "Alright, Sunshine, have a good day."

"You too." Sunshine watched as he walked back in without another word. He was indeed a man of few words who got his point across without needing to tell you a hundred different ways. Ugh, why couldn't she get her shit together? She knew she could juggle a man, her business, and parents, but she was going to have work smarter not harder.

Sunshine continued checking out the herd on the four-wheeler when she found the cow she'd been looking for in the back corner of the pasture. She was trying to give birth, but it didn't look to be going well. Damn it, that wasn't what she needed on an already busy day.

Sunshine tried to force it, but the calf wouldn't come. It was too big, and she didn't have the strength to pull any longer than she had. She was gonna have to get the pullers, damn it. She would more than likely lose the calf now. That wasn't the outcome she wanted for the heifer, the calf, or herself.

Sunshine felt the sweat roll down between her breasts, and the sun beat down on her back. Considering it was fall, it sure was hot as hell, but she may have overdressed for the warmer than normal day. She patted the momma cow's head as she hurried into the hay barn to get the calf pullers out. She called Atticus as she maneuvered her way through the barn towards her goal. She heard him answer on the first ring.

"Hurry back out here. There is a calf stuck in the birth canal, and I am gonna need your help." Sunshine heard his grunt before sliding her phone back into her jeans.

She brought the calf pullers back out of the barn in time to see Atticus striding across the field towards the catch lot. She had been able to entice the heifer into the portable head catch so she couldn't move on them. She slipped everything into place in time for Atticus to come beside her and slip the chains on the calf's hooves. They cranked the calf jack one leg at a time to mimic the way of pulling by hand and walking the shoulders through the pelvis. They made sure to pull downwards to not cause the calf any undue hardship or paralysis.

When the calf came free, Sunshine breathed a pent-up sigh and stretched her aching back. She tilted her heads towards the sky and took a deep breath to cleanse the stress. Sunshine could smell the afterbirth as she bent down to the calf and checked him over. Atticus released the momma from the head catch and they both exited the catch lot to allow the heifer and calf to bond. It was imperative that the calf get some colostrum from his momma's milk bag into his belly quickly to get the bowels functioning, and put some strength in him.

"Thank you. I couldn't have done it without your help." Sunshine gave the gruff old man a quick side hug. He would pretend to hate her show of affection. Atticus shrugged away from her.

"Anytime, Sunshine." He patted her hand, as affectionate as he got towards anyone, and headed back across the pasture towards his mobile home.

Sunshine moved her gaze over to the nursing calf. The aching in her chest released at the sight of the calf nuzzling at his momma's udders. The heifer and calf would both live to see another day it appeared. She would have to come back and check them over good tomorrow and let them out of the catch pen to integrate back into the herd. Sunshine looked everyone over once more before making her way back home for a bath and some rest.

She was relieved to feel the warm water from the shower rush over her as she scrubbed the sweat and stink from the day off. She hadn't talked to Drake since she'd left him in bed this morning aside from a couple of short, quick texts back and forth. Both of their days had been busy.

Sunshine walked downstairs and lay on the couch, exhausted but relieved that her earlier wrestle with the young calf's life was a success. All too often you lost calves, but today she was on the lucky side of things. She fell into a light slumber, then woke up to someone putting a key in her door. She had enough energy to peek her head over the couch when she saw John Wayne open.

Drake came strolling through in sweatpants and a T-shirt with a ball cap pulled low. Looked as if he intended to stay the night. Drake exuded sexual energy. He only had to walk into a room for anyone to see the sensual way he carried himself. He gave her a slow grin as he threw his ball cap on the counter and jerked his shirt over his head. His sweatpants hung low on his hips. She was almost too tired to be concerned with what he was cooking up, but her traitorous vagina wasn't. Damn thing perked up every time he came into view. She felt his arms slide underneath her and her cowboy took her to bed.

Sunshine juggled Moonshine, work, and Drake the best she could over the next few weeks. Drake would sneak over to stay with her most every night, and then get up early to leave. She would head out in the mornings after he was gone and spend a couple of hours at Moonshine. She'd check everything over with the herd and talk to Atticus about what he would do. She had some heifers she needed to watch closely over the next couple of weeks. He told her he would call if he saw anything out of the way. Her cattle herd was growing by the week with every new calf that dropped, but she was afraid it still wouldn't be enough.

Sunshine lay awake. She could hear Drake breathing deeply beside her. She glanced over her shoulder at him. The moonlight coming in the room was bright enough that she could see the outline of his shoulders above the quilt and sheets. He was devastatingly handsome. It was still a jolt to roll over and find him in bed with her. A nice, hard, sexy shock, but a shock nonetheless.

She snuggled back down into her blankets to try and get some rest, but her mind wouldn't turn off. Sunshine was in a transition phase. There wasn't much else she could accomplish with her herd if she sold except to build up another, and she didn't know if that was something she wanted to do. She bought into what cattle her Dad already had and contributed her labor and money. Her and her Daddy's cattle were maxed out on ground. He wouldn't have let her buy in, and just given it to her, but she demanded he let her pay her way.

Her Dad was busy running his construction business, therefore Sunshine took on most of the day-to-day of their cattle operations. She made the house payments easily on what she made, along with her other expenses. The loan she took out for Moonshine, however, was maxing her out. She didn't want to live paycheck to paycheck. She wanted to breathe.

She wasn't going to quit giving Moonshine her all, but she may be forced to give it up sooner rather than later while it was still her choice. She had to figure out how to pay for the loan this year, or it would be sooner. She had to keep reminding herself she was entitled to change her mind.

Sunshine rolled back over to Drake. She had changed her mind about him. Things were good, but sometimes she had the tiniest urge for them to be more than what they were. Then she would panic and try to erase that feeling. It didn't help that they were better together than she ever could have her imagined. Who knew they'd get along so well and be such a good team? She sure the hell wouldn't have thought it, but it seemed to work.

Somehow, he helped level her out. Drake certainly gave her

the impression that he cared for her as more than a friend some days. She was beginning to wonder if things were becoming deeper for the both of them. Sunshine was afraid to think too heavy on that though, and willed herself to quit overanalyzing and get some much-needed sleep before the day's activities came calling.

Morning rolled around and differed from prior morning routines. Drake had gotten a wild hair it appeared. He was trying his best to make her leave her bed, but so far she didn't feel the least inclined.

"No, I refuse. I won't do it." Sunshine pulled the covers back over her head and rolled over.

"Come on, baby, it won't be that bad. Just try it." Drake said, trying to sound as sweet as possible as he rolled her back over towards him, giving her his best smile.

Sunshine clamped her eyes shut and mumbled, "I will not do it. It's against my religion."

Drake sighed and tried to kiss her lips, but she wasn't having any of it. "Alright, but you are missing out on a chance to make me happy."

"How is me not being able to breathe and my knees hurtin' goin' to make you happy?" Sunshine glared at him, questioning his sanity. He looked akin to a big puppy on the side of the bed, trying to get her to agree. The man was often too sexy for her own good but looking at his grin was softening her resolve. "I don't see how you can have the energy or stamina to think about it. We had sex twice last night." Not to mention, she was up for a while having unwanted deep inward thoughts and reflection about who she was as a person.

235

"Because it gives me a type of release—not as great as when I'm inside you—but I want you to get to experience that. You're just scared you aren't going to be good at it." Drake had changed tactics on her, the sly dog.

"I am good at whatever I do. The fact that I haven't done it in a long time doesn't mean anything." Sunshine groaned and rolled out of bed. She hated him in this moment. The bed had wrapped its fluffiness around her and held her body. "Fine, but I swear to Bob if you break out singing 'Eye of the Tiger' I will punch you in the dick."

"Thank you." Drake already had his running shoes on. He smacked Sunshine on the ass. "Get to moving, hot stuff."

She glared daggers at him. "Hurry me again and I will murder you." She turned her back to him and pulled out her gym shorts and a sports bra. Without another word, she walked into the bathroom, shutting the door and locking it.

Sunshine pulled her hair up from where it had fallen in the night. Her boobs were trying to spill out the top of her bra, and her shorts were a little more snug than normal. She'd put on some happy weight. She may have to cut back on those peanut butter milkshakes and Oreos. Damn it.

She must be getting close to starting her period because she felt bloated and lethargic. It was five o'clock in the morning but it felt more threeish. She should go back to bed, then later on, head over to Moonshine, but when he'd looked at her with his pleading gaze, she'd caved. Sunshine picked up her toothbrush and noticed it was wet. The bastard had used it again. He had his own there now, but it seemed he took great enjoyment in using hers, the ass.

Sunshine finished up and met him downstairs. He had a cup of coffee ready for her on the counter. Good man. She picked up her cup and inhaled a deep breath of the delicious aroma.

She hadn't bothered with a shirt that morning. It was early September but it was still hot and humid. He let her drink her coffee and then tugged her out the door.

"We are going to train for this 5k. Come on, you will enjoy the competition," Drake encouraged her as she stretched.

"Drake, shut up. You are too happy about this. The only reason I am doing it at all is because it's for a good cause." Sunshine tried to kill him with her eyes.

"Come on. Everybody's gonna be there—Belle, Willow, Brice, even your new friend, Emerson. Reece called me the other day and said he was too. It wouldn't be right if you didn't," Drake said. Then he made her jog a mile.

She made it back to the house without having a heart attack, while he wasn't even breathing hard.

"Drake, am I getting fat? I think I've gained some weight."

"No, baby, you look great. A little weight gain fills out all those curves I love so much."

She glared at him. "So you have noticed that I've gained weight?"

"No, I was meaning that if you did gain weight, it would look good on you."

She stripped off her shoes and socks. "Okay, let me get a quick shower, and then I'll take you home." She had stopped by his drive the previous night and picked him up. She had to get him back.

"Okay, that's fine. Whatever you need to do. I will sit down here and imagine you peeling off those shorts and that sports bra."

Sunshine whipped her head around. "What do you mean peel off? You think my shorts are too tight? You think I look like a banana that needs to be peeled out of my clothes?"

"What the hell, Sunshine? Get the stick out of your ass. I was meaning I was going to think about you taking your clothes off, that was it. I will be waiting out in the truck. I ain't listening to this shit anymore this morning. You went on a run. So what? Get the hell over it." Drake grabbed the bag he'd thrown by the door and headed out to the truck.

"Well, shit," Sunshine said aloud. She felt her eyes begin to tear up. She and Drake had been getting along so well the past few weeks. She didn't want to screw that up, but she was mad as hell this morning. She couldn't stand herself.

Sunshine looked over at Drake in the passenger's seat as she climbed in. He was studying his phone and not paying her a bit of attention. He filled up the entire seat and his visibly tanned legs, arms, and chest were turning her on. She could slip her hand inside his gym shorts to grab ahold of her favorite appendage of his. She needed to apologize or he may deny her.

Sunshine cleared her throat. "I'm sorry. I don't know what's wrong with me this morning, but I shouldn't have taken it out on you."

"I believe that is one of the rare times I have ever heard you utter the word *sorry* in my direction." Drake pulled her towards him and gave her a kiss. "Let's head out."

She was glad he had accepted her apology, but she still felt like a bitch. And horny. She would have to make it up to him—and her—later. Sunshine pulled into the Caldwells' drive at a creep and Drake gave her a kiss before he got out at the barn.

"Bye," Drake said before shutting the door. Sunshine waved as she pulled out. She was creeping out the drive when Brice waved her down from the porch with a worried look. She rolled the window down for him to tell her whatever was so important.

Brice's face was set in a grimace. "The parents know."

"How much?"

"All of it."

Sunshine hung her head at his answer. "How did they find out?"

"Seems our parents keep a much closer eye on us at this age than anticipated," Brice said.

"Screw a goose."

# CHAPTER 24

# Drinkin' Beer and Tellin' Lies

Drake walked into his living quarters in the barn to find his Dad sitting on his couch. Ben was quite the imposing figure. He was a bear of a man with salt-and-pepper hair and steel-blue eyes that matched his son's. He smirked over at him, trying not to seem skittish since Sunshine had dropped him off. "Mom giving you fits already this morning?"

Ben shook his head. "No, not yet, but it's early. I came out here to talk to you." He motioned for Drake to sit down beside him.

Drake's stomach plummeted as he sat and turned towards his Dad. "Alright, what is this about?"

His Dad looked him straight in the eye and stated, "We know."

Playing dumb wouldn't work, but he tried anyway. "Know what?" He tried to look confused and innocent. He knew his Dad wouldn't fall for that.

Ben sighed. "You have been staying with Sunshine. We aren't sure for how long or how often, but we know. Brice may be home, but you're still your mother's baby, and she does come out here to check on you. Not only do we know, but Mac and Sophia know too."

Drake felt the color drain from his face. He, and probably

Sunshine even more so, was in deep shit. Not that he would have minded his parents and Sunshine's knowing about them if they were in a normal relationship, but hell, he and Sunshine had been almost living together as of late. Who was he kidding? He did live there 99 percent of the time, now that he took the time to think about it. He didn't know how they hadn't been found out before now. Their parents would expect something more from them, which would be damned odd since they were in a sexual relationship and not a normal one. Not that he didn't like being with Sunshine and spending time with her, but a relationship and possible marriage on the table was a whole different ball game. That was a commitment.

"I don't know what you want me to say." Drake glanced over at his Dad. "Sunshine and I wanted to keep this between us. I don't think either of us thought we would even make it this long without killing the other. We never meant for y'all to find out about this. We didn't want this coming between our families, or for there to be any awkwardness."

Ben shook his head. "You plan on ending things with her?"

Drake felt his chest get tight. "I don't plan on ending it right now, no. I'm sure we will decide to go our separate ways before long. There were never any promises made between the two of us."

"How can there not be awkwardness when I look my best friends in the eye and know that my son is screwing their daughter? Hell, Drake, you are living with her, with no intention of commitment and by the sounds of it, every intention of leaving her. I've taught you things are either right or wrong, and I think you know what side of the line this falls on." Ben got up and walked out the door with those ominous words hanging between them.

Drake went to his bedroom, stripped off his clothes, and headed to the shower. He turned on the side jets and rain showerhead, standing there, letting the warm water relax his muscles. He was crazy about Sunshine. She was fun, sexy, and hot in bed, damn it. She was the best he'd ever had, but being in a real, committed relationship with her seemed far-fetched. There was a part of him that worried that when she found out about his suspicions—the suspicions he had about them raising competing herds—the suspicions he'd kept from her—Sunshine would leave him.

She was hot and last night she had been wild. Damn, but if she didn't look his every dream come true when he had her bent over the bed. Drake reached down and began to stroke himself when he saw movement out of the corner of his eye.

Drake looked Sunshine over while he continued stroking. "Who's the pervert now?"

She shrugged and pulled off her clothes. "You made me this way, and now I can't seem to help myself." She slipped out of her bra and panties and walked in behind him. She wrapped her arms around his stomach and hugged him for a moment.

Drake felt the tension of his thoughts leave him and a different tension enter. He pulled Sunshine around to face him and moved them out from under the shower. She smiled. "We will figure it out."

Then the talking stopped because Sunshine dropped down to kneel in front of him. He reached over to the towel bar and threw a towel down for her to put under her knees. He was a gentleman after all. For the most part.

He was fast losing what tiny bit of restraint he had. He looked down to see Sunshine working him in and out. Her hair was wet down her back. Drake's resolve to enjoy the moment snapped. He reached down and pulled her hair up in his hand and titled her head back a bit for him to angle better.

Drake watched as Sunshine took everything he was giving her. He pulled her up and guided her to the bench in the shower. It had been built tall enough for him, so it was the perfect height. He pulled Sunshine's legs to the edge and spread them. He didn't waste any time getting her ready. He knew she would already be soaking wet, so he shoved right into her almost to the hilt. Every time he thrust, she was able to take a little more of him.

Her head fell forward as he pushed in. Nothing and no one had ever felt as good as her. It was hard and fast and it wasn't long before her orgasm was bowing her back. He tensed when his own release hit him. He stayed in that position for a moment before he pulled her up to kiss her and hold her for a bit.

Drake pulled her back under the showerhead and looked down at her. Her face was flushed and she looked dazed. "Was I too rough?" he asked, rubbing his hands down her back and massaging her ass.

"You know I love it when it gets hot between us."

Drake kissed her again and stepped out of the shower so she could wash up in peace. He dried off and was standing at the sink with his towel around his waist when Sunshine stepped up beside him.

"I passed your Dad in the stairway in the barn. He gave me a hug, but otherwise didn't say a word." A frown marred her face.

He gave her the quick rundown of what his Dad had said. "He's disappointed in me."

"We will have to face our parents. I don't know how long I can avoid all of them. No more than a day or two if I'm lucky." He nodded at her, but knew her parents may come for his head before then.

"We didn't kill anyone, Drake. Quit looking as if we're headed to the gallows. I don't know if either of us is ready for a long-term commitment, and they are going to have to be okay with what we do have goin' on."

Everything his Dad had said and left unsaid made a loop through his mind. He felt like shit. He knew how to read between the lines. "It sure as hell feels as if we've done something wrong. Our parents are going to want an explanation. We've been raised well enough to give them one. Even though it isn't any of their business what we do." Drake ran his fingers through his hair and leaned against the sink. He felt as if everything with Sunshine was going to fall apart any minute. He was trying to push too much down and hide things from her and himself.

"You're making this out to be more complicated than it is. We won't have to hide it from them anymore, and we will continue on as we have been no matter what they say. I love my parents, but I will do as I please in my home. Chill out. Everything is going to be fine." Sunshine kissed him on the shoulder and walked out of the bathroom.

"You are underestimating our parents." Drake followed her into the bedroom and watched as she pulled her clothes on. He felt punched in the gut over how beautiful she was.

"I think you are being weird and acting guilty when there isn't anything to feel guilty about. Now, I've got to go get some work done." Sunshine gave him a kiss and headed out. "Remember we are meeting everyone tonight at the Badmoon."

Drake watched her walk out of his bedroom and heard the front door shut. He didn't know when she became the calm and logical one in this whatever their situation was, but after what his Dad said, he didn't think what he and Sunshine were doing was right for her. Something felt off, and his gut told him keeping Duck and Cover a secret was going to bite him in the ass.

The hours zoomed by, and it wasn't long before the speakers at the Badmoon assaulted Drake's ears. Sunshine walked out of his door this morning, and now he was having to watch as she danced in another man's arms. It was Reece dancing with Sunshine, but he didn't have to like it. He huffed when Reece bent down and gave her a peck on the cheek. That was the last straw.

"Pulling me out of a good-lookin' man's arms while I'm enjoying a dance is becoming a habit for you." She grinned at him when he cut in.

"Savin' you from horny bastards is what I've been doing." Drake smirked at her. He shot a glare at Reece over Sunshine's shoulder. The bastard grinned back at him. Drake had been played.

Sunshine laughed. "If that was the case, I wouldn't be dancing with you. You're the one who seems to always be trying to get in my pants. I don't think you have to worry about Reece." Sunshine glanced over to where Reece and Emerson were dancing. "I do believe he has his sights set on other prey."

Drake looked over to see one of his oldest friends trying to lay the charm on. "She will give him something to chase. Maybe he won't get so damned stir-crazy and leave again. Coming back to your earlier statement. I don't try to get in your pants, I succeed, and you want me there."

"Damn right I do, darlin'." Sunshine grinned at him. You could get a big head going real quick when a woman looked at you that way.

Drake didn't think about his next move. He leaned down and kissed those plump smiling lips. It was a sweet, quick kiss between two people who were familiar with one another. They were both smiling at one another when he pulled back. It took Drake a moment to realize what he had done. He took a quick glance around and noticed everyone from Lawrence County had stopped what they were engaged in and stared.

Drake looked at Sunshine and hung his head for a moment. "Shit."

Sunshine shrugged her shoulders. "It would have come out. If we're going to continue to see each other, we can't stay hidden forever."

Drake pulled Sunshine close and continued to dance with her. "Maybe this will get Dad off my back. Let him know I'm not ashamed of you, or just shacking up." Drake had false hope in his voice.

"Wishful thinking, but it may help." She moved her hands up and down his back while they swayed to the music. He felt her hands play across the muscles in his back.

"At least everyone will know we're together now. We ain't got to worry about where we go out to, or who sees my truck in the yard and at what time," Drake said, hugging her in reassurance. They would have to handle their parents' disappointment over the fact that they weren't running down the aisle only because they were sleeping together.

"We are together?" Sunshine asked, raising her eyebrow. "We doing this because we want to, or because it will make our life easier with our parents?"

Drake stopped dancing. "Yeah, I believe we are. I wouldn't make this type of decision on what anyone else wanted, but us. You want to be with anybody else?"

"No, I don't."

Drake nodded his head. "Looks like we are together then."

Sunshine grinned at him. "Looks like."

He guided her back over to the table and took the seat beside hers. Everyone at the table was giving them a golf clap.

Willow spoke first. "'Bout damn time, you asshole. I was beginning to think you were using one of my best friends."

Drake made a face at Willow. "I'm not. We didn't want everyone in our business."

"I think y'all make a beautiful couple. No matter how ugly Drake is. Sunshine's beauty more than makes up for it," Emerson said, batting her eyelashes at them.

"I second that. You're ugly as homemade sin," Reece added. Drake watched as he pulled a smooth one and slipped his arm across the back of Emerson's chair.

"You're welcome, Sunshine. I told him he needed to make an honest woman out of you." Brice winked at her.

"Yes, Brice, our decision was made upon your recommendation."

"I'm happy for the both of you. Y'all deserve one another. I've never met two more stubborn people," Belle told him.

"I have. I'm looking at them." Sunshine gave Belle and Brice a pointed look. Seems like Drake had missed something important.

"Sunshine, your titties look huge tonight, even bigger than normal. Did you get a new bra?" Willow asked. He watched as Sunshine tried to shove her boobs back down into submission, but there was no use. They were spilling out of the boob jail she'd insisted on putting his babies in.

"No, the damn things have grown a cup size I swear. I've put on some happy weight. I hate to say this, but I may have to start exercising." Sunshine put her head down on the table and shook it in misery. He would love for her to come work out with him in the mornings. She'd enjoy it once she got in the swing of it.

Drake patted her thigh. "Babe, you are sexy in your clothes, and even sexier out of them. Don't worry about it—that is unless you start getting a spare tire. Then we may need to talk."

Sunshine rose from the table and slapped him in the chest. "Ass."

"Sunshine, let me buy you one drink, something light so you can still drive, and we'll have us a toast to your and Drake's newfound whatever the hell it is," Reece told her, waving for the waitress.

Sunshine shook her head no. "No thanks, I'm good. I need to go to the bathroom."

"Me too."

Drake watched as all the women at the table hurried out of their chairs.

"Is it me, or was that some weird woman mind meld thing happening at the table?" Brice asked.

"The bathroom is a magical place for women to commune from what I've gathered," Reece said, sipping his beer.

"I'm sure my dick is the main conversation piece," Drake said with a smug grin.

# CHAPTER 25

# The Shit Hits the Fan

"Sunshine, snap out of it. How long has it been?" Sunshine heard Belle, but she didn't answer because she felt a tad light-headed at the moment. Belle went through and checked all the stalls to make sure they were alone before giving the all clear to talk.

"Let's give her a minute," Willow said. Sunshine could feel them staring at her, waiting on her answer. Sunshine pulled out her phone and looked at the app. She tried not to panic. Her periods were late sometimes, even on the pill. Her life had been hectic, and stressful. She had missed a few days here and there but had doubled up as the doctors recommended when you forgot.

Sunshine muttered, "Three weeks."

Emerson spoke first. "Okay. Well, you need to get a pregnancy test. If it is positive, we've got your back."

"Sunshine, it isn't the end of the world if you are. Stop looking as if you've seen a damn ghost." Willow snapped her fingers in front of her face.

Sunshine walked to a stall and sank down to sit on the toilet. "I'm not ready for that. Neither is Drake. Hell, neither one of us was even ready to make a commitment to the other before now. I am bat shit crazy. Drake and I drive each other insane. We are immature. We have only now been able to stay in the same room together without trying to pants the other one. What kind of parents would we make?" Sunshine's heart raced at the thought that they might have created a baby together.

"Y'all would make the best kind. The fun kind that raises insane children that go on to be amazing adults," Emerson said as she patted her back.

Sunshine straightened up and looked at all of them. "My life has been stressful and that is why I am late, okay?"

Belle pulled her up off the toilet. "That is disgusting. Get up. Now pull your crap together, woman. We have a fun night ahead of us, and as you said, you're late because of stress."

Emerson and Willow nodded too, but Sunshine could feel the unease. She had a gut feeling that stress truly wasn't the cause as she walked back to their table.

She smiled as Bishop walked in and sat himself down. "Evenin'. What are y'all celebrating?"

"Seems my brother and Sunshine are a couple after years of dancing around one another, and a few months spent playing hide Drake's—" Brice didn't get to finish that statement before Drake reached over and slapped him in the back of the head.

"Shut your mouth. That's Sunshine you're talkin' about."

Brice grinned at Bishop. "Big brother's a one-woman man now, as you can see."

Drake threw an arm around Sunshine's shoulders.

"You're damn right. Who wouldn't want to be with someone as sexy as Sunshine?" Drake stole a quick kiss from her. "It's good to be king."

"You are still an ass, even if you are my ass." Sunshine shook her head. It gave her a thrill. She couldn't deny it. No more having to hide they were seeing one another.

"Bishop, have you met everyone?" Sunshine asked him.

"One of them, but not all of them. Women as beautiful as your friends here a man wouldn't forget."

Sunshine made the introductions. "Our vivacious local bookstore owner and resident pin-up girl look-alike is Ms. Magnolia Emerson Caraway, who goes by Emerson or Em." Emerson smiled and held her hand out across the table. "Nice to meet you."

"Likewise." Bishop shook her hand and Sunshine continued.

"Beside her we have our beautiful brainiac and resident genius Lily Belle Ivy, Belle to everyone."

Belle rolled her eyes at Sunshine's dramatics. "Hello, Bishop, but we've met."

"Hello, Belle, good to see you again. How's the training going?"

"Not so good these days," Belle said.

"And last, but never least, is the devilish, delightful, and glamorous Willow Scarlett Sullivan, or Will." Sunshine waved her hand towards Willow.

"Charmed, I'm sure," Willow said.

"That I am, Willow."

"You know all the guys, dumb, dumber, and dumbest," Sunshine said, pointing to Drake, Bishop, and Reece.

"Hey, why do I have to be dumbest?" Reece asked.

"Because you left us," Sunshine snapped at him. "That title belongs to you until either Brice or Drake messes up, or you get back in my good graces."

"I love all of you assholes; it was never about leaving y'all."

Drake reached over and slapped Reece on the back. "We know, man, but we have the right to worry about one of our best buds. Even when he acts like a horse's ass."

Sunshine turned her attention back over to Bishop, giving Reece a break. "What brings you to the party tonight, Bishop?"

"Drake invited me, told me it might be good for me to mingle instead of studying stock portfolios, and I happen to agree with him." Bishop got his beer from the waitress and tipped her.

Drake nodded his head. "Smart man. It is always best to agree with Drake. If ever in doubt of anything, channel your inner Drake and things will work out."

Sunshine slapped Drake in the stomach and he grunted for effect. She had given him a small swat.

"While I'm here, and have you both together, I'll finish up our business before I get to drinking. It is all said and done and Mr. Alexander has made his choice. He chose Drake's herd. We can celebrate the fact that at least one of you got it." Bishop turned to her. "I'm sorry, Sunshine. Drake had more depth in his herd than you did, and a year more of statistics to back it up, but that doesn't mean the next time someone contacts me about an up-and-coming registered line, you won't have built up your numbers. I'll be working at giving you first shot next go-around. I'm glad this is all over now. It was hard not talking about business with both of you, but Drake said that's how y'all wanted it."

Sunshine felt light-headed and turned towards Drake. His face looked pale. "You figured out I was raising registered cattle and mentioned it to Bishop, but you never told me?"

Sunshine's heart was breaking into a million pieces. She had lost, but his deceit hurt far worse. He had kept his involvement from her on purpose.

"How long did you think it would be before I found out? How damn stupid can you be, Drake?"

"Oh shit," Bishop muttered. Bishop looked between Drake and Sunshine. "I didn't mean to cause trouble between y'all. I assumed you both knew."

Drake still hadn't answered her.

Sunshine looked over at Bishop, and then Drake. "There is no longer a y'all. There's a me and him, and that is how it will now continue to stay." The table went silent as she, Willow, Belle, and Emerson got up to leave.

She got to the truck and, damn it, realized she forgot the keys inside the bar.

"How in the hell do you do screw someone over that you love?" she heard Brice ask Drake as she neared the table.

"Hell, it was never supposed to get out of hand. We were supposed to sleep together and that was it. Break things off when we got ready to. And I don't love her."

Sunshine walked back to the table in time to hear the words that felt more devastating than losing the stock contract. "It's a damn good thing I don't love you either then, isn't it?"

Drake's head flew around towards her. "Sunshine, I didn't mean that how it sounded."

She snatched her keys off the table and walked back to the truck. No one said a word on the ride to her house. Sunshine headed upstairs to her bathroom. She stopped and got Willow,

Belle, and Emerson some pj's out of her dresser.

She looked no different as she stared at herself in the mirror. It was divine intervention that the scars of the heart weren't shown on the skin. She had would have been a terrible sight to behold after the night's events.

First, she and Drake had become a couple. Second, she might be pregnant. Third, she discovers she lost out on selling her entire herd and that Drake sold his. Fourth, he was hiding that he knew they were competing. And fifth, she broke up with him.

She heard a soft tap on the door to the bathroom. She opened the door to her friends' solemn faces. She moved to snuggle into the bed.

"Give me a minute. I don't want to talk yet." She told them and rolled over onto her side to try and sleep. It never came, but the tears did.

Her friends were gone the following morning when she woke up. She looked at her phone and slid her finger across the screen to clear the call and text from Drake. He wasn't the type to blow up your phone. He would show up at her doorstep. Sunshine called her Daddy and told him she was sick and wouldn't be able to make it to work today. And truthfully, she was sick. She didn't make the sale.

She'd make the loan payments for Moonshine, but it'd be based on what price she could get at the registered stockyard sale. That would change weekly, and be based on the current market value of cattle. She would stretch a dollar and make it work. It'd take more time and energy, having to haul cattle to Tennessee multiple times a week. She would come clean with her parents. That was a stress she didn't need, but she shouldn't have kept it from them in the first place.

Her belly turned over. She didn't have time to be pregnant. She wanted to refuse the fact that she had morning sickness, but she was smarter than that. She drove over to the next county and went to Target to pick up some pregnancy tests. She had dressed in a ball cap, baggy sweat shirt, and sunglasses. Sunshine reckoned she was about as incognito as she could get.

Her palms were sweating as she went towards the feminine aisle. She headed to her destination and selected a few different tests. After she put her picks in her basket, she went over to the grocery section and snagged a pack of Oreos, reasons being because she was craving them, she needed to cover up the tests, and she needed help easing her misery. Sunshine's stomach dropped to her feet. There was G-Momma in the aisle. She couldn't catch a damn break. She peeked down at her basket to make sure her tests were covered up before she approached.

"Hey, G-Momma. What are you doing out this way?" Sunshine hugged her and stepped back and turned to the side to hide her basket the best she could.

"Hey, baby girl. I was in town visiting some friends and thought I would stop by and get a few groceries. What are you doin'?"

"I wasn't feeling well, needed to come grab some medicine, and a few pick-me-ups."

G-Momma looked her granddaughter up and down. "You go on home then, baby girl, and get some rest. Things will look better in the morning. Love you." G-Momma pulled Sunshine in for a hug.

Sunshine pulled out of her G-Momma's arms. "Bye. Love you." She headed to the cash register.

Sunshine went through the checkout process in a haze and headed home. She tried not to think about what her future was going to look akin to without having sold the majority of the Moonshine herd, not to mention the possibility of a baby. How was she going to work all the cattle? Atticus was helpful, but he had his own things to do. She also didn't know if you could ride horses while pregnant. She didn't know anything about being pregnant, or babies. Sunshine knew about livestock.

Bishop was fair in business. Drake must have a larger selection of cattle, but what she didn't understand is why he didn't come out and tell her that he was the one she was up against? Where had he been keeping them? He'd obviously been keeping what he was doing, and where he was at times, a secret from her, same as she had. That part stung some, even knowing she was doing the same to him.

Sunshine was trying not to get hysterical, but she was close to it. She was twenty-six damn years old. She knew how to not get pregnant. She rushed into the house and upstairs to her bathroom. She opened all the boxes—five so there couldn't be a tie—and laid them out on the counter. She grabbed a disposable cup from the sink and sat on the toilet to fill it up with her pee. Then she started the process of dipping each test. She recapped all of them and went into the bedroom to wait.

The timer went off on her phone and she walked to the bathroom to look at the five tests she'd laid out. All five were positive. She fell to the floor and curled into a ball to cry. Cry over the loss of the sale, over the loss of Drake, and the surprising joy of carrying a baby. She never had been a weepy woman, but this baby seemed to be opening her tear ducts. That was how her Momma found her.

She watched as her Momma picked up the tests. "I've screwed up. I'm so sorry. I never meant to disappoint you and Daddy." Sunshine sniffled. "Everyone will think I'm a whore."

"Roll over, Sunshine Grace." Sophia waited for her to obey before she continued. "Don't you ever apologize to me, or anyone else for that matter, for being pregnant with my first grandchild. Am I happy about the way this pregnancy came about? No. Am I happy that you are bringing a life into this world? Yes. And never, ever let me hear you refer to yourself as a whore again. You got caught doing what everyone else does behind closed doors. Now your Daddy is going to be upset at first because he is going to one hundred percent know that you have had sex, and that is not going to go over well. After that initial shock, he will be as happy as I am about having a grandchild. That goes for Mac and Claire also. I don't know how you and Drake are going to handle this, but I do know y'all will be wonderful parents. You have both had wonderful examples in all of us."

Sunshine's belly dropped at the mention of Drake's name. She hugged her Momma while they continued to lie on the floor. "Momma, it's not that I don't want babies—or this baby—I just feel so young, and not ready. There is a part of me that is excited, then another part that is terrified."

She felt her Mom's hand stroke her hair. "Welcome to motherhood."

Sunshine pulled back to look at her Momma. "Drake doesn't know yet. We broke up last night and I'm scared to tell him. He doesn't love me, and neither of us wanted anything but a causal commitment, I am now ashamed to say. We didn't anticipate this crap."

Her mother patted her hand. "Why did you and Drake break up?"

Sunshine told her Momma the whole sordid story from her and Drake deciding to take their relationship to the next level to her overhearing he didn't love her, all in one night.

"Oh sweetheart, that is an emotional roller coaster of a night. Even without being pregnant. I know you feel as if you have been dragged over barbwire. Why didn't you tell me or your Daddy about this contract?"

Sunshine shrugged her shoulders. "I needed to do it on my own, separate from the family. I had to know if I could make it without Daddy to guide my business moves or be there to smooth the way."

Sophia smiled at her only child and daughter. "Baby, you are independent. How could a daughter of mine not be? We have helped you, but that does not change the fact that you make the decisions when it comes to your money, and your stock. You have made your money and parts of your life separate from us. We are proud of you, Sunshine Grace; don't you forget that."

Sunshine hugged her Momma again and they got off the floor. "I love you."

"I love you too, but you need to talk to Drake. G-Momma wants to know if you think you are going to be craving Oreos during the entire pregnancy."

# CHAPTER 26

## Bless His Heart

Drake's heart hurt in a way that he hadn't expected. Sunshine had always had an important place in his life, even more so now, but it looked as if he'd screwed that up in a major way. He didn't know if he could fix this, or how to even start.

Hell, there wasn't any way he was going to talk himself out of this one. He had planned on breaking it to her eventually, that he thought it was her and him against one another, he just hadn't gotten around to it.

He threw bale after bale of hay off the barn loft to his brother down below. He hadn't slept last night and he was exhausted. Brice was shooting daggers at him with every other throw, and it was pissing him off. He knew he had screwed up. He didn't need Brice or anyone else to tell him that.

"Man, you are in deep shit," Brice told him.

"No, really? Thanks, Sherlock." Drake put his hands over his face and rubbed, hoping this was a bad dream, but he wasn't that damn lucky.

"Why hadn't you already told her about it? Why not be up front?" Brice asked.

"Hell, I don't know. I thought it might give her another reason not to get in bed with me." Now that he said it out loud, it sounded even worse than he imagined.

"Go ahead and say it."

Brice shook his head at his brother. "Not only did I tell you not to mess with her, but then you bend her over the barrel in a business deal. She is one of our best friends."

Drake didn't bother answering. There was nothing he could say in return. Brice was right. His brother kept staring at him.

"Quit lookin' at me with murder in your eyes," Drake told him, throwing the next bale down harder than necessary. Brice caught it and didn't budge. His little brother kept up the subtle reminders that he was a man.

"How do you think our whole friend group is going to work now? You think everything is going to go back to normal overnight?" Brice asked him, stacking the bales on the back of the truck. Five more to go.

"No, I don't. I don't know how this shit is going to play out."

Brice turned from stacking and looked at his brother. "You'll be lucky if Belle, Willow, and Emerson don't castrate you. There ain't no telling what they are cooking up."

"Makes me nervous. I ain't afraid to admit it," Drake told him. They finished the last few minutes, throwing bales in silence. Drake climbed down the ladder and stood beside his brother, leaning up against the truck.

"I don't know how to fix this," Drake admitted to Brice. He knew he did want to fix it. He wanted to work things out with Sunshine. She was his partner in crime, and he missed her something awful last night, lying in his bed alone.

"Getting a cup and protecting the boys would be a good start, and then grovel," Brice offered up.

"Don't believe it's going to be that easy. Sunshine doesn't hold well with being lied to. Remember when we were in high school and you told her that she had blood on the back of her shorts?"

Brice winced and nodded. "She then somehow got to my football pants and stained the back of them red. I didn't know till we were out on the field and Sunshine was in the stands holding a sign that read, 'What's wrong, Brice? Did you finally start your period?' The whole stadium laughed at me."

"You never know where payback is going to come from with her." Drake hoped his balls and dick were safe. "I do love her. I've been running from it for a long while." He noticed Brice didn't seem shocked. "You're not surprised?"

Brice laughed. "Hell no. You've loved her since we were little. That's why no one else ever stuck. Some people just fit, and y'all fit."

Drake sat there for a while longer. He wasn't sorry he was able to sell his herd, but he was sorry about how she found out. "We got any cups lying around? I believe it is time for me to grovel."

"No, but get your ass to Sunshine's. I'll finish putting out hay," Brice told him. "And congratulations on your big sale. I'm sure you worked hard for it. Not that I would know about it."

"Thanks, B," Drake said over his shoulder, heading for his truck. Seemed he had also hurt his brother with his deception. He may have more than one person to make it up to. He needed to make a stop by the house.

His Momma was standing in the kitchen at the stove. She was there more often than not. His Momma had cooked for them for as long as he could remember. Not so much these days, but she still liked for him to come over and eat a home-cooked meal once a week at the least. His Mom was the softness to his Dad's gruff nature. That didn't stop her from telling him and Brice when they had messed up, but she did it with a hug.

"Hey, baby." She gave him a hug and stretched to give him a kiss on the cheek. She was tall for most women, but he still had about six inches on her in height.

"Hey, Momma." He sat down at the table while she went back to the stove to stir something in a pot that smelled delicious.

"What's on your mind?" She sat down in the chair beside him.

"I'll tell Dad I'm sorry later on, but you I needed to tell today. Mom, I'm sorry. If I embarrassed you and Dad, or made you think less of me, please forgive me. You did an excellent job raising me and Brice. My recent selfish decisions do not reflect on your parenting." Drake hung his head, waiting on his Mom to speak.

"Drake, baby, look at me." His Mom gave him a smile. "I love you, and I am not happy about the way in which you and Sunshine have been carrying on behind our backs, but you're grown. You are responsible for your decisions. They now reflect on you, not me and your Daddy."

"I've been raising registered cattle on the side also. I needed you to know that. I want to expand the stockyard's resume to include a registered sale night. I'll be talking to Brice and Dad about that. I just wanted to come clean about everything."

She gave a small laugh. "Baby, how dumb do you think your Daddy and I are? We've known the whole time. You live in the barn. We know your comings and goings. I swear you boys think we are dumber than a box of rocks somedays. You give yourselves entirely too much credit."

"Yes, ma'am. You have indeed proven you are the smartest of us all on more than one occasion, even smarter than Dad, but don't tell him."

"I don't have to. He knows." His Mom shrugged her shoulders at him. "Do you love Sunshine?" His Mom's question threw him.

"Well, yeah. Of course, I do."

"Remember when y'all were little? I believe Sunshine was about four, you were five fixin' to turn six, and Brice was three. You had Brice marry you and Sunshine even though Sunshine said no when you asked her."

He laughed. "Yes, I believe her words were, 'You're a poopy head, Drake, and I don't won't to marry you and have poopy-headed babies.'"

"You wouldn't take no for an answer and bribed her with the promise of giving her all your Reese's Cups when y'all went trick-or-treating. Sunshine's emotions have always been attached to her stomach." His Mom gave him a soft smile. It couldn't get any worse at this point. He hoped.

"I'm not above bribing her with food to get her back."

"Baby, I don't think you ever really had her. When you have someone, you are honest and forthcoming with them. You share things. It isn't only about sex."

Drake looked at his Momma in horror when she said "sex."

"Yes, Drake, I said 'sex.' I raised two boys. I'm not blind to your and Brice's late nights and what those mean at y'all's age." She gave him a glare.

"Okay." He didn't know what else to say. Whenever he was scolded by his Momma, he still felt like her little boy. "I've hurt

265

her enough by being stubborn. I don't want to continue to do that."

"I'm sure you have hurt her. But if you want her more than anyone else, if you love her, and respect her, you will find a way to make it right, no matter what. I'm not tellin' you it'll be easy, because Sunshine isn't any easy woman, but you keep trying."

"I don't deserve a Momma like you." He laid his head over on her shoulder, and she ruffled his hair.

"No, you don't, but you got me anyway." He felt his Momma kiss his head. He may be twenty-eight years old, but his Momma's kiss could still make his battle wounds some better. Her support and forgiveness soothed his soul where his parents were concerned.

"Thank you, Momma, I love you." He got up and pulled her into a hug.

"If wooing her doesn't work, you could always try sexing her up. That's what your Dad did to me."

"Eww, Mom. No." Drake ran out of the house at her laughter. Parents were weird as hell sometimes.

He went to the catch lot where he had kept the bull that had started it all. He would have never thought that Sunshine and him would end up where they were now. Not speaking, hurting, and angry. Damn it he was miserable, and so was she, and none of this shit was supposed to ever have happened. He should have kept his damn mouth shut and not popped off that he didn't love Sunshine. Hell, he loved her. Words weren't going to be good enough. There were going to have to be actions, and he was ready to cowboy up. A little too late, but he couldn't give up hope that he still had a shot.

His resolve pushed him towards his truck for a quick drive. Drake swallowed the knot in his throat as he stared at the Blackwells' house. He had been welcome there whenever he had walked through the door. Today was a different matter. He didn't know how he would be received. He knocked on the front door and waited.

"Drake." Sunshine's Momma answered the door. He saw that she didn't have her normal smile on her face when she greeted him.

"Sophia, I would like to talk to you and Mac if y'all have a minute." Drake rocked back on his heels and shoved his hands in his pockets while Sophia judged him.

"Come in." She didn't bother holding the door for him.

He followed her to the kitchen. Mac was sitting there eating a cookie. He tried not to shy away from the harsh look Mac gave him.

"First off, I would like to apologize. I'm sorry for disrespecting you both. Sunshine and I should have been up-front with you and my parents. I hope you both can forgive me." Sophia gave him a small smile. Mac continued to stare a hole through him.

"Second, I came to ask both of you for your permission to ask for Sunshine's hand in marriage." Drake watched as Sophia wiped at a tear that came to her eyes. Mac put his hand over his wife's.

"Why do you want to marry Sunshine?" Mac asked, not giving him a hint as to which way he would decide.

"I've loved her our whole lives, and it has taken on different forms. At first it was as a friend, then it evolved into lovers, and now I want it to turn into a lifetime of partnership. I want Sunshine by my side, day in and day out, helping me, yelling at me, and loving me. She is my other crazy, insane half and she keeps me in check."

Mac gave him a nod and looked at Sophia. "What do you say?"

Sophia looked at Mac and then back at Drake. "I love you, Drake. I have since the moment I laid eyes on you in the hospital. I've loved you and your brother like my own, and now you will be my son, if Sunshine says yes." Sophia gave him a bright smile.

"I want to tell you no and keep my baby girl to myself from here on out, but I know that isn't possible. You both have belonged to one another for a long time. We all could see it, even when you two ran from it. It's like Sophia said, I've loved you and Brice like my own. I'd be proud to call you my son." Drake stood up and hugged them both.

"Y'all are two of the most important people in my life besides my own family and Sunshine. I love you both. Thank you for your blessing." Drake pulled out of their embrace.

"Now I've gotta convince y'all's stubborn daughter to give me a chance."

Drake's phone started ringing when he got in his truck. He was shocked to see Sunshine's name pop up, but was grateful it had. He jumped one hurdle; it was time for another. "Hello?"

"Hey," Drake heard her respond, but she sounded hesitant. He hated that they'd done this to one another. He ran his fingers back and forth through his hair. If he kept this up, he was going to be bald.

"I would like for you to come over today and for us to talk," Sunshine told him.

"Yeah, I'd like that. I'll be there soon," Drake said.

Drake heard her say, "Okay, bye," and then the line went dead.

# CHAPTER 27

## Bless Her Heart

Sunshine headed out to the barn to try and work out her anger. She was brushing and washing Deacon when she heard Drake's truck pull in the drive. Her heart felt as if it were breaking all over again and she was pissed about it. Sunshine watched as he walked through the barn doors. He looked good as always. He had his work clothes on, a white thermal on tight enough that she could make out the outlines of his muscles, tight blue jeans, and a ball cap. Her vagina wanted her to tell him everything was fine, beg him to come and kiss her, but her pride said hell to the no. Shut up, vajayjay.

"I'm sorry, Sunshine," he blurted. "I didn't know how to ask you or tell you about it."

"Something along the lines of, 'Hey, Sunshine, I decided to raise registered cattle, I'm fixing to sell out my herd to Mr. Alexander. I have suspicions you may also be doing that on the side. I thought you should know.'" Sunshine stared straight through him.

"When you put it that way, it does sound simple." Drake sighed, taking his ball cap off and tapping it against his leg. "It wouldn't have been though."

"You're right. It wouldn't have made things simple between us, because all you wanted was uncomplicated sex and telling me this might have muddied the waters a bit more."

"At first, yes. I ain't goin' to lie about it. That was what I thought, but then things became more between us, and I didn't want to screw it up," Drake said. He sat down on a stool across from her while she continued brushing Deacon.

"I trusted you enough to let things happen between us, and you didn't even let me know you had suspicions." Sunshine turned to stare him down again. "I talked to you about how I was working on something for myself. That I needed to branch out and do something separate from my family. I craved to prove I wasn't having everything handed to me in the cattle business. I needed that because I am a woman, and I needed everyone to know I could make it on my own in this male-dominated industry. You may not have known what I was doing, you may have only suspected, but you should have brought it up with me." Sunshine was shouting at him by the end. She held back the tears that wanted to stream down her face.

"Do you not think I want the same damn thing?" Drake shouted back. "You think you're the only one living in their family's shadow? Get your head out of your ass, Sunshine, and quit being so selfish. You're not the only person in existence in this business."

Sunshine felt his barb strike her heart. He'd hit too close to home. Being an only child sometimes blinded her to her own selfish faults. "Don't try and turn this on me. This is about you keeping this from me and lying to me. I may be selfish sometimes, and I now realize you would want the same thing, but that doesn't mean that you couldn't have told me about it."

"Yeah, it did, Sunshine. There would have been an automatic wall between us. Nothin' would have developed the way it has. No becoming close. Both of us had our walls up in the beginning and they would have stayed that way. Had you known about the contract, we wouldn't have had the time to develop feelings for one another."

"What feelings? You made it crystal clear to our friends, and me, when you said you didn't love me at the bar." Sunshine could still hear the words ringing in her head and her heart.

"Sunshine, I wasn't about to admit anything to them before I even admitted it to myself or you. Hell, we had decided to make it official only a few minutes before, instead of tryin' to keep it a secret that were sleeping together. I didn't believe that declarations of love were necessary yet."

"They weren't, but hearing that things went further than we initially wanted and you being adamant that you don't love me was another slap in the face after finding out about you suspecting I was also up for the contract. What were you doing? Stringing me along so you could know all my plans for my herd, and stay one step ahead of me?" Sunshine saw the hardness come into Drake's eyes.

"You crossed the line. I would never use anything you would have told me to get ahead in business over you." Drake turned and walked towards the barn door. "You called me to come over here, but I won't be yelled at or talked down to."

Sunshine couldn't keep her mouth shut. She had to have the last word. "It wouldn't be the first time I've crossed the line. I crossed it when I started sleeping with you. That's been my biggest mistake yet." Sunshine knew she had hurt him with those words. She meant to and had hurt herself in the process.

He turned back towards her before he walked out the barn doors. "We weren't a mistake, Sunshine, and when you get your head outta your ass, we can talk about this again. I expect you to act like an adult about it next time."

Sunshine heard his door shut followed by the sound of him pulling away from the barn. She sat down on the stool and hung her head and cried. All the anger left her and was replaced by a deep loneliness and sadness. She was a fool. She should have told him about the baby.

She heard a knock on John Wayne a short while later, but didn't bother gettin up to get it. Whoever it was could either let themselves in or go away. She wasn't suitable company after her and Drake's talk. She heard whoever it was set something down in the kitchen, and she rolled over on her side to see her G-Momma standing at the end of the couch. She was stunning as always in black leather leggings, knee-high boots, and a red draping top.

"Hey, G-Momma, did you bring me some Oreos?" Sunshine asked, trying to sound even more pitiful. She wanted to milk this free food thing for all it was worth. Although the baby would probably be as huge as Drake. Maybe she needed to rethink the whole eat till she was big as a barn idea.

"That I did, baby girl. Brought you something you and the baby are wanting. There were a few containers left on the table on the front porch too. Bo didn't bother them. Looks as if your friends dropped them off." G-Momma moved her legs and sat down. Sunshine stretched them back out in her G-Momma's lap.

"That was nice of them. I am not ready to talk to them yet." Sunshine didn't know what else to say to break the silence. She lay there and waited for G-Momma to say something surprising and wasn't disappointed.

"How good is he in the sack?" G-Momma asked Sunshine with a sly smile.

"Superior. I didn't even know sex could be that fantastic," Sunshine told her truthfully. This wasn't Sunshine's first talk about sex with her. G-Momma had told Sunshine her own version of the birds and the bees. Traumatizing was what that conversation had been.

G-Momma smiled and then said something even more shocking. "I was pregnant when your G-Daddy and I got married, and I miscarried shortly after. I was lucky in the fact that I loved your G-Daddy senseless."

G-Momma had been crossing boundaries and breaking rules for years, but back then, that would have made her a complete social outcast. G-Momma continued, "Your G-Daddy was a man, um, you talkin' about a man. Amazin' in the sack, haven't had one yet that has measured up to him."

Sunshine covered her face with her hands. "G-Momma, I don't want to hear about your and G-Daddy's sex life."

"Anyway, you know it is still frowned up on now, and we still have shotgun weddings, not as frequent, but back then it was rough on women. Your G-Daddy and I immediately married, and we had fifty-two wonderful years together. I have loved him from the moment I laid eyes on him and will till they bury me in the ground beside him. There is no one that could ever come close to him. The others after he passed have only been because

I'm lonely. After having someone with you all day every day then suddenly having no one, that's hard." G-Momma sighed. "I know your mother frowns upon my gallivanting, but G-Daddy would have wanted me to try and find some happiness on this earth without him. As I would have him, and that has been a hard thing to do." G-Momma patted Sunshine's feet. "I want that for you. I want you to have a man that rocks your world in the sack and fills your heart so full of love that there could never be a replacement. If Drake is that person, then you need to forgive and fight for that type of love. There is a lot of forgiveness that has to happen in any relationship on both sides. If Drake is not that person, you do not settle, baby girl, just because you are having his child. That doesn't mean that there are no other men out there. This isn't the fifties."

Sunshine moved around on the couch and laid her head in G-Momma's lap, crying. "I want that, G-Momma. I want that type of love, everything seems insurmountable right now with Drake, but he's my person . I can't imagine life without him." That was the truth, and it was staring Sunshine in the face. She couldn't imagine a life without Drake in it daily. She wanted him by her. She wanted him to be there every day, helping raise their child.

"Enough with the twenty-five-cent words. There ain't a thing that can't be overcome with enough determination," G-Momma told her. "Now get up, and get a shower, and put some clothes on besides pajamas. You want to lie here in this house and stew in self-pity, fine, but that doesn't mean you can't look good doin' it. You are made of sterner stuff, and it is time you start actin' like it. I don't want my great-grandchild coming out with a weak personality because he or she may absorb it by osmosis or something."

Sunshine smiled. "Who's using the twenty-five-cent words now?"

G-Momma turned towards Sunshine and raised her brows. "I don't care that you're pregnant, your butt isn't, and back talk me one more time and I will reintroduce you to a wooden spoon, missy."

"Yes, ma'am," Sunshine said and jumped up from the couch, headed upstairs in the direction of the shower. Damn woman could still scare the shit out of her. She had a mean swing with that wooden spoon. Her backside could remember the sting from her childhood. Sunshine tried to let the shower rinse away the tension and the worries.

She looked down at her belly and patted her tiny pudge. "You may not have been planned, but you are loved. Loved by a bunch of crazy weirdos, but don't worry, we will make you one us and you won't be sane enough to know the difference. I love you, pudge."

Sunshine felt better talking to the baby, letting him or her know they were loved in case the baby could feel her stress. Sunshine put on a pair of jeans and put a hair band around the loop and button to give her some more room—she had found that trick on Pinterest. She put on a dark green sweater that was comfortable, but still attractive, and she felt better already. G-Momma was right. There was not any sense in looking bad, but makeup wasn't happening. She went back downstairs to find G-Momma had left while she was in the shower, but she left a note taped to the top of the dirt cake bowl.

*Baby girl,*

*Call him. Don't let anger and pride steal your chance at a once in a lifetime friendship and love. Also, I made you some dirt cake. You're welcome. There's a fresh pack of Oreos in the pantry. Don't be a puss. Go after what you want. You are not a weak woman. You are strong. Remember there are two ways to win a man's heart—his stomach and his dick. If you're any granddaughter of mine, you know how to make both happy. You're welcome, again.*

*I love you and my future great-grandchild,*
*G-Momma*

Sunshine couldn't help but laugh. She pulled out a large serving spoon to eat with. There was no one there to judge her, and she'd be damned if anyone tried.

# CHAPTER 28

Damn it, he hated arguing. He headed to the safe his parents' kept in their bedroom closet and pulled out some cash he'd been saving up. He shut it, then turned to finish out his plan.

"That big of a grovel?" Brice asked as he stood in the doorway of their parents' bedroom.

"Yes, and it isn't about groveling. It's about getting the woman I love to marry me. You want to ride with?" Drake headed towards the door.

"Yeah, you don't need to mess this up."

It was a quick drive over to the jewelry store. Drake heard the gravel crunch as he hit the drive to Billy Mitchell Jewelry.

"You nervous?" Brice asked as they got out of the truck.

"Nervous about how much money I'm gonna end up spending." Drake walked to the counter and was greeted by a sales associate.

"What are you looking to spend?" The guy must have recognized his dumbfounded expression. "Do you want a small, medium, or large diamond?"

"Man talk. I can understand that." Drake laughed at the guy. "I don't want to have to break the bank, but I'd like to get her a bigger than average diamond. I want the setting to be thin and delicate." Sunshine's frame was slim and delicate, but her personality was big. She needed a ring to suit her.

Drake was schooled on cut, clarity, and carat. His eyebrows raised at the prices that were thrown out. That was a hell of a lot of cattle he could buy with what he was spending on her ring.

"Hell, I like that one." Drake pointed to what he thought the guy said was an asscher cut diamond. It was two and a half carats, and some kinda good clarity. Whatever the guy said. It was supposed to be a good one.

"That's the diamond, huh?" Brice came up behind him looking at it. "I like it. Not the usual round or princess cut. A little different like our Sunshine. Good taste." Brice nodded his approval.

"Now what about the setting?"

"Delicate, nothing gaudy. She has small hands."

"Do you know what size she wears?" Drake froze. "Hell no." He picked up the phone.

"Hey, Sophia, what size ring does Sunshine wear?" He told her a quick thank-you and hung up.

"She wears a size five."

He got the ring setting picked out, and the money squared away. He choose to wait on the diamond to be set. He wanted to give it to her as soon as possible.

When he got in the truck, he sat there for a minute trying to absorb the hit his pocket took. He felt as if he'd been robbed. Damn it, but she was gonna love the ring. He took it out of his pocket and looked at it again. It was gorgeous, but not as gorgeous as Sunshine. He loved her, and she was gonna love this ring, and him. He was gonna wear her down till she forgave him and wanted him for the rest of her life.

"Drake buddy, you gonna be okay?" Brice gave him a look.

Drake glared at his brother. "Why didn't you warn me rings were that expensive?"

"I don't think they have to be that expensive. It was more so your expensive taste that had you spending so much."

"Let's go get insurance on this thing right now." He drove as fast as he could to get the dang thing insured. He wasn't taking any chances on losing something that expensive. After he took care of that, he dropped Brice back off at home.

"Good luck, Drake!" Brice yelled as he drove off. He would need it with Sunshine.

His stomach was in knots as her drove to her house. She may not want to marry him. But if she loved him half as much as he loved her, she would want to marry him. Hell, the more he thought about being married to her, the more excited he got.

He got the spare key and opened John Wayne to find Sunshine asleep on the couch. He'd been in a rush to come over, and here she'd been sleeping away. He ran his hands up and down her hip and laid soft kisses to her neck. She stretched into his touch. He gave her a small kiss on the forehead when he picked her up. There were things he needed to talk to her about, but he didn't want to talk right then. He didn't want to argue anymore. He wanted to hold her.

She gave him a small smile. "Let's go to bed." He was more than ready to agree to that.

Drake laid her out on the bed and pinned her hands above her head. His sanity left and all he could think about was how he wanted this, he needed this, and he needed Sunshine. She belonged to him, she did, and she always had. Her hands grazed along his back. She stopped kissing him long enough to pull his shirt over his head. He stared into her eyes for a moment before leaning his head back down to hers. She began to rub her body against his, straining for something he could and would give her, but he was keeping it out of reach.

Drake pulled away from Sunshine's mouth. "Sunshine, I can't wait." His voice sounded rough. She was beautiful lying under him with her hair spread around her head. Her face was void of makeup and her eyes shined with unshed tears. He hated the tears. He wanted to make up for every one of them, and he would. He would make love to her and show her he loved her until she didn't remember the hurt anymore.

She ran her fingers through his hair, and he looked down into eyes that had darkened from lust. "I didn't want anything less," she answered.

Drake slammed his mouth to hers and jerked her head back to give him better access to her mouth. He continued to ravage her mouth, but he didn't worry that he was hurting her because the more excited and rough he got with Sunshine, the more she wanted. She was his perfect match on every level when it came to sex. Hell, she was his perfect match on every level outside of sex. She arched into him and he was gone. Drake slid his hands up her sides and felt goosebumps break out as he pulled her shirt off over her head. He was going to give her what she wanted. What she needed. What he also needed.

He noticed her breasts were spilling out over her bra and were beautiful and full.

"How is that you get more beautiful every time I see you. I've seen you thousands of times in the past, and in my dreams, but now every time feels new, different, better."

Drake sat up on his knees and looked down at her. He noticed there was a hair band holding her pants together, something tickled his brain, but his brain had recently relocated to his dick. "What's this contraption?" Drake asked her, undoing them and getting down off the bed to slide them and her panties off her legs.

She shook her head at him. "Let's not talk about that right now. I want to see you."

Drake didn't need to be told twice. He jerked his pants and boxer briefs down and climbed back on to the bed. He lay down on his side beside Sunshine and pulled her close to him to hold her for a second. He would wait. He needed to make love to Sunshine tonight, and it was pertinent for him to get ahold of himself. He was being as gentle as he could with her. He loved her, but the hurt was there under the surface. After they made love, there would have to be a talk.

Drake caught her lips with his and devoured her mouth. He wanted to worship her body tonight and soothe her heart. He grazed her breast with his hand and felt her nipple harden. She was incredibly responsive to his touch. He never had to guess with her. He moved his lips from Sunshine's and kissed her cheeks, her nose, her neck, and moved with slowness down her breasts to her stomach and then down between her legs.

He said he couldn't wait, but he was waiting. Her gave her a slow lick of his tongue. He heard her moan at his teasing. There wasn't anything hotter on earth than going down on her. It was a selfless act in lovemaking, and one he could say he was excellent at if her reactions were enough to go by. She arched into his mouth when he gave a low groan, and he felt her legs begin to quiver.

"Drake, I don't want to come undone without you." Sunshine moaned and he felt her pull at his hair before he sent her over the edge.

Drake moved her legs further apart and placed one upon his shoulder. She had voiced on more than one occasion that she liked it deep. He worked himself in, inch by inch, till he was almost all the way there and then he pulled back. Sunshine whimpered. "Don't worry, baby, I've got you," he murmured and thrust back into her, making the headboard hit the wall with the motion. Sunshine moaned even louder. Damn woman was perfect. He watched as she arched her hips, trying to take more of him in. He placed her other leg on his shoulder and grabbed a spare pillow and put it under her ass to give him a deeper angle. Drake started driving into her over and over. He could feel her getting tighter as he got her closer to the edge.

"Harder, Drake. I need more." He gave her what she asked for. He had wanted to be gentler, but she wouldn't have that. He heard her cry out as her back arched up off the bed and her legs began shaking, her body clenching. Her nails dug into his back.

He couldn't hold back any longer and with one more thrust he emptied himself inside her, moaning her name. He lay down on top of her for a moment before rolling over.

Drake wrapped her in his arms. He didn't want to let her go yet. They lay in bed and

Sunshine snuggled into his arms.

"Can we wait a bit longer before talking?" she asked. "Let

me lie here and enjoy this moment for a little while."

Drake's heart broke a fraction more at her words. "Yeah, whatever you need." He felt her breath even out and her body relax a few minutes later. He kissed her cheek and enjoyed holding her. Home, this was home, she was home. Drake was sorry it had taken him so long to realize.

He studied her face and body. He wanted to memorize every detail of the night he asked her to marry him. After a while, his belly started to growl loud enough that he was afraid it was going to wake Sunshine. He slipped his arm out from under her as gently as possible, got up, and slipped on his underwear and headed downstairs.

He opened the fridge and saw a clear bowl with what he knew was dirt cake. Hell yeah. Drake put the bowl on the counter and noticed the note taped to the top. He read G-Momma's words, and his heart soared, same as a damn eagle, when he read the first few lines. He laughed at the next few and felt his heart drop at the end. What in the hell? Great-grandchild?

Drake sat down on a bar stool, his mind racing. Sunshine's mood swings. Damn it, those didn't count. That was normal. But her boobs had to be at least a cup size bigger, and she had gained weight, but it hadn't all been in her belly. That damn hair band trick. He knew where he had seen that now. Clint's wife, Trisha, had done that when she was pregnant. Drake put his hands in his hair. Sunshine was pregnant with his baby.

He didn't know what to feel. On the one hand, he was thrilled. He had always wanted kids, later on, but still, he wanted them. Now he was going to have one with the woman he loved. The woman he was going to spend the rest of his life with. On the other hand, he was pissed because how the hell did G-Momma know before him? He was the daddy. He should know first. Why hadn't she told him?

# CHAPTER 29

# Their Beginnin'

Sunshine rolled over in bed and didn't feel Drake. She looked out the windows to see that it was dark. She headed down the stairs and her heart stopped. She saw the lid and note lying in front of Drake. Oh shit, this was not going to happen as she thought it would.

She cleared her throat. "This is not exactly how I planned to tell you, or for you to find out. I'm sorry about that."

Drake turned towards her, placing her legs between his. Sunshine studied his face. He was so handsome, his beard stubble was evident and those eyes, Lord, what they did to her. She felt undone. He looked sad and helpless. She hoped that wasn't the reaction to her being pregnant, but rather the reaction to how he found out.

"When did you find out?" Drake asked her, his voice low and strained.

"Yesterday morning. I went to Target and got five tests. All of them were positive." She watched him nod.

"Who all knows?" he asked. She felt her heart sink. She knew he would be hurt he wasn't the first to know.

"Momma and G-Momma know for sure, but that is because

G-Momma happened to be in Target and saw me. Damn my luck. I thought I had the tests hidden in my basket, but she must have seen them and called Momma. Belle, Willow, and Emerson suspect that I am, but that's because they brought it up to me the other night at the bar. They put my symptoms together before I did, and then with the way things happened with the contract and everything else…" Sunshine let her sentence drag off.

"You knew when we were fighting this morning, but you didn't tell me?"

Sunshine felt a tear roll down her cheek. Her keeping this from him had hurt him in the same manner as him keeping the cattle deal from her. She might not have kept it from him as long, but this was of more importance. G-Momma was wise. There would have to be forgiveness on both sides.

"Yes, I did, but I didn't want to tell you then. Not when we were both angry. This was going to be a big shock, and I didn't want there to be words said in anger about the baby that could never be forgotten or taken back. It wasn't meant as leverage or to hurt you."

"What about you being on birth control?"

Sunshine had a feeling that question would come up. She would have asked too if she were him. "I was on birth control. I must have forgotten a day or two. That's the only thing I can think of. Maybe when I stayed over at the barn with you or something. I don't know. I've asked myself the same thing. It wasn't planned on my part; I want you to believe that. This baby was destined to be." Sunshine flashed a slight smile.

"Stubborn. Same as us already. How far along are you?"

"Between six and eight weeks is what one of the tests said.

I'll have to get an appointment with my OB/GYN, and then we will know more." She couldn't read his face.

"Let me know when that is," Drake said. Sunshine watched in shock and dismay as he got up and headed upstairs. He came down a moment later with clothes, and her heart broke.

"Come one, let's go for a ride," Drake said and held out pants and a jacket to her.

"This is new, trying to put me in pants instead of getting me out them." Sunshine tried to smile and make a joke as she tugged them on.

Drake walked out the door and she was on his heels. She followed him to the barn where he saddled Sugar Baby. He didn't bother saddling Deacon. Drake got on up and pulled Sunshine up sideways into his lap. When they got to the gate, he leaned down to pull it open using the handle she'd installed to allow passage without dismounting.

Sunshine was enjoying riding in Drake's lap. He held her close and kept her warm. The ride was clearing her mind, as it always did. There wasn't anything akin to riding a horse on the night of a full moon. Sunshine didn't know if she was supposed to ride horses pregnant, but at that moment it seemed to be what she and Drake needed to do.

He pulled Sugar Baby to a stop in the middle of the pasture and pulled her closer to him, holding her tight.

"I am sorry about the cattle. I didn't want to know for sure if it was you I was up against. It would have been a roadblock between us. I was selfish not to come out and ask you or tell you my thoughts on it," Drake said, breaking the silence. His body tensed with the admission.

Sunshine wrapped her arms around his waist, her head on his chest. "You're right. I would have used it as an excuse to put some distance between us, but it still wasn't right."

"Nope, it wasn't, and it wasn't right for me not to be the first to know you were pregnant either."

Sunshine tried to swallow the lump in her throat. "No, it wasn't." They sat in silence for a few minutes, taking in the full moon.

"I don't want to hide where I'm at with you. You know the land I live on was given to me by G-Daddy and G-Momma." He nodded. "The house I'm making the payments on fine with what I make off Dad's and my cattle. That income covers my needs, and most of my wants."

She ran her hand across Sugar Baby's coat to help calm her nerves. She took a deep breath before continuing. "The registered herd, however, I took out a large loan to buy. I've paid over half of it off. I'm making that payment, but not by much. The artificial insemination I did, plus the feed, land rent, and all that, was more than I anticipated. I'm telling you because I'm gonna find a seller for the herd, and get out from under that. You were right the other day when you said I needed to spend more time at the construction company if I was going to run it one day. I enjoy the cattle, but I think long term, I want to make sure my Dad's business continues to flourish. I believe building on his legacy will be more important to me. I want to be able to hand that down to our child."

"I'm glad you were honest with me and sounds as if you have it all figured out. If you need my help or want it, you know where to find me. What if our baby wants to run the stockyard?" He gave her a grin.

"Then he or she can pick."

"What if I want more kids?" She felt the shock to her soul at his question.

"I guess after this baby, if you want more, we can talk about it, if we're still together."

"We'll still be together."

She raised a disbelieving eyebrow at that statement.

"Sunshine, I'm not mad that you're pregnant. I'm surprised and shocked, but not mad or upset."

Sunshine felt the weight of the world lift off her shoulders. "I'm happy to hear you say that. I've been concerned." She gave him a hug.

"You thought I was going to be an ass about it?"

"Don't get your undies in a wad. No, I didn't think you would be an ass. I didn't think you would handle it this well."

"Sunshine, look at me." Drake stared into her eyes. "I am handling this news well because I am happy that you are pregnant with our baby. You are the only person I could imagine having a child with. These last couple of months have showed me there isn't a person out there who will ever know me, or put up with my shit as well as you do."

Sunshine kissed him and said, "Thank you. I feel the same way, and there is a lot of shit to put up with on both sides."

"I hope you continue to feel the same way because"—Drake took a deep breath—"I love you, Sunshine, and that isn't ever gonna change. I love that you're a stubborn ass. I love the noises you make when I'm inside you. I love the way your forehead wrinkles when you think hard. I love the way you laugh. I love how amazin' we are together in the sack. I love that no matter what life has thrown my way, you have had my back. I love that you are the mother to our baby, and most of all, I love that I have loved you my entire life and that I will love you till it ends."

Sunshine held back her tears. Her throat would barely work. "I love you too, Drake. I love it when you run your hands through your hair and mess it up. I love when you hold me close. I love how confident you are. I love how amazing you are to me. I love how you rock my world every time we have sex. I love waking up beside you and knowing you have always been there for me. I love that you are the father to our baby, and most of all, I love that I have loved you my entire life and that I will love you till it ends."

Drake kissed her till the tears stopped flowing.

"Sunshine, I asked you when you were four if you would marry me, and at first you said no because I was a poopy head, and you didn't want to have my poopy-headed children, and I bribed you with promises of Reese's Cups and you said yes. Tonight, I am going to ask you again." Drake reached into the saddle bag on Sugar Baby's saddle. He had slipped some Reese's Cups in there along with a little something else earlier. He pulled out a black jeweler's box.

Sunshine's heart was pounding. She wanted this. She wanted this to be true. She hoped she wasn't dreaming.

"Sunshine, will you marry me? I'll support you in your business venture and try my best not to stick my nose in where it doesn't belong. I'll give you all my Reese's Cups every Halloween and make you peanut butter milkshakes. If you want, I will even give you my bull. I promise I will love you till death do us part, be the best husband I can be to you, and the best Daddy I can be to our child," Drake finished and waited for her to answer.

Sunshine could see the diamonds sparkling in the moonlight. It looked to be an asscher cut in a thin antique setting. It was beautiful in the soft glowing light, but she bet it would be even more stunning when she could see the details.

Sunshine couldn't go too easy on him. "When did you get this gorgeous ring?"

"This morning. I drove to Billy Mitchell Jewelry and picked this out for you after our fight. I thought we might be over for good, but I wasn't going to give up. If I wanted you in my life, I knew you were going to need more than words to prove I loved you. I was going to try to get you back no matter what."

Sunshine nodded and pretended to think hard, but it wasn't a hard decision at all. He had wanted to marry her even before the baby, and now she knew he'd be there by her side, supporting her. She didn't get to make the big sale like she had wanted to, but Drake did, and that was as good as her getting it. There would be others buyers for her herd, but there would never be another Drake.

"All your Reese's Cups and your bull? The bull that was supposed to be mine anyway?"

"Yes. Okay, more like three-fourths of my Reese's Cups, but I will give most of them to you, and yes, the bull that was supposed to be yours. You can have whatever you want of mine, because you are my Southern Sunshine. You seeped into my bones over the years, and one day I woke up, never wanting the warmth to leave. You make me feel energized and relaxed all at the same time. Without you in it, any day would seem cold and dim. You bring light and laughter to me and everyone else."

"You drive a hard bargain, but a love that lasts a lifetime sold me. You didn't even have to sacrifice your Reese's Cups, but I will let you keep the bull." Sunshine let the tears stream down her face. Never would she have thought Drake would have all the answers to her heart, but he did. She wouldn't be letting him go again.

Drake kissed her. "Let's go back to the house."

"Yes, please. I'm about to freeze my ass off out here." Sunshine tried to snuggle in closer.

"Can't have that, your ass is one of my favorite things about you," Drake said and slipped his hand down to squeeze it.

Sunshine was pleased with herself when Drake made an *ump* sound when she punched him in the stomach for that remark. "Watch it."

"We will have to tell our parents tomorrow. They will have a shit ton of questions," Drake said.

"Screw a goose," Sunshine said in response. They would be excited, but Lord help her, Claire and her mother were gonna make her life hell with wedding plans. She was going to make sure they stuck to what she wanted, simple and outdoors. She didn't care where or what kinda wedding they had as long as it was Drake she was walking down the aisle to.

They made it back into the house and crawled into bed beside one another. Drake threw his arm over her waist and pulled her against him. She felt him grow hard against her. She was the luckiest woman in the world. Drake kissed her neck, and she felt herself shiver.

"You gonna let this go to waste?" he whispered into her

ear and then bit down on it enough to make her moan. Her soon-to-be husband was a dream in the bedroom.

"My vagina is staging a damn mutiny," she muttered as she turned towards her future.

# Epilogue

"I hate every one of you," Sunshine told Belle, Willow, Emerson, and G-Momma.

"No, you don't," Belle said.

"You love us," Emerson told her.

"You are going to look back on this and laugh," Belle exclaimed, pulling her hand into her lap.

"Imagine the story we have to tell," Willow tried to calm her.

Sunshine heard G-Momma yell out, "You hoo, Clint. Could you come here and take our picture, darlin'?"

Sunshine watched in horror as Clint walked in front of them to do just that. "Smile big for the camera." They all huddled around Sunshine and smiled, looking like the demented people they were.

"The baby's first trip to jail, and we have it documented," G-Momma squealed, and asked Clint if she could see the picture. "Looks pretty good considerin' the cell bars are in the way, but you can see us all. This will be great in the baby book."

Sunshine wanted to crawl under the cot in the cell. She didn't understand how they seemed to end up here. She was three months pregnant for crying out loud. Sunshine heard heavy boot steps coming down the hall. She looked up when they stopped to see Drake and Brice standing in front of the cell looking at them with resignation and what she hoped was amusement. Drake, damn him, looked as handsome as always.

Brice spoke first. "I'm afraid to ask."

Drake nodded. "Me too, but what happened?"

Sunshine pointed to Belle. "It's all her fault this time, I swear."

# Acknowledgements:

I would first like to say thank you to my husband. He deals with me talking to myself, having to repeat himself twenty times as I stay in my own head, my random bouts of frenzied writing, as well as occasionally being my note taker when an idea strikes. He is also the man that gets locked in a room with our twins as I creep away to write. Big Daddy, I love you.

To my babies, I love you more than life. Thank you both for giving me the courage to show you how to work hard for your dreams.

To my mom, who has always stood behind me, pushed me forward, kept me from running away from difficult tasks, and given me endless love, thank you.

To my step-dad, who indulged me by taking me to book stores and buying me limited edition books off E-Bay, thank you.

To my crazy aunts, who are an incredible source of support, nonsense, and good fodder, thanks for the laughs.

To Granny, who always flamed the fan of my love to read and write, thank you.

To my family and best friends who have been my support system and helped me push and market this book, thank you so much.

Thank you to the editors and designer who helped make this book possible. To everyone that shared, liked, posted, and took any other action to help me promote *Southern Sunshine*, thank you so much. You have all had a hand in making this country girl's dream come true, and I couldn't be more grateful.

Made in the USA
Lexington, KY
21 July 2019